A Pro..... Keep

Book 2 in the Out of Time series

Loretta Livingstone

ISBN-10: 1537714147
ISBN-13: 978-1537714141

For my lovely dad, Ian David Robinson, without whose legacy, I may never have started writing books. Also, my wonderful mother, Margaret Robinson, whose encouragement has been a constant support.

Acknowledgements

My grateful thanks and appreciation to Phil Pembridge of the Plantagenet Medieval Society who kindly spent some time advising me where to find clothing and accessories for the twelfth century. Also to Alexandra Arden of the Museum of London who was kind enough to advise me which museums would have the items I was interested in finding out more about. And especial thanks to the lovely Helen Hollick for her help with all things equestrian and for her kind encouragement which means such a lot to me.

Thanks, also, to my cousin, Claire Robinson, for her help with 21st century medical matters, and my wonderful beta readers, Marie Cockburn, Marie Godley and Heidi Peltier. Their help has been invaluable. I couldn't have done this without them.

I also want to express my appreciation to Nicky Galliers for her brilliant editing and research skills. She made me dig deeper than I thought I was able. It may have made me howl a bit at the time, but I am very grateful she pushed me that little bit harder.

And last, but never least, special thanks to Iain, my wonderful husband, who has endured many a late or burnt meal without complaint and listened patiently as I tried to herd my ideas into some kind of order.

INTRODUCTION

In 2006, Marion was visiting the Abbey of Sparnstow in southern England, an abbey that, like so many, owed its destruction to Henry VIII. Thanks to him, it was now little more than a romantic ruin.

Accompanied by her two daughters, Marion was distracted by a strange buzzing which alarmed her since one of her daughters is allergic to bee stings. The buzzing, combined with the heat of the day, so disorientated her that she stumbled into a huge beech tree nearby, passing out and coming round to see a very different version of Sparnstow Abbey – the original twelfth century building.

Despite her caution, Marion found herself the centre of attention when a young man was brought to the abbey, close to death. Marion, recognising the symptoms of anaphylactic shock, administered her daughter's EpiPen, saving his life.

That's when she discovered she had saved Prince John, untrustworthy brother of King Richard I, who was embroiled in yet another treasonous plot, accompanied by his household knights who were led by Giles de Soutenay. Unfortunately, although his men had not seen Marion intervene, John had and was determined to acquire both her and her mystical device. It fell to Giles to bring Marion to him; the price of failure would be unthinkable.

Hildegarde, Abbess of Sparnstow, herself a refugee from a different age, was determined to thwart Prince John and return Marion to her own time. She needed to convince Giles to aid her. That, however, would put his life in peril. He consented, so long as Marion would agree to deliver two EpiPens every year at Whitsuntide via the beech tree.

So far, she has kept her promise, but this year there is a problem.

PROLOGUE

Marion shifted restlessly. The pain was still there – it was what had woken her. That and her unquiet dreams. Her mouth was so dry. She reached for her water with hands that shook slightly and sipped a little before remembering she wasn't supposed to drink; her operation was scheduled for first thing tomorrow. Guiltily, she replaced the cup hoping one mouthful wouldn't hurt.

The ward was in semi-darkness. Somewhere, a machine bleeped urgently; soft moans and snuffles came from the other patients. Was it worth her trying to get back to sleep? She checked her watch. Her meds had worn off, and the next dose wasn't due for another hour.

It was bad enough worrying about Giles and Hildegarde without having to enlist the help of her younger daughter, whose dark, haunted eyes disturbed her. But Shannon was the only one who would have believed her.

Marion shook her head. No, Shannon wouldn't do anything stupid; she was the sensible one, not like Chloe. Besides, Shannon was going to France with friends as soon as she'd delivered the EpiPens. No, she wouldn't miss that for anything; she'd been talking about it for months, and wasn't that boyfriend of hers going too? What was his name? Jackson? Yes, that was the one.

Anyway, she knew she could trust Shannon; she'd promised. And tomorrow, at last, she would have her op.

Finally, Marion relaxed; the pain eased a little, and she fell into a dreamless sleep, the quiet of the ward punctuated only by the occasional gentle snore from the bed next to hers.

CHAPTER ONE

Whit Monday 2012

"Promise me you won't go through. Just leave the injectors and walk away." Marion had grasped Shannon's wrist so tightly, it made her wince. "It's dangerous. Promise me, Shannon!"

Shannon had promised. And she'd meant it – at the time. But that was before she'd caught the man she'd thought was the love of her life cheating on her. That was when she thought they had a holiday in the Alps to look forward to. Hurt and angry, now, she was considering the unthinkable.

It can't be that dangerous; Mum did it. She got back okay and she wasn't even prepared. Shannon surveyed her own well-stuffed bags complacently.

It was only a holiday, Mum would be none the wiser. To cover her tracks, Shannon had told her the connections would really bad – well, that was true enough.

So, last chance to change my mind then. But she wouldn't – she knew that. Pulling out her mobile, she sent one final message. *All done,* she lied. *Off to the airport now. U won't b able 2 reach me but don't worry, I'll b fine. See u in 3 weeks.*

Her mother must have been waiting for her text. Immediately, an answer pinged back. *Thanks, love. Have a gr8 time, x.*

Shannon's brown hair was braided; her long, plain dress would pass as a shift. She glanced around – good, nobody in sight; she'd better be quick. Pulling on a dark grey undergown and a deep red bliaut that laced at the sides, she dragged the wimple over her head and pinned a veil around it. Then, she turned her mobile off, put it into one of her bags and took a deep breath.

The tree was just yards away. Already, she could hear it starting to buzz. Mum had hated the sound; she said it had made her feel ill, yet to Shannon, it was mellifluous, soothing. And it was like a gift really, wasn't it? This chance had come just when she needed an excuse to get away. *You can't get much further away than the twelfth century,* she thought with a grin. Then, taking another deep breath and crossing her fingers, she put one hand on the rippled bark. The vibrations beneath her palm felt as though they would go right through her. Fascinated, she watched her hand disappear into the trunk of the tree. *This is it then.*

Pulling her hand back, she picked up her bags and walked forward, legs shaking a little. She felt a slight resistance but kept going, closing her eyes and holding her breath as she pushed her face through. At first, she thought she might suffocate. The tree seemed to turn almost liquid but thick, a bit like walking through soup.

As she wondered how long before she dared breathe, she heard a sort of popping sound, and her face came free. She put her hands up to her cheeks to wipe away the stuff she had just come through, but there was nothing there; her skin was dry and clear.

Opening her eyes, she stared about her. The scene was the same as the one she had just left, apart from the car park, which, obviously, wasn't here now. A meadow to her right, woodland ahead of her, a stream to her left and a track alongside that. But the tree! The tree was half the size – well, that made sense. How old was it anyway? Did beeches even live that long?

A frisson of excitement shivered through her. *Awesome! Shannon Hart – time traveller!* And still, she felt as though she was in a dream.

She looked across the meadow away from the woodland, gasping as she saw Sparnstow Abbey as it used to be, its graceful structure soaring in pale-coloured stone. It was magnificent! *Wow! I've done it! I've really done it!* A wild joy surged through her.

Shannon stared at the abbey, entranced. Taking a step towards it, she caught her foot in the unaccustomed fabric swirling round her ankles. She dropped her bags and flailed her arms to save herself – too late. Over she went, as her trapped foot propelled her inexorably forward, landing awkwardly with a sickening thud. She sprawled on the ground for a moment, dazed, before trying to rise to her feet.

As she pushed herself up, a sharp pain shot through her ankle, making her wince. She tried again to stand; the pain was too much, and she allowed herself to sink back down.

What to do? There was no one about, although that was probably a good thing, bearing in mind how she'd arrived, but it meant there was no one to help her, either. Well, she couldn't sit here all day. It was a bit of a distance to crawl, and she could hardly arrive on her hands and knees anyway.

If I can make it to the woods, I might be able to find a branch I can use to help me walk. And I could use my spare veil for strapping. That'll help.

Tensing against the pain, Shannon reached for her bags. Then, taking out the veil, she eased off her shoe and probed her ankle with cautious fingers, yelping sharply as she touched the injury. Wrapping the fabric tightly round her foot and ankle, she secured it, gritting her teeth as she pushed her foot back into her shoe.

Now, all I have to do is get to the woods. Yeah, right. That's going to hurt. First though, she rummaged in her bag again and pulled out the EpiPens she'd brought with her.

She turned back to the tree and grubbed around the roots until she found the hollow her mum had told her about, pushing the devices deep inside and covering them with grass and leaves. When she'd finished, she surveyed her hands in dismay – her fingernails had mud beneath them, and her hands were grimy, more peasant than lady. *Oh well, I can wipe them on the grass for now and wash them later.*

That job done, she crawled painfully across the grass, dragging her bags with her. At least away from the tree, the ground was dry. Once at the woods, Shannon rolled over and sat for a few moments holding her ankle. *Now, let's see if I can find a decent bit of wood.*

Spotting a fallen branch which looked to be a useful size, she stretched as far as she could without moving her legs until her fingers just touched the tip. Inching carefully sideways so she could grasp it, she pulled it towards her. She reckoned it would just about do. There was even a knobbly bit at the top she could hold it by.

She eased to her feet, trying not to yelp again and leaned experimentally on the branch. It held her weight and, with it, she could manage to shuffle along. It hurt, but she could bear it – just.

Limping heavily, she struggled over to the track by the stream. The straightest route would seem to be across the meadow, but this would be easiest for her, she thought.

The path, such as it was, had been worn smooth by the passage of feet. It was wider than she remembered it to be back in 2012, but it was probably used more now than then – or was it then than now? Trying to ignore the increasing pain in her ankle by puzzling over which tense she should be using, the past or the present, she was lost in her thoughts and didn't hear the party of riders coming up behind her.

CHAPTER TWO

April 1197

Isabella pressed her lips together mutinously. Reluctant though she had been to wed Giles, she'd been permitted no choice in the matter. Married to Baldwin at just fourteen, widowhood had come as a great relief to her three years later. Indeed, she had considered taking holy vows. Her heart had sunk when the Queen had taken an interest in her welfare. *Welfare!* Her lips had twisted in derision. And just who was this impoverished knight who was to become her lord and have the right to plunder her estate? But there had been no escape.

On her wedding day, she had gritted her teeth, held her head high and responded to the priest in colourless tones. But Giles, she discovered, was a very different man to Baldwin, who had expected nothing from her save duty.

She'd learnt and learnt speedily. Baldwin had known nothing of love, had not been beyond bruising her or sending her tumbling to the floor with a powerful backhanded blow if she had not pleased him quickly enough. Mayhap it was a sin, but when he died, she rejoiced. Surely, God would understand. Surely, He had freed her from her cage. And then, she had been promised in wedlock again. And again to someone not of her choosing.

Baldwin had been well-favoured, although he stank. He had rarely bathed, believing it was not healthy, and was careless of his dress. Heaven only knew why her elegant father had chosen him for her. The love of rank and fortune must have overpowered any finer feelings.

She had wept and pined when told of her first betrothal, to no avail. And had discovered beyond that easy smile had been a cold heart, a ready fist.

And now, her father was less than satisfied with Giles, a knight with but one manor, whose liege lord was Prince John, not Richard, England's King. It was that which had given her some satisfaction. She knew Eleanor had selected her for this very reason; the Queen was not always so quick to take revenge but Isabella's father had displeased her more than once. His annoyance had been the one thing in Giles' favour. And her lands and portion had enhanced Giles' own.

Before her betrothal, she had seen Giles but twice. Once when she was eight, and John had paid a brief visit to her father's largest manor. John had been positively avuncular, producing a silver ring from her ear, flipping it to her with careless charm as she gawped in amazement, chucking her under the chin while Giles de Soutenay stood behind him. Giles' hawkish face had contrasted ill with John's smiling charm.

The next time she had encountered both men had been at her wedding to Baldwin. On that inauspicious day, John had been far different from the delightful magician who had teased a small girl. He had ogled her lasciviously during the feast, leering and making lewd jokes, as she huddled on the bed sick with fear while the priest performed the blessing.

Giles had remained in the hall, unsmiling, disapproving; a fact which had both pleased and displeased her. He had not joined his liege in the bedchamber, which had been a mark in his favour. Beyond that, she had known nothing of him.

Two years on from her second marriage, she knew him to be a good and honourable man. Away from John's employ, he no longer looked grim and unyielding; indeed, if not precisely handsome, he was far from unattractive to her.

His temper was equable; he had never shown any inclination to beat her. There was warmth between them, and he talked to her as though her opinion mattered, something she still found strange but refreshing. She had slowly blossomed and learnt to care for him. But his Whitsuntide duty to John she could not understand, nor would he explain it to her. It stood like a wall between them. John she hated with her whole being. She shook her head almost imperceptibly. She would not think of it. Would not recall the memory. And now, as the date for his annual duty approached, he wanted her to come with him? No, she *could not.*

Giles, watching her expression close, shook his head in exasperation. "Isabella, I know you like John not, know you like court company not, but you are my wife. I would have your presence there this year. Maude will be attending. She will look to you whilst I am with John. This year, I would have you bear me company. It will be only for a short while; I have little taste for court life either."

Giles could not have explained why he wanted her there, only that he did, and it would keep Heloise, one of the court whores, from him. She'd taken a fancy to him, seeming determined to seduce him, constantly sidling up and whispering softly in his ear. He had no problem resisting her, provocative though she might be, but it would give her less encouragement if Isabella were at his side.

He suspected his indifference was the draw; also, he wondered if John was behind it. *That troublemaking hellspawn.* Giles thought John held a grudge against Isabella and was probably trying to repay her in kind for the expression of revulsion she had given him on their wedding day. John nursed his grievances overlong – Giles should know. He gave her a conciliatory look. "Come now, give me a smile and cry peace."

"My lord." Isabella dipped her head, reluctantly obedient; what choice had she?

He stayed her as she turned from him. "Isabella, it would mean much to me if you would come willingly."

She gave him a wan smile, for how could she tell him it was John she feared? John, handsome, suave and utterly loathsome. She felt nauseated as she remembered how, having decided to honour their wedding with his presence, he had then demanded a kiss from the new bride – and not a decorous one. The memory of that kiss had tainted the remainder of the day and made her dread the coming night even more. She never wanted to set eyes on him again, and now... Ah well, the die was cast, and she must accept it or risk raising Giles' ire.

"I will need a court gown, my lord."

"I'll escort you to the cloth merchant myself. We'll take the boy; your maid can have a care to him. A visit to the market will be a fine treat for him." Giles was willing to do his part to bring a softening back to her face. In truth, he had wondered whether or not Eleanor would keep her promise to him, wondered which heiress she would find him. He need not have worried.

Isabella, newly widowed, had been biddable, sweet-faced and mild; although now she was gaining trust in him, she was beginning to show some spirit, test the boundaries. He minded that not. In truth, at first she had been so docile, it had been like living with a puppet. She was obedient, compliant and utterly colourless. Clearly, being married to Baldwin had taught her to hide her real nature. Beneath that mouse-like exterior, he was just beginning to glimpse the true woman – a woman with a bewitching smile, an earthy warmth. Giles had grown to have an affection for her, which was starting to blossom into something deeper.

He smiled at Isabella. "We need only be present at court a few days. We will stay with Ralph and Maude until after Whit Monday. We can travel with them."

Isabella's own smile grew warmer, less dutiful. At least she wouldn't be left alone while Giles' other obligations kept him from her; she should have trusted he would have a care for her. She would make him a new tunic. Maybe deep red wool with gold thread. And for herself? She had a fancy for light blue with silver lozenges of 'broidery, but Maude always wore those colours, knowing they complemented her soft blue eyes. Besides, blue was expensive. Mayhap something in bright tawny with saffron thread? It would suit her own colouring and brown eyes well. And mayhap, with Giles at her side, she would find some pleasure in this trip. It would be a delight to have a new gown. She turned a sunnier face to Giles and took heart at the warmth of his response.

Dickon leaned against Jehane's ample bosom, clutching the neck of her shift with one hand, chewing on the thumb of his other hand, eyes wide as he took in the sights and sounds. A roar scythed through the air, and he pressed his head into her neck as a chained bear swiped at a hound, which whimpered and then lay still. Isabella, alert to his fears, removed him from his nurse and settled him on her hip. "Go, Jehane. I'll take him." She smiled at Dickon's nurse. "You may take some time for yourself." She slipped her a coin. Jehane grinned broadly, showing her missing eye tooth, and bobbed a curtsy before disappearing into the throng.

Isabella soothed her small son, who was now bawling in earnest, buying him a sticky sweetmeat from a stall, successfully distracting him. At least the day, for once, was fair, and boards, on which their pattens clacked loudly despite a covering of straw, had been laid down to cover the mud.

The mass of people swirled like some ungainly, disorganised dance, although Giles' men kept Isabella and her women from being jostled.

Hawkers yelled, children were cuffed by exasperated stallholders as they whined and begged for alms, and music drifted over from where a small group of jongleurs were playing pipes, tabor, shawm and rebec. Isabella bounced Dickon in time to the rhythm, and, fears forgotten, he waved his sweetmeat, laughing.

Giles turned from the swordsmith, where he had been admiring a weapon with an amber-topped pommel, its blade intriguingly engraved. "You'll not need me, I think. Adam, take charge of my lady's purchases, if you please."

Adam, Giles' youngest hearth knight, who'd been hoping to find his own amusements, inclined his head and turned grudgingly to Isabella, his lips set in a thin, tight line which made his displeasure clear, until he realised Beatrice was to accompany them. His eyes lit up; Beatrice was comely and young. She batted him a glance, blue eyes half hidden by her long lashes, and instantly, his sulky air abated.

Isabella made for the mercer's stall where, passing Dickon over to Mahelt, her senior maid, she began to finger the fabrics. Picking out a fine wool in a deep red, she watched as the mercer cut the lengths she required. Dickon should have a tunic in the same, she decided.

She admired the glowing silks and brocades with Beatrice, then discarded them for the less expensive, more practical wools, and searched for the shade she favoured, but the aurnolas reminded her of the flesh of a trout, the greens were too dark, and the paler shades, she feared, might make her appear sallow.

She winced at the reddish-violet the mercer held out and shook her head at an over-bright popinjay blue. As she dithered over one in her favourite shade of bright tawny, she felt a hand on her arm. Giles had returned, and now, he took the bolt of cloth from her, handing it back to the mercer. He pointed at a much more finely woven fabric in a deep, rich blue-green verdulet, which the stall holder lifted down and spread out with eager enthusiasm, his eye on a better sale now.

Isabella gave Giles a sidelong glance. He met her eyes. "You need not retain too tight a grip on my finances, sweeting. This would look well on you."

Isabella was torn between the pleasure of wearing it and the desire to remain unremarked by John, should he be there. No doubt the colour would suit her only too well; she did not wish to attract John's notice. She hovered, drawn by the fabric, pleased by Giles' generosity but unsure how to respond.

Giles noticed her hesitation and, assuming she was mentally calculating the cost, he handed over the price himself. "I would not want you thinking I hold you too cheaply, Wife."

Still, she paused, and he tried to quell the impatience he felt. Why did she continue to hold part of herself back? Surely, he had proved he was no Baldwin. Exasperated, he handed over the package to her maid and was moving away when her hand reached out and grasped his. He turned back to her, and she smiled tremulously, saying, "Thank you, my lord. You are kind." His irritation disappeared as swiftly as it had come, and he caressed her cheek lightly with the back of his fingers before leaving her to make the rest of her purchases.

Isabella and her maids had been sewing all afternoon. Her eyes ached, for the sky had clouded with rain yet again, and they were working by torch and candlelight. Two court tunics for Giles were already hanging on the clothes poles, one in dark red wool, the other in a deep vert, the shade of a yew needle, ready to be embellished with braid and embroidery, and her own gown was nearly finished. She put down the cloth and stretched, arching her back, then picked up her work again, admiring the fine texture of the fabric, holding it up against herself and trying to see her reflection in the disc of polished metal Mahelt was holding up to her.

Beatrice, who had been plying her needle with decreasing enthusiasm and many sighs, brightened visibly and put down her own sewing. "Shall I fetch wine, my lady?"

Isabella considered. "No, Beatrice, I think not; I have the headache." She rubbed her temples. "I think a willow bark tisane would be a better choice.

And Beatrice?" Her maid raised an enquiring eyebrow. "Be wary of Adam. I know he has charm, but he is inconstant. And for all his flattering words, he will marry higher than you, my dear. I am sorry, but it has to be said, for I would not have you taken in by his cozening ways."

Beatrice flushed and bit her lip. Isabella reached out and touched her hand. "I know you think I'm meddling, but I have a care for you. He will hurt you, and your parents would not be pleased to find you paying the price for his pleasure. There are fish aplenty in the sea and far better than he, for all he is a knight. I promise you, you will be better not setting your eyes on him. The knight truly only marries the maid in the jongleur's airs, not in real life. We shall find you a husband, dear Beatrice, and one who'll be kind to you. Adam will not wed you."

She released her hand, and the maid scuttled away without saying a word. Isabella sighed. It would be necessary to have words with Giles over Adam, for she would not have any of her maids compromised. She was fond of Beatrice, even though the girl was dizzy with dreams. Closing her eyes for a moment, she gave thought to the young men of their household. It was best she made a match for Beatrice before the girl got herself into trouble. Filbert, their steward's son, might be a possibility. Twenty, well-favoured, and showing no preference for her other maids, she thought she had caught him casting sly glances in the girl's direction. It would be worth finding out if Oswin, his father, was agreeable. And Beatrice was not a bad match for Filbert. Fifteen, comely and of a respectable background.

She gazed at the dreary scene outside the solar, made more dismal by the slightly greenish hue of the glass panes, one nail tapping on the narrow stone sill. The window had been a wedding gift from Giles' brother; whilst Isabella's dower had added considerably to Giles' income, a glass-paned window would have been beyond their means. It added consequence, and Isabella delighted in having this one window which need not be shuttered against the cold.

Nibbling the tip of a fingernail, she considered. Yes, she believed it might work. She would endeavour to turn the girl's thoughts in Filbert's direction. Adam would not marry her, that was certain, but Isabella was not sure how far his flirtation would take him. Beatrice was not to be used and cast off. She would speak to Oswin once she had approached Giles.

The wind blew a flurry of rain against the panes, the draft that filtered through making the candles gutter. Isabella shivered, calling for braziers to be lit as she thought more on her plan.

Beatrice was far more eager to be wed than she herself had been, but that was likely because her father would give her some say in the matter. He was a kindly man so, as long as Beatrice did not look too high or low for her station, would be unlikely to balk. Filbert would be an excellent choice.

In Baldwin's household, she had been allowed no responsibility, mostly left to her needlework in the bower, surrounded by maids who had no real care for her, a grim, sour-faced mother-in-law, rigid with disapproval, and a husband whose only interest in her was to grace his table and appease his appetites.

As she mused, Giles came in, towelling his wet hair and shaking himself like a dog. "In truth, I shall develop webbed feet if this rain does not soon cease," he grumbled. Unable to throw off the nervous habit of her time with Baldwin, she jumped to her feet ready to assist him, but he waved her away.

"No, lass, no need to get you wet too; I'm drenched through and chilled to the marrow." He threw the cloth he'd been using to dry his hair onto the floor. "Ah, it's useless. I may as well dunk my head in the tub along with the rest of me and be done with it."

Isabella dismissed her maids; now would be her best opportunity to speak about Adam and Beatrice. Giles pulled off his sodden clothing and wrapped himself in a warm mantle while he waited for the servants to bring in the tub. Isabella poured him wine and picked up the garments he had scattered heedlessly over the floor rushes.

When the tub was hauled into the room, Isabella supervised its filling, scattering herbs into the steaming water. Giles sniffed appreciatively as the fragrance of rosemary drifted up, then dropped his mantle and stepped into the large half barrel which he had ordered padded around the edges, groaning with pleasure as the warmth seeped its way into his bones. Isabella fetched the bay-scented soap she saved for him and began to rub it into his hair.

"Ah, Bella, that feels good." He wriggled his shoulders and, after sluicing his head, she moved to knead the knots out of them. Her fingers had cramped while she sewed; she hadn't noticed how cold they were getting, and now, the hot water felt soothing to her also.

"If this rain does not let up, I fear for the harvests again this year. The ground was still sodden from last year. Another poor yield will bring much hardship."

Isabella still found it disconcerting to have things like harvests discussed with her. Whenever she had timidly ventured an opinion to Baldwin, he had backhanded her and instructed her to mind her distaff. She enjoyed times like this with Giles but still found herself tongue-tied. God grant he didn't think her a lack-wit. She racked her brain, trying to think of something useful to say, then remembered she needed to speak to him about Beatrice and, by reason of that, Adam.

"Husband," she began. Giles raised his head and caught at her hand as she continued to work on his shoulders.

"Enough, my love. Whilst I am enjoying your efforts, I would rather speak to your face. Come, pull up a stool, and sit in front of me." He grinned, wanting to invite her into the tub with him, but forbore; she would be shocked. "Mayhap you're wishing we'd bought the thicker wool after all. If this weather continues, you'll be chilled in that fine fabric."

Isabella smiled. "My pride will keep me warm. The colour is beautiful; I thank you for it, my lord."

Giles put his head on one side, considering. "Isabella, will you not try to call me by my given name more often, at least in private? Formality is all well and good in public, but I sometimes feel you do not even remember how I am called."

Isabella flushed, and Giles sighed. Was she embarrassed or angered? He was trying to be patient, trying to give her time, but she was still like a nervous filly on occasion.

Why was she biting her lip like that? He was about to speak again when she flung up her head and looked him full in the face with those dark-honey coloured eyes of hers which so enchanted him.

"My l..." As he flashed her an exasperated glance, she stopped and tried again. "Giles?"

"You see, it was not so hard."

She smiled absently at him. "Giles, I need to speak to you about Adam."

He narrowed his eyes, and she quailed. It did not escape his notice. "Do not be so fearful, Bella; I am not angered with you. What has that scapegrace been doing now? Which of your maids is he bedazzling?"

She raised her eyebrows. "You know?"

"I know Adam. The lad is oversure of himself, although I think there's no real harm in him. I'll watch him if that would please you."

Visibly sagging with relief, her lips curved into the generous, open smile which he was beginning to see more often these days.

How much had it cost her to come to me? he wondered. *Still, we are making progress.*

"Thank you, my l..." He cocked an eyebrow at her, and she laughed. "Giles, then. You see, I am learning, my husband." Rising from her stool, she pushed up her sleeves. "Shall we return to the other important matter?" She moved behind him, and then, Giles felt her small, firm hands kneading his lower back muscles and gave himself up to the pleasures of his bath.

CHAPTER THREE

It had been dry for three weeks. The gloom that had been almost constant since Saint Guthlac's day, in early April, was lifting as the ground began to turn from a thick morass into something more firm. Still muddy in the bailey but dry in places, a brisk wind had helped take some of the moisture from the earth, and the sunshine had lifted everyone's spirits. Even Isabella was looking forward to the trip more than she was dreading it now.

She loved Maude, Giles' brother's wife, as though she was her own sister. Maude, it was, who had first made her feel she might be able to trust Giles.

She was in her twenties, a little older than Isabella, ten years younger than Giles, and considerably younger than her husband, Ralph. Maude was the one who had enveloped her in a hug of welcome at their wedding and whispered in her ear how fortunate she was to have a good man this time, for Maude had known of Baldwin.

Giles' sister, Petronilla, had also greeted her warmly and called her sister, but there was more of an aloofness about her which Isabella could not find her way through. It didn't help that Isabella hid her own feelings. Only Maude had been able to penetrate her shields. Maude, who for all her ethereal beauty and her cool silvery-blonde colouring, had a tangible warmth which thawed the ice from Isabella and drew her to let down her guard. She treated Giles like a favoured brother, standing on tiptoe to kiss him and cuffing him over pretended slights. Isabella had been nervous of Giles' brother, Ralph, to start with, for his bluff geniality had repelled her, but when she saw how he treated his wife, she thawed to him as well.

Isabella's spirits rose higher at the thought of the week they would spend there before proceeding to court. At court, Giles would not be able to stay beside her, protecting her, but with Maude to bear her company, she might be able to face even John.

The ride was very pleasant. Giles, astride Troubadour, his favourite horse, was in high good humour, and Isabella was completely at ease on her dainty grey jennet, Merlin. She turned a laughing face to him as he teased her over her new gown, and even ventured to taunt him for his vanity about his new tunic. They rode ahead of the entourage of men and maids, and, without the constant company, Isabella began to respond in kind to Giles' gentle flirtations.

Far behind them, unnoticed, Adam rode with a scowl, for Isabella had sent Beatrice back to her parents for the time they would be gone, and the maids who accompanied her today were wiser to his antics than she. Doubtless, he would be in a better mood once they arrived at Oakley. Maude was his sister and had a decided tendency to favour her younger brother. For certès, she would mend any fraying seams for him, probably provide him with new clothing, mayhap even a mantle. Though he would have to refrain from flirting with her maids – her spoiling of him did not go so far as turning a blind eye to that.

They stopped halfway to Oakley, sitting outside an alehouse to eat and rest, and even Adam brightened when it became apparent that the serving wench welcomed his advances. It was a merry group who arrived at Oakley some three hours later. However, as they clattered into the bailey, Isabella saw Maude standing amidst total chaos. Men and beasts milled around, coffers were being unloaded, maids and squires were scurrying hither and yon, and the general hubbub was nearly deafening. Maude rolled her eyes at their arrival and held up her hands exasperatedly as she moved towards them.

Giles dismounted, striding over to Maude who wore a frown instead of a smile of greeting. Isabella waited in vain for him to return and help her down. She could hear Maude's raised tones and Giles' annoyed response but could not make out what they were saying. Giles scowled in the direction of the manor and, kissing Maude, returned to his wife with drawn brows and a grim set to his mouth. Isabella lifted one delicate eyebrow in question; Giles' scowl grew blacker.

"We cannot stay. Maude's entire family have arrived unannounced. They are packed to the rafters; Maude is seething, and Ralph has managed to disappear himself."

Isabella felt the colour draining from her face. Twisting to speak to Giles as he remounted, she asked in tones as cold as death if that meant they would be going straight to court.

"No, sweeting, I will not take you there yet. Any time spent at court will feel overlong; I think neither of us would find pleasure in it. We'll try the abbey first. I would have had to pay my respects to Abbess Hildegarde while we were at Ralph's anyway, so we may as well seek lodging there. I know you wished to have Maude with us, but, in truth, I think you would not enjoy the company of her family. It's not something I've enjoyed myself, and even Maude would prefer for them not to be here. Her overbearing father and his cantankerous wife alone are enough to drive a man to the nearest alehouse. Add her brother and that stiff-necked wife of his, and that would be the furthest alehouse." He turned to see Adam coming towards him. "Adam, do you wish to spend time with your family? If so, I give you leave to remain."

The young man's horrified face raised a smile even from Isabella. "No, my lord, I do not. Enough that I pay them my duty visits; I do not wish to spend more time with them than necessary, I thank you."

Doubtless, his father's watch and that of his older brother would curtail his pleasures even more than Giles. And neither of the women were any pleasure to be with. Despite his irritation with the young man, Giles felt some sympathy with him. He nodded. His main concern now was for his wife, and at least, since Beatrice was not of their party, Bella would not have that to fret over.

As the group turned and left the manor behind them, he moved forward to ride beside Isabella. She turned a white face up to him, and he felt a surge of irritation. It had been so pleasant earlier; now, she had retreated back into her shell again. *Damn and blast.* He smiled into her worried face. "Don't fret, sweeting. I promise we shall not stay at court beyond a day and a half. Trust me to take a good care of you."

She nodded, her heart sinking. He would fully intend to keep his word, but she knew how it would go. Within the hour of their arrival, he would be jostled from her, and that snake, John, would doubtless soon find her to torment. She gritted her teeth into the semblance of a smile, took a deep breath and tried to find comfort in the fact that it would not be for long.

CHAPTER FOUR

Shannon started and looked up, alarmed, as a horse suddenly reined in beside her. *Stupid!* She should have been more aware of her surroundings. Too late to conceal herself and let them ride by; she'd have to brazen it out.

The rider was male, tall, well-built with a neat black beard, holding a small boy up in front of him, who waved a chubby fist. Behind him, a woman gazed at her in concern. Following were others – some of them might be knights, she thought, some other men, and a couple more women, which made her feel safer. Surely, with them there, she was in no danger. She swallowed nervously as the black-bearded man stared at her with an unreadable expression before saying, "Demoiselle, what do you here alone? May we assist you?"

Shannon was wary. Her ankle was painful and the abbey still far enough away to make her glad of help, but could she carry this off? Would they know she was odd as soon as she opened her mouth? Oh well, now was the time to find out. "My lord, my lady." She inclined her head in what she imagined to be a gracious manner. Better not try to curtsy, but maybe she could bob a bit. "My ankle. I turned it. I'm on my way to visit my aunt, the Abbess." That should sound reasonable. She crossed her fingers and hoped they wouldn't pursue the fact that she was unaccompanied. Maybe if she could squeeze out a tear, they would be so busy trying to help, they'd forget the rest. She pressed her eyelids together and, thankfully, found she could manage just enough moisture to wet her lashes.

The man on the large horse stared at her hard, almost as though he was searching for something. "Demoiselle, have we met before? You seem vaguely familiar to me."

"No, sir." She shook her head. It was hardly likely, was it?

He nodded, with a slightly puzzled expression, saying, "If you will allow, we can at least help you to the abbey." Then he turned to a younger man with chestnut hair shot through with hints of red, and luminous green eyes which twinkled at her now. "Adam, take the lady up behind you; she may travel with us."

Adam grinned. "It would be my great pleasure, Mistress."

Shannon looked at him doubtfully; she had no idea how to get up behind him. Her problem was solved when he called, "Eustace!" and a strapping lad dismounted and came over to her. Before she had time to realise what was happening, he grasped her around the waist, lifting her with more ease than she thought was possible, to sit behind Adam, who twisted in the saddle to slide an arm about her.

Casting her a glance that made her blush, he steadied her until she had her balance. Then, he released her, saying, "Hold tight, Mistress, we'll go slowly so you're not jolted."

Shannon, still flushed with embarrassment, sat bolt upright, not allowing herself to lean against his back. Should she hold him round the waist or not? The problem was solved when the horse started to move again. She felt herself slip and automatically looped her fingers around his belt, gripping tightly. He turned and gave her a flirtatious wink. She grinned back; she couldn't help it. Some things never changed, it seemed.

The woman rode up beside her. "Mistress, I am the Lady Isabella. We also are on our way to the abbey. I look forward to spending a little time with you whilst we are there, since you are kin to our dear Abbess. My husband will have much to do, and it will be pleasant to have your company, if you so wish."

Shannon nodded. Isabella eyed her with compassion. "Forgive me, you are in pain. We shall speak later." Smiling again, she moved her horse away and returned to her husband who inclined his head towards her as though in conversation.

The ride was not comfortable; Shannon's ankle stabbed with pain each time the horse jogged it, which was often, and her mind was going in circles. She'd expected not to have much need for speech until she had met Hildegarde and explained herself. This was not going according to plan. She needed to get her mind geared up to the twelfth century, and fast. First off, how did she address these people? 'My lord' and 'my lady' was perhaps safest. Isabella was friendly enough. What about Adam? What was he? She peeked at his heels – he was wearing spurs. Did that make him a knight? What about the older man? He appeared to be in charge. Maybe he was a baron or something. It had seemed so easy when she imagined how it would be, but it really wasn't. And she was here now, at least until she could get back to the tree.

Oh well, her prosaic nature kicked in. She'd wanted a change, and she'd certainly got one. She'd get by. *Oh, come on, Shannon,* she told herself. *It'll be fun. It's just a bit awkward to start with. On the plus side, you're making friends already.* She couldn't call herself Shannon, though; she'd better be Rohese from now on.

Hildegarde was sitting in silent contemplation. She loved the Whitsuntide rituals; they spoke to her so clearly of the coming of the Holy Spirit. The rites of this century were so much more evocative than those of her original time. Today, she was still feeling the rapture of the previous day, her heart swelling with private praise to the One she loved above all others.

When a soft tapping came at the door, she jumped, but her frown at the disturbance turned to a smile as Sister Prioress poked her head around the door followed by Giles de Soutenay. Her delight increased as his wife entered hesitantly behind him.

Rising to her feet, she held out both hands in greeting. "Sir Giles, Lady Isabella!" She moved towards them, ready words of welcome on her tongue. Before she could utter them, Giles spoke.

"My Lady Abbess, we crave your indulgence and also a chamber for a few days." Hildegarde opened her mouth again but, before she could say anything, Giles continued, "And, Abbess, we bring a surprise for you, for we encountered your niece on our journey."

Hildegarde stopped in her tracks. "My...?" She had seldom found herself speechless, but as she met the worried face of the young woman who was limping silently into the room, she trailed off in confusion.

"Aunt Hildegarde?" The girl gave her a look of desperate entreaty. Hildegarde read the unvoiced plea in her eyes and responded instinctively.

"Truly, Sir Giles, a surprise indeed. As you see, I am…quite lost for words." She took the young woman's hands in her own and led her to a padded settle in the window alcove.

"Sit you there, child, whilst I speak with Sir Giles and Lady Isabella." She gave her a repressive look. "We have much to catch up on." Hildegarde turned to the nun who hesitated by the door, as though she would like to be invited to linger. "Sister Prioress, my thanks. Pray, bid Sister Joan prepare a chamber for my niece, if you would be so kind."

Thus dismissed, the Prioress had no choice but to turn away, disappointment and frustration writ clear on her face.

Hildegarde turned to her guests once more. "Sir Giles, we have your chamber prepared, as always, and there is room aplenty in the guest-hall for your household. Allow me to escort you." She turned then, addressing the girl on the settle. "Stay you here, child; I shall return shortly."

Left alone, Shannon saw a small stool. She limped over, pulled it to the settle and sat down again, resting her injured foot on the stool, for it was hurting quite badly by now. She screwed up her face partly from the pain, partly from annoyance. Only she would have managed to damage herself before her time here had even started. She bet Chloe wouldn't have been so clumsy.

She stared about her, a cold dread replacing the thrill she had felt when she had woken a few hours earlier. This was a mistake; she couldn't cut it here. But here she was, and until she could get to the tree, here she must stay.

No! She wasn't going back. She *would* have her adventure. And her ankle would probably heal quickly. It wouldn't spoil things. She shook her head, determined. She wouldn't let it. She'd rest up for a couple of days which would give her time to suss the people out and get her act together.

Hildegarde, returning to her chamber, took one look at the whey-faced girl in front of her, and a dim light began to flicker in her brain along with an unwelcome idea, which she quickly dismissed – *ridiculous*! "And now, my child," she said gravely as she sat beside her on the settle, "perhaps we had better start at the beginning. Pray, tell me your name and who you are, for," she paused, "I have no niece."

"My name is Shannon, and you *are* my aunt – sort of." Hildegarde's face was expressionless; Shannon leaned towards her. "Well, we're related. My mother's name is Marion."

Hildegarde's jaw actually dropped as the name registered. "Ma...Marion?" she said faintly. Now, she knew why the face seemed familiar.

"Yes, and you *are* my aunt. You're my Grandma Ann's cousin."

"Child, that would make me your cousin, not an aunt, but that is immaterial. What are you *doing* here?"

"Mum was ill; she couldn't come. She asked me to deliver–"

"Shannon," Hildegarde cut in sharply, "did your mother ask you to deliver them in person? Truly?"

The girl blushed and fidgeted. "Er..."

"No, I thought not. In fact, I feel sure your mother gave you strict instructions *not* to come here."

Shannon's mouth turned down. If Hildegarde hadn't been so horrified, she would have found it comical. "So, child, what maggot came into your head? Why did you come? I doubt not you had your reasons, so, since you've named me your aunt, treat me as an aunt, and tell me all."

Shannon moved closer to Hildegarde and drooped, her head resting on her hands. "Oh, Auntie!"

Hildegarde, still slightly in shock, patted her shoulder, and Shannon started her tale. Hildegarde frowned in sympathy as she heard about Marion, and then, Shannon gave a gasp and a sob and poured out the rest of it, ending with, "So you see, I had to get away. I was so miserable, and everyone would have pitied me; I couldn't bear it."

As the tears poured down Shannon's cheeks, Hildegarde passed her a large kerchief saying with a smile, "I have brought a few inventions forward. I simply could not imagine life without these." Then she sat quietly, waiting for the storm to pass. Once the weeping had eased into a few sniffs, she spoke again. "But child, you cannot stay here; you must return. You know that."

"I know I can't stay long, but, oh, Auntie H, please, oh please, just let me stay a couple of weeks. Please."

Hildegarde steepled her hands and closed her eyes in thought, then, "Shannon, do you have any idea of the dangers?"

Shannon's lips compressed. "Not if I stay here with you, Auntie H, surely? And…and…I can't go back yet, I just can't." She narrowed her eyes, and a mutinous expression settled on her face. "I won't."

Hildegarde was stunned in the face of Shannon's intransigence. It had been thirty years and more since she had been in contact with modern young women, apart from the odd wanderer. She was, once again, lost for words. She gazed steadily into Shannon's eyes. Shannon glared back unrepentant, but slowly the mulish look dropped from her face.

"I'm sorry, Aunt Hildegarde. I was rude. But, please, let me stay. I won't go back, so please let me stay here."

Hildegarde couldn't resist her pleading. Besides, if Shannon would not return home, she could not be left to wander the countryside. A thought struck her. "Shannon, where does Marion think you are now?"

Shannon shifted in her seat, a flush starting from the depths of her wimple and rising to her veil. "Er, she thinks I'm in France with my friends."

"I see. And will she not be expecting to hear from you while you are away?" She hadn't thought the girl could be any more uncomfortable; now, Shannon was practically squirming.

"I told her she won't be able to contact me where we are."

"And do you not think that would worry her? I know of your allergy, Shannon."

"No. She thinks I'm with my friend, Dani. Mum trusts her. Dani knows exactly what to do if I get stung."

Hildegarde tapped her teeth with one fingernail. "Shannon, you did bring your injector, did you not?"

"Of course I did. And a spare. I never take any chances."

"Except for the fact that we cannot get you to hospital should you be stung here."

Shannon leaned forward, her face earnest. "Honestly, I know they always say get to a hospital, but the couple of times it's happened to me, my injector was enough. Hospital is only a precaution for me. And that was when I was a kid. I haven't been stung for years. You never know, I might have even grown out of it by now. Besides, it's only for a little while. How often have you been stung in your life? How about the nuns? Do they get stung often?"

She has me there, thought Hildegarde, *but wait.* "Shannon, were you aware we keep beehives here?"

For a moment, Shannon looked taken aback before rallying with, "Yes, but how often have you been stung?"

Hildegarde admitted defeat, and her lips curved into a reluctant smile. "I must confess, most of my nuns have never been stung, and neither have I. Very well; however, you must stay well away from the beehives. Do you have a portable phone thing such as your mother carried?"

Shannon nodded.

"Then, show me how to use it, and let us say that, if the worst happens, I inject you, get you back through the tree as fast as I can and phone for an ambulance."

Shannon's grin lit up the room. She got unsteadily to her feet and threw her arms about Hildegarde. "Oh, thank you, *thank you.* I'll behave, I promise. And see, here's my mobile. You can keep it with you." She rummaged in the pouch at her side, pulled out her mobile, turned it on and a cacophony of noise jangled out. Hildegarde jumped.

"Shannon, can we turn it down? I can explain many things to my nuns, but that…that appalling din may be beyond even my capabilities."

"Oops, sorry, yes." She put the phone in front of Hildegarde. "It won't work here, at least I don't think it will, so you can't practise. This is what you do."

Hildegarde studied the screen in front of her, trying to commit the instructions to memory. She just hoped it wouldn't be needed. "Very well, let me try. So, I press this, then this? Yes, I think I have it. Now, give it to me, and I shall keep it. If you get stung and I am not by you, send someone to find me urgently."

"Okay."

"And now, I think we need to provide you with a background. What have you told Sir Giles and Lady Isabella?"

"Nothing yet. I did do some research before I came, but I wanted to see what you said first. Look." Shannon rummaged in one of her bags and pulled out a crumpled piece of paper which she thrust at Hildegarde. "I printed this out from the internet." Ignoring Hildegarde's baffled expression, she continued, "Back in 1231, a group of princes

44

called the Bolohoveni fought as allies with the Hungarians. I think they came from near Romania and the Ukraine. Now, I know people in this time are familiar with East European countries but in everything I read, I never heard much about that area. I thought we could say my mother is ill; well, that will be true enough, anyway. And, if we live in Bolohovenia, it's so obscure, no one will have heard of it, will they? Have you ever heard of it?"

Hildegarde felt another reluctant smile tug at her lips. Shannon had certainly been thorough. "I must confess, I have not. And, like you, I have never come across anyone who has been in that region. That was clever of you, Shannon. And we can use it to account for anything which may seem strange about you, any odd turns of phrase or any slips you may make." She nodded, satisfied. "Yes, I think it will do. We do have one other problem though."

Shannon cocked her head. "Yes, I know. Isabella didn't say anything, but I think she was wondering why I'm travelling alone. She's going to ask. I'm sure she is. What can I say? I didn't expect to meet anyone before I got to the abbey."

"Foolish child, how did you think you would explain your arrival to my porteress and prioress?"

Shannon looked rather sheepish.

"You didn't think, did you?"

"No. Sorry, I was so excited, and I thought I had everything covered. I forgot that bit." She fiddled with her veil, her eyes distant. "I know, how about, isn't there an outbreak of spotted fever at the moment? Couldn't I say my escort went down with that?"

"You have done your homework, haven't you?" Hildegarde had to admire her; she hadn't missed much of the minutiae. Even her clothing appeared pretty much correct. "In fact, our last outbreak of that locally was last year. Please God, there won't be another." She thought for a moment before asking wryly, "And just where will you say you left your escort? Have you, metaphorically speaking, left their dying bodies strewn across the shire?"

"Well, perhaps I could say I've come on a pilgrimage? Maybe they escorted me to the fringes of the village then followed my instructions to leave me?"

"It's a little thin, Shannon. Perhaps you could combine both stories. You know," she leaned her chin on her hand meditatively, "when I became a nun, I had hoped to be always only speaking the truth. Your mother has already pushed my construction of 'truth' to its limits. I would prefer you to think up this story on your own if you are able."

"Sure." She seemed dubious though. "But you'll tell me if it won't work, won't you?"

"Of course." Hildegarde patted her hand. "Continue. You're doing well so far. We will hope you don't have to explain yourself to more than

Lady Isabella. For certès, arriving with them means you haven't aroused the curiosity of my nuns." She paused, remembering her prioress hovering like some stray cat in search of a dish of cream. "Well, only by the way you blithely announced I was your aunt. Ah well, that is one obstacle which is easily overcome, and we may be able to turn it to our advantage. It certainly gives you a reason for visiting. Why shall you say your mother sent you, though?"

"To ask for your prayers and your care of me whilst she's sick," Shannon said promptly.

"And what of your father and your household? Could they not have cared for you?"

"Oh no. They're all sick with spotted fever. My parents were so afraid I might catch it."

"So they sent you here, where we also have spotted fever?"

"Oh, not like it is in Bolohovenia! It's as bad as the plague over there, you know. Why, nothing else is heard of the Bolohovenians after the thirteenth century. It's so bad over there, it must have killed everyone off by then."

She had an answer for everything, Hildegarde had to give her that.

"And that's why I'm on a pilgrimage, you see. For my whole family. And it's why I needed to be sent to the care of my aunt. I'll try to avoid going into detail to Isabella; I'm very good at being evasive."

"So you are." And very determined. Hildegarde bowed to the inevitable. Shannon was here, and here she would stay – at least until she could be convinced to go home. She hid a smile. Shannon might find the twelfth century was not so much fun as she imagined. She could help with that, she thought. An abbey wasn't the most exciting place for a teenager from the twenty-first century.

"Auntie H, may I ask you a question?"

Hildegarde wore an expression which might have been pained but for the tell-tale quiver at the corners of her mouth. "Shannon, much as I enjoy the novelty of being called Auntie H, I think it would be more seemly for you to refer to me as Aunt Hildegarde or merely Abbess. If you should be overheard addressing me as aught else, I'm afraid it would rather, er…"

"Blow my cover?"

"Quite. And by the same token, I think it better that I call you Rohese. Or was it Eleanor? Those were the names your mother used when she was here. If we use the same names in private, we will not err in public."

"Rohese. Chloe was Eleanor. We used to play at being medieval when we were kids. Mum told you? How clever of you to remember." Shannon grinned brightly. "Okay." Hildegarde winced, and Shannon clapped her hand to her mouth. "Oops, I mean of course, Aunt Hildegarde."

"It's harder to stay in character than you realised, my child, is it not? Vital though, if you are to pass unnoticed. If you slip, you put yourself and all connected with you in grave danger. Please, do not underestimate the risks; this may seem like a game to you, but, in truth, it's a perilous one."

"Oka…I mean, yes, Aunt, I'll do my best."

"See that you do." Hildegarde relaxed the stern set of her mouth, and her lips twitched into a warm smile. "I confess, despite the difficulties of having you here, the pleasure of being with kin is something I never expected to enjoy again. I know not how short our time together will be; however, since I cannot remove you, I intend to enjoy your company for as long as you remain. Truly, I never expected to see any of my family again. Now, what was it you wanted to ask me?"

"Auntie…I mean Aunt, why did you become a nun? I mean, you weren't going to be one in our time, were you?"

Hildegarde steepled her hands together and closed her eyes for a moment. "In truth, it was not my intention, but consider the options open to me here. I arrived from nowhere, with no family, no background, no protector and no means of providing for myself. I did not fit into any of the classes here. With no history, it would have been impossible to find acceptance.

"Sister Ursel saw me arrive. Bless her, she coped admirably, for my wits were wandering so much, I would have blundered my way straight into peril. She took me to Abbess Bertrille."

She paused again, as if the memories had overwhelmed her. "Two wonderfully adaptive women. They shielded me, helped me fit in, as it were. At first, I was just grateful to be safe, wished only to return to my own time, then, something strange happened." She laughed. "Stranger even than falling into another time, I mean." Hildegarde looked at her hands, then at Shannon. Shannon gazed back intently.

"Gradually, and quite unexpectedly, I found I had developed a relationship not just with the other sisters but with God."

"You could have kept that even if you'd gone home, couldn't you?"

"I could, of course, but that relationship became so sweet, so intense, I found it didn't matter to me to return. Then, too, I began to understand the good I could do serving Him here. And almost without my noticing, the abbey became my home; the sisters truly became my sisters, and I knew that, unless God called me to return home, I would remain here."

"All that prayer, though! I mean, there's loads of it, isn't there? Don't you get bored?"

Not really such a surprising question, Hildegarde mused, though for her, the answer was as simple as breathing. She continued, "At its essence, prayer is simply talking to God as though He is your friend. Yes, as Creator, but as infinitely more than that. In finding Him, I found a safe place for my heart to dwell."

50

Shannon sat spellbound, for, as Hildegarde spoke, her words resonated with what felt like a supernatural power, and the peace of the abbey took on an intensity which was almost physical. Despite the austerity of her habit, an inner radiance shone from her.

At last, Shannon found her voice. "Didn't you miss Gran, though? She told Mum she was so upset when you disappeared. Didn't you ever want to see her again?"

"Oh, Rohese, of *course* I missed her. But she had your grandfather, your uncle, your mother. I had no close family other than her, and the longer I was here, the more that century faded. I could have a ministry here. I was happy. I missed Ann, but it was impossible to have both her and my life here. We can rarely have everything we want. We all have to make choices; this was mine.

"And now, child, you had better show me what you have brought with you to wear, and we'll make sure you will pass scrutiny."

Shannon was complacent. "Oh, I will. I bought stuff from a re-enactment society. I even got the right shoes. They cost me a fortune," she said virtuously, thrusting one foot out from beneath her gown, showing a tan leather shoe, tied at the ankle.

"I am impressed. And what of your other garments?"

"Well, this is what Mum bought for a medieval banquet. She wore it when she was here last." She indicated the deep red bliaut and the dark grey undergown she was wearing beneath her russet travelling cloak, then tugged at her veil and wimple. "I don't know about this though. Do I really need to wear one? I couldn't find anything definite about when they came in."

"Indeed not; you are unwed and young enough that you may wear just a veil with a circlet or braid to secure it, and I would suggest one in a lighter fabric than that. I think you were wise though, to wear the wimple for travelling, alone as you were. The more respectable you appear, the safer."

"I have another veil." Shannon's face fell as she untied her shoe and saw the state of her spare veil. "At least, I thought I had. I fell and twisted my ankle and used it for a bandage."

"Ah yes, I noticed you limping. Well, that veil won't do either, I'm afraid. We'll settle you in a chamber shortly and have Sister Ursel or Sister Etheldreda take a look at you." She knelt and expertly examined Shannon's foot. Shannon winced. "I'm sorry, I'm being as gentle as I can, but I need to check there are no bones broken. Bear with me a moment longer."

Shannon caught her lower lip between her teeth as Hildegarde probed again with her long, slender fingers then sat back on her heels. "No, just a bad sprain; it will be painful for a few days yet, I'm afraid, but it could have been worse. You did a good job with that bandage.

"Now," Hildegarde got to her feet and lifted Shannon's bags onto her desk, "what do we have here?" She pulled out a yellow gown and unfolded it, spreading it across the wood. "Very nice; you won't be wearing it with that grey undergown, will you?"

"No, I have a pale mauve one here for beneath that, and a plain white shift for spare. And see!" She rummaged in the same bag and pulled out two more gowns, one of fine linen in a shade of deep rose with a pale pink undergown and, less suitably, a peacock-blue silk gown, with orange embroidery and glass beads stitched onto it, which she laid down carefully before shaking out an orange undergown. "It's not a combo I'd wear at home, but they like bright colours here, don't they?"

Hildegarde looked dubious. "Sha...I mean Rohese, my dear, I'm afraid this is too fine if you wish to avoid making yourself the subject of speculation. We want people to know you are well bred; however, to appear too nobly born or wealthy might attract more attention than would be wise. Now, I know you are disappointed, but this is more of a court gown."

Shannon's mouth took on that stubborn pout which Hildegarde had noticed earlier. Then she sighed, resignedly. "I suppose. It cost me so much though. Maybe I can wear it at one of the re-enactment things when I get home or to a medieval banquet or something."

Hildegarde took pity on her. "Ah well, as you are my 'niece', I suppose I might be expected to indulge you a little. Would it cheer you if I were to procure you something in a more suitable fabric? We can stitch it together. I'm sure some of my nimble-fingered sisters would enjoy helping you. It will make a change from embroidering altar cloths."

The mobile mouth quirked back up. *Not a face suitable for playing poker,* Hildegarde thought. *I hope she can cover her feelings better than that when she is not with me.* "Now," she continued, holding up a pair of briefs, "I'm afraid these really will not do – but you knew that, didn't you?" *Doubtless she didn't expect me to go through her bags. A good job I did, though.*

"But...but–"

Hildegarde shook her head. "According to the history books I read, women of this era do not wear undergarments such as knickers." Shannon opened her mouth to protest. Hildegarde forestalled her, holding up her hand for silence. "Do not be so hasty child, allow me to continue. History, in my opinion, came to that conclusion because so few items of underclothing from this period have survived. I have found some women do wear a form of undergarment, although not all, and it's said men frown upon it." She smiled. "In my situation, I am not able to be entirely sure about this; certainly, we wear something when our menses are upon us. So, you may not wear the undergarments you have brought with you, for they may be discovered when you change or bathe. I will find you something more suitable."

Turning her attention to the bag again, she pulled out a pair of shoes made from pale, soft pigskin decorated with embroidery with buckled straps to fasten them across the instep. "Now, these are very nice. You may wear them so long as it does not rain. This is the first period of good weather we have enjoyed since Saint Guthlac's Day. I truly thought the relentless downpour would never cease. Happily, the ground has mostly dried now; we may even manage a better harvest than expected. By the saints, we need it." She sighed. "We've done our best to help ease the deprivations of the last few years, but even our storehouse is not endless."

Shannon nodded. "I read about that, and I thought, since I can't pay you for my keep, I could bring something useful." She reached for the other bag and, with the air of a conjuror, pulled out two small sacks. "Here! There's some meds in there I thought you could use, and these. One of lentils and one of split peas. I bought as many as I could carry. I didn't think you'd want them left in plastic bags though." She grinned.

"Rohese, my dear, how thoughtful. We can certainly put these to good use."

"I just wish I could have brought more; that was all I could manage, but they go a long way, don't they? Mum makes loads of soup from just a small pack."

"They certainly do go a long way. You chose wisely. They're a most acceptable gift, thank you, my dear. And now, I suggest we put all your garments back into your bag and allow you to rest." She twitched the other bag out of Shannon's reach. "I will look through this later. I suspect Sister Joan will be knocking on my door at any moment to tell you she has prepared you a chamber. As my niece, you'll be allotted a small room to yourself, so at least you won't be sharing one of the guest-halls – and that will be a great relief to both of us. It means you'll not have to be on your guard all the time."

Shannon reached across the table and made a grab at the bag Hildegarde had moved. "I need the stuff in there. I won't unpack it; I'll keep it hidden, but it's my *stuff.*" She held it tightly. "I'll make sure no one sees it."

At that moment, there was a tap on the door, and a dumpy little nun poked her head in. Hildegarde gave up temporarily. Rohese needn't think she had won though.

CHAPTER FIVE

Hildegarde left Shannon – no, she must think of her as Rohese, if her tongue was not to betray her – safely bestowed in a small room in the guest-house with her injured foot and ankle being tended and strapped by Etheldreda. Giving strict instructions for Rohese not to even attempt to cross the threshold but to wait until Hildegarde could return, the Abbess sent Sister Matilda to find Sister Ursel and returned to her own chamber, grateful the position of Abbess afforded her some privacy. At this moment, she longed for nothing more than to cast off her veil and wimple and thrust her fingers through her cropped hair to massage away the tension in her scalp. Ursel would bring her an infusion of willow bark and some lavender unguent for her temples.

She picked through the bag she had confiscated from Rohese. *That girl!* For all she knew her twelfth century history far better than had her mother, she lacked Marion's native caution. Marion had known to think before she spoke, had known the items she carried were best kept hidden; Hildegarde had no such confidence in Rohese. If Marion had known she would end up here, Hildegarde believed she would not have taken the risks Rohese had.

She pulled the items from the bag. Soap, deodorant, a spray can, no less! Face cream, a tube of lip balm, toothbrush, toothpaste, – really! These things Marion would either have known to accept substitutes for or acknowledge she must go without. Not Rohese. Prising her possessions from her had been a battle, and as for this…this phone thing! What had Rohese called it? A mobile? She turned it over in her hand, accidentally pressing something, and dropped it as it lit up and that awful racket jangled from it again.

Fumbling urgently, she tried to find whatever it was she had pressed before. Ah, a small catch on the side. The phone turned itself off with another jangle of 'music' which grated on her raw nerves.

Hildegarde was thankful she'd left instructions not to be disturbed by anyone other than Ursel; thankful also for the thick stone walls and solid oak door which, she hoped, had muffled that dreadful cacophony. She picked the mobile up gingerly, being careful not to touch the side again, and, stowing it in a casket along with the other possessions she had culled from the protesting Rohese, she continued to look through the bag. Bottles of paracetamol, ibuprofen and aspirin. *Oh!*

Hildegarde felt no compunction about helping herself to the aspirin. Since Rohese had given her a headache the like of which she hadn't had in years, it seemed fitting she should also provide the cure. She swallowed them with a small sip of well-water from the flagon on her desk.

Now, what else had that foolish girl brought with her apart from her adrenaline pen, which she would need to keep hidden about her person? At least Hildegarde had approved of the small pouch Rohese had made and strapped to her leg so she could reach it quickly in case of need.

Continuing to sift through what appeared to be half the contents of a chemist shop, she smiled. The girl had a good heart. They had herbal substitutes for many of these but by no means all, and it was kind of her to bring things she thought would be useful. And then, Hildegarde breathed a sigh of relief; Marion had not forgotten the tea. A cup of tea and an aspirin – the two things she craved most and expected least.

She tumbled the other things into the casket and locked it with one of the keys which hung from a chain on the belt she wore. Then, she put the casket into a coffer and locked that. Later, she could hide them securely in the secret cell, the door to which was now concealed behind a wall hanging, but they would be safe enough here for the present.

Knuckling her aching eyes and rubbing her forehead, she left her chamber with a twist of tea-leaves in a scrap of linen, locking the door behind her. She made her way to the kitchens, where her sudden appearance so startled the sisters there that one of the novices dropped a dish which shattered loudly as it hit the stone flags, making Hildegarde wince.

She gave the flustered sisters a warm smile and knelt to help them pick up the broken pieces, despite their protestations. "For it was my fault for alarming Sister Euphemia so." Then, she asked if she might have a cup of freshly boiled water and a little milk.

They bustled and clucked around her, delighted to serve, exclaiming at her wan face and generally behaving like a coop of hens with all their anxious fussing, which only served to further increase the throb in her temples. At last, the cup of water was handed to her, and she tipped a small amount of milk into it along with the surreptitiously added tea-leaves.

Hildegarde left the kitchens thankfully, unable to bear their fluttering for another second. She groped her way back, half blinded with pain by now, and sank onto the settle, watching the liquid take on the colour and fragrance she loved so much. Then, closing her eyes, she sipped thankfully at the scalding brew. A shame it could not be strained, but the sediment had mostly settled in the bottom of the cup anyway.

The tea was heavenly. Drinking it slowly, savouring the flavour, she felt the tension leave her scalp.

Resisting the temptation to drain it to the dregs, she opened her eyes and placed the cup carefully on the floor then, leaning her head against the wall hanging, shut her eyes again and waited for the pain to recede, drifting into a light doze.

A tap on the door made her jerk sharply to wakefulness as Sister Ursel's wrinkled, rosy face appeared, hazel eyes watching her with concern. She tendered her nostrum to Hildegarde who shook her head. "It seems my young visitor has a satchel full of remedies from her own time. My headache is easing, Sister, dear. My thanks anyway."

Ursel picked up the discarded cup of tea and sniffed at the remaining liquid. "An enterprising young lady, your niece, Mother." Her old eyes twinkled shrewdly. "But then, she isn't your niece, is she? Would I be wrong in thinking she is Marion's daughter? There is a certain likeness." Hildegarde's eyes widened. "Fear not, my lady, that chattering tongue of hers has not given her away." She paused. "Yet! I left her in her chamber with Etheldreda to guard her; although, Lady Isabella seems determined to while away some time with her. They are of an age, I think, and the lass seems in need of friends."

"Isabella is a little older. Rohese – her real name is Shannon, by the way – although she has wider knowledge than the young women of our time, seems much more of a child. In her time, young women are a law unto themselves. They are also taught to believe they can do anything they set their minds to.

"When I was of their world, Ursel, I thought it to be a good thing; here, it becomes less of a blessing, for her behaviour makes her seem little more than a spoilt child. It's strange, for I felt Marion worried less about this chick than her older one. I had the impression Rohese was the sensible one."

Ursel nodded. "Ah, but she's been betrayed by someone dear to her, I suspect. There's nothing like a humiliation to put a stumbling block in the way of the most sensible girl. And, mayhap, her wits flew out of the door when disappointment flew in. The two together may cause the most unlikely of lasses to commit indiscretions."

Hildegarde patted the hand that reached for her own. "You're very wise, Sister. What should I ever do without you?"

Ursel grimaced. "Tush! You'd manage. Happen you'll have to soon enough. I'm getting no younger, as these aching bones remind me often."

Hildegarde was immediately contrite. Ursel, interpreting her dipped head correctly, said with some asperity, "And don't you be looking like that, my lady; it's not the walking, for I can still manage that well enough."

Hildegarde regarded Ursel, her expression rueful. "Yes, indeed, but the constant standing and kneeling when we are at worship does you no good, Sister. I have seen your pain, which is why I gave you dispensation to be seated, though still you refuse to refrain. I think you are as wilful as our young visitor. In future, I do not merely give you dispensation – I command you to seat yourself during worship, and I forbid you to kneel."

Ursel opened her mouth to protest. Hildegarde forestalled her. "No, Sister Ursel, I will hear no more on this matter. If you do not wish to cripple yourself, you will do as I say."

A martial light flared briefly in Ursel's eyes, but the obedience of a lifetime won. She bowed her head, murmuring, "Yes, Mother Abbess."

Hildegarde smiled. "It's for your own good, Sister, and for the good of our house, for we still have great need of you."

Ursel said nothing; the sniff she gave conveyed volumes.

Hildegarde got to her feet. "I suppose I had best get back to this 'niece' of mine. I had thought to insist she accompanies me to Divine Office as often as is possible. That will keep her out of mischief. Unfortunately, I suspect she requires far more instruction than our youngest novice if she is not to instantly give rise to suspicion. Now, is Magda in the laundry today?"

Ursel nodded. Most of the work here was done by the nuns and lay brethren, but villagers were also employed. Some worked the fields, some were tenant farmers for the abbey, and some worked in other areas. Magda, the abbey laundress, was a bustling woman of middle age with a stout frame and brawny arms. Hildegarde found her a most useful person. She had a sensible attitude, and, more importantly, Hildegarde judged her able to keep a still tongue. She did not gossip. Abbey business did not get bandied about the village by Magda.

"Then, I must speak with her. I must get the girl a few items and some fabric. Magda can procure what I need. Rohese will need a couple of lengths of silk for veils. I may purchase one length of fine linen for her also." As Ursel raised her brows, Hildegarde sighed softly. "I know, Sister; however, I find I am unable to resist her the small indulgence of silk. For two veils, such a little amount would be needed, and I've not had the chance to be an aunt for many a year. It's certain, too, I never shall again. I fear I am also indulging myself." She gave Ursel an almost pleading look. Ursel smiled and patted her hand.

"And I'm afraid, dear Ursel, the coins used in her time would not be recognised here, so she cannot pay for her keep either; however, she has brought us some food and medical supplies, so we shall call that recompense. Now, what think you? Shall some of our sisters enjoy helping her to stitch?"

Ursel laughed. "Mother Abbess, I think there will be a glut of helpers. It's a long time since any of them have dealt with anything fancy other than altar cloths and embroidery. Most will enjoy a vicarious pleasure in clothing your niece. Indeed, you may struggle to control their excitement."

"Well and good then. As for that wimple she wears!" She threw her hands up. "It is an unnecessary restriction for an unmarried young woman, barring our sisters, of course. To be honest," she paused, giving Ursel a speculative glance, "I strongly suspect the Queen's attachment to her own wimples increased as age began to catch up with her. She was a great beauty, so I understand, and it must be hard to watch yourself fade into old age." She laughed. "That's one problem we do not have to concern ourselves with, Sister. Never having been a beauty myself, even if I were not a nun, a wimple more or less would make no difference."

Ursel merely gazed at her, a muscle twitching in her jaw the only indication she was swallowing a grin. Mother Abbess had no idea that the serene lines of her face coupled with that aristocratic nose and high cheekbones gave her an austere beauty all her own. The light shining from those untroubled grey eyes only enhanced the overall effect. At times, she appeared almost saintly.

Hildegarde bent to pick up Shannon's bag, but suddenly jerked upright, one hand flying to her mouth. Ursel looked at her quizzically. "Mother Abbess?"

"Oh, Ursel, in all the confusion of Rohese's arrival, I forgot something of great import. You'll excuse me, Sister. I have need to speak to her most urgently. Pray send Magda to me here; I shall return shortly."

Leaving Ursel, Hildegarde's feet almost flew through the cloisters. Rohese had arrived with Giles and Isabella. Marion had told her of their relationship, but had she explained that Giles was also an ancestor? This visit was testing all her inner resources.

CHAPTER SIX

As Sister Etheldreda tutted over her ankle, removing the veil with which Shannon had bound it, anointing it with salve and binding it again, Shannon was thinking. What had Hildegarde called Isabella's husband?

"Is that too tight, Mistress?" Etheldreda looked up from her kneeling position, disturbing her thoughts.

"No, that's fine, thank you."

The nun's forehead crinkled. "Fine?"

"Sorry, I mean comfortable. Fine is something we say in Bolohovenia."

"Is it far away, this Bolohovenia?"

"Many, many miles."

"And yet, apart from a few strange words, you speak as we do. You have no accent." The nun must have suddenly realised she was showing an unseemly curiosity for she dipped her head. "I'm sorry, my lady, it's none of my business."

"That's true."

Etheldreda looked mortified; Shannon hastily corrected herself. "Oh, not that, I don't mind you asking. Sorry. I meant that I have no accent." What was she speaking now? She had no idea, still she must be doing it right or no one would have understood her. How weird; she felt as though she was speaking English, just with some odd turns of phrase. Mum had said the same thing. Your language must adjust when you go through the tree.

Etheldreda was standing now, gazing at her with undisguised curiosity. Shannon met her eyes, and she flushed. "Forgive me, Mistress, for a moment you appeared familiar to me."

Shannon coughed to hide her confusion, and Etheldreda turned her attention to the bag.

"Do you wish me to help you?"

"Please."

The nun unpacked her bag, shaking the creases from Shannon's gowns, smoothing them and hanging them on poles in the corner of the room. "Mistress, I'll leave you to rest now." She bobbed her head and turned, closing the door behind her, and Shannon was left to her own thoughts.

At first, she passed the time by studying her surroundings. The novelty soon wore off though, and she found herself longing for her mobile, her music, or at least something to read.

She put experimental pressure on her ankle. It hurt, but she could bear it, so she stood up, leaning heavily on the stick she had brought with her, and hobbled to one of the narrow windows which looked out onto a garden and a boundary wall. The glass, if it *was* glass, was distorted and so thick in places as to be almost opaque but, leaning against the stone sill for support, she could just make out a small pond with some ducks going about their business.

Their antics amused her at first, though they palled after a while and her ankle started aching again, so she limped back to her chair and propped her foot on a low stool. Of all the things she'd expected, boredom was not on the list. If only there was something to do.

Just as she was beginning to feel the urge to scream, shout, sing – anything to break the tedium, the door opened and Hildegarde entered, followed by another nun bearing a flagon and cups.

Shannon's eyes lit up. *Thank goodness!* The nun put the flagon down on the small table next to Shannon's chair then, as Shannon thanked her, raised her eyes shyly, smiled and left the room. Hildegarde pulled up another stool and sat, pouring Shannon a cup of wine from the flagon.

"It's watered, Rohese. I suspect you aren't used to much alcohol at this time of day."

Well, she'd had one or two moments, but overindulgence here would not really be wise. Besides, she hated hangovers. A few heavy sessions had more or less cured her of that.

"Child, how does your ankle now?"

She grimaced, feeling anew the throb as she considered. Thinking about it made it worse.

"It aches, though it feels better than it did. I don't notice it so much when I'm talking, but oh, Auntie H…I mean Aunt, I'm so bored."

Hildegarde looked sympathetic, but Shannon felt as though she was trying to hide amusement.

"Poor Rohese. It's not quite as you expected, is it?"

"You can say that again. I thought it would be a bit more fun."

"My dear, this is an abbey. What did you expect to find? Here, though the rule is more relaxed than many, we are still nuns; we go to Divine Service throughout the day."

"Yes, but aren't there supposed to be games and stuff going on over Whitsun? That's what it said on the internet."

"There are, it's true; not here in the abbey, though. The games are all in the village. We do not have them here, and even if it were our custom to attend them, you would find it uncomfortable to travel."

Shannon's face fell. "I hadn't expected that to happen, had I? Trust me to hurt my ankle and get stuck in my room." She put her head on one side with a winsome smile. "Aunt, couldn't I have my mobile back, please? I could listen to the music with my earbuds, or at least, I could read." *While the battery lasts,* she thought. *And I'd better not tell Auntie that, or she'll stress. I expect she thinks it has the sort of batteries that can be changed. She's probably assumed I have spares somewhere.*

Hildegarde was astonished. "Music? Read? You can do all this on your phone?"

"Yeah, it's pretty cool when you think about it, isn't it?"

"Very, er, cool. Though how would you explain it away if someone should enter your chamber unexpectedly?"

"I could hide it in my lap. Or I could put my head under the sheets, so if they saw me, they'd think I was asleep."

Shannon was sounding a little desperate; Hildegarde felt for her but couldn't take the risk.

"I could say–"

"No, Rohese, you could not. I'm sorry, I know you're bored. After we have eaten, the sisters take their midday rest period and then recreation. During that time, I will help you walk to the gardens, where you may sit awhile."

"Could I borrow a book?"

"You could; however, I'm afraid, even if you could read it, which I think is improbable, we have nothing which would appeal to you."

"But you have illuminated books, don't you? I could just look at the pictures; it would be something to do."

The desperation in her voice was becoming more strident, and Hildegarde capitulated. "Very well, later. For now, be still, my dear, and listen, for I have things I need to ask you."

She took a sip from her own cup then raised her head. "Rohese, what did your mother tell you about the time she spent with us? I need to know what you know."

"She told me she'd helped save Prince John's life." Shannon's eyes grew wide. "I thought she'd gone crazy."

"As indeed you might," Hildegarde murmured.

"He was really lucky though. I mean, sometimes the epinephrine just buys time to get to hospital. Anyway, he saw her, and she had a really bad time getting away. And then this Sir Giles–" She broke off, hand to her mouth.

"Yes, Rohese, this Sir Giles is the same one who pursued your mother."

"Wow! She said Prince John threatened him if he didn't get more epinephrine, so to save his life, she promised to get him a couple every year. And that's why I came," she said, nodding virtuously. "I didn't want to let Mum and Sir Giles down."

"Do not look so innocent, Rohese; I think I have already discussed the fact that your visit was not for his sake but your own."

Shannon flushed deep crimson, and Hildegarde patted her hand. "Never mind, child; what's done is done, and, I confess, it brings me great pleasure to get to know you."

Pleasure yes, but Hildegarde's trepidation, she felt, was not without reason. Shannon was not Marion; she possessed far less innate caution.

"And now, we come to the crux of the matter. Did your mother tell you Sir Giles is your ancestor?"

Shannon nodded. "Yes, she did. I can't wait to tell him. I wonder what–"

Hildegarde's blood ran cold as she interrupted. "Rohese, you may not tell him. I forbid it absolutely."

"Forbid? Why?" Again, her mouth took on that mulish pout Hildegarde was beginning to dread. She straightened her spine, compressed her lips and prepared to do battle, but Shannon shrugged and said, "Oh well, I suppose it's safer. The more who know, the more likely it is they'll let something slip accidentally. It seems a shame for us never to meet as relatives, though."

Hildegarde said a silent prayer of thanks. "Now my dear, I have brought your ibuprofen and paracetamol, but you will be drinking wine or ale often during the day, so save them until tonight. I think you'll find you'll be more aware of your ankle then, and they will help you sleep." She drew out a small box made of leather with a painted lid.

Shannon looked enchanted. "Oh, isn't that pretty? Thank you."

"Now, dinner is shortly to be eaten. Normally, I would dine with you privately in my chambers or in the guest-refectory–"

Before she could finish speaking, Shannon's eyes lit up. "Oh, I don't mind where we dine. I just want to get out of this room."

Hildegarde held up her hand for silence, and Shannon checked herself. *Dear Lord, this child is so impatient. Please grant me the tact to deal with her.*

"Please, child, let me continue. I was going to say, but today, we feast. I must eat with my daughter nuns in the frater; it will be expected of me. Will you dine in our guest-refectory or would you rather eat here?" *Lord, is it too much to ask that she will decide to remain here?*

Shannon hesitated. Hildegarde was about to relax when she said, "Well, I guess I have to learn to mix with people sometime." She grinned, and the Abbess felt her heart sink. "It may as well be today. If I get it wrong, we can just tell people there are different customs in Bolohovenia. Is it far to the refectory? Will I be able to hobble there? Where's my stick?"

Hildegarde knew when she was beaten. She picked up Shannon's stick and looked at it critically. "I'm sure we can find you something better than this but, for today, it will suffice. Now, prepare your mind. You are not Shannon; you are

Rohese. Try for a little more composure and try," *oh, please let her remember,* "try not to speak too much today. Listen and learn. I have brought you knife and spoon. Attach them to your girdle, so."

"Oka...yes, Aunt." Shannon eased herself up and leaned heavily on her stick. Hildegarde took her other arm, and she hobbled, wincing a little, to the door.

"Are you sure you can manage? We don't want to damage that ankle further."

"Yes, Aunt."

"Very well. Come then."

CHAPTER SEVEN

As they entered the refectory, Shannon gazed around her. There were rather more people than she'd expected. She hadn't really considered eating here, thinking she'd be permitted to eat with the nuns. How would she manage alone? The idea was daunting, and Shannon was considering whether she should return to her room after all when a short, rotund monk caught sight of Hildegarde and came to greet her. "Abbess." He bowed his head, then noticed Shannon, and his eyes widened.

"My niece. She is paying a most unexpected visit from Bolohovenia. Rohese, this is Father Dominic, our confessor."

Father Dominic may have been a priest, but he was clearly not averse to the opposite sex. He gave Shannon a courtly bow. "Demoiselle Rohese, the pleasure is all mine. Abbess, I know you will be eating in the frater; perhaps you will allow me to accompany your niece at the table?"

Shannon looked questioningly at Hildegarde; there was no choice but to accept, and Hildegarde bestowed a gracious smile on the priest.

"Father, Rohese is yet to become familiar with our ways, so I trust you'll be patient with her and bear with her prattle. I'm afraid she has also damaged her ankle, so haply you would be kind enough to assist her to a bench." She transferred Shannon's arm to him, as she spoke. "I leave her in your good hands."

Turning to Shannon, she dropped a kiss on her forehead, murmuring "Rohese, do try to remember what I told you." She lingered hesitantly for a moment before walking away, pausing again briefly at the door to turn back with a worried frown.

Shannon was on her own. She gripped the head of her stick, stomach tight with nerves as she waited for the priest to speak, then noticed, with relief, the twinkle in his eyes. "So, Demoiselle, I have you all to myself. I also have travelled somewhat but not, I regret to, er, where did you come from? You must tell me all about it." He appeared rather proud of himself. "I enjoy so much to hear of foreign realms and customs."

They were still standing, and at this point, Shannon wobbled slightly which recalled him to his duties, for he said, "My dear, your ankle is paining you?" She nodded pathetically – better to look pathetic; sympathy might be helpful – and he shepherded her across to the table at the top of the room, pulling out a bench and settling her, fussing like an old woman. Other people who looked to be poorer than Giles and his household were seated further down the hall.

She discovered that to be the little priest's dining partner meant sharing a trencher and cup with him. It also meant him cutting up meat for her and selecting morsels from the serving platter. And how he talked! Thankfully, that meant she didn't have to say much.

It seemed he was inordinately proud of his travels and pilgrimages, and, rather than hear about Bolohovenia and its customs, he was evidently delighted to expound every detail of every trip he had ever taken.

As the main courses were removed and honeyed fruits and custards brought in, he finally paused for breath, wiping his mouth on a linen napkin and dabbling his fingers in the bowl of scented water, before passing it to Shannon. "And now, my dear, you must tell me all about your own land. I confess, I had no idea our good Abbess had any relatives at all, let alone a niece."

"I'm not exactly a niece, I suppose. More of a distant cousin; my family always speak of Cousin Hildegarde as our aunt, though." She dipped her head in what she hoped was a demure manner.

"But you'll be bored with my life soon enough. Please, Father, do continue your own tales; they are *so* fascinating."

Father Dominic was not proof against the invitation to talk some more. Shannon barely had to speak for the rest of the meal to her great relief. At last, the dishes were all taken away, and he got up, stretching his short arms luxuriously. "Well, well, my dear, it has been most pleasant; however, I must leave you now. Duties to attend to, you know." As he strutted away, Shannon started to give a huge sigh, then remembered where she was and caught herself up short, jumping as a hand touched her arm and a pair of sparkling eyes looked down at her.

"Lady Rohese, did you enjoy your speech with good Father Dominic?" Isabella's muted laugh showed she was very well aware of how tedious the little priest could be.

"Oh, um, he's very kind, but, er…"

"I know; I met him earlier. How does your ankle now? Giles has business to attend," for a moment, those soft eyes hardened, "and I would be so glad of your company. Should you like to sit outside for a while? It's so pleasant to have sunshine at last after all those weeks of rain." Then, as Shannon tried to struggle to her feet, she said, "Wait, I'll fetch you help." She moved gracefully across the hall and spoke to Adam, the young knight who had ridden before her earlier.

He glanced rather coolly at Isabella at first, Shannon thought, then decided she had been mistaken as he bent to listen, nodded and came back across the hall.

"Demoiselle, may I assist you?" His smile was warm, and Shannon decided she must have imagined his earlier expression. She blushed and dipped her head. He was so handsome, she felt quite flustered.

Don't be so stupid, she chided herself. *Of course you don't fancy him. You're heartbroken, remember?* But, maybe she wasn't. Certainly, she hadn't given a minute's thought to Jackson once she had sobbed her heart out to Hildegarde. Anyway, nothing was going to come of it, so she saw no reason why she shouldn't enjoy the moment. She dimpled up at him, and he took both hands, helping her to rise. Then, with one arm about her, he helped her outside, Isabella at her other side.

Shannon managed to hobble across the herb garden a short way, then gasped with pain, her ankle throbbing. "Please, I'm sorry…I need…I can't…" He looked down at her, saw her distress and swept her lightly off her feet. Despite the pain, Shannon almost laughed; this felt as unreal as some kind of romantic novel. Chloe would be so jealous.

Clutching at his tunic, she was aware of a faint fragrance of rosemary and bay and breathed in, savouring the masculinity of it as he carried her past hedges and into another part of the garden.

Depositing her gently on a bench beneath an apple tree, he said, "Here, Mistress, a fine place to sit," before fetching a small wooden stool from against the cloister wall and placing it so she could rest her ankle, all the time watching her.

Oh, those eyes! She could not drop her gaze; they were hypnotic, with laughter lurking in their depths. He gave her a lazy smile before turning to Isabella. "My lady."

Shannon thought his tone had cooled, and when Isabella replied, hers was almost frigid.

"Thank you, Adam. I'll call you when Mistress Rohese has need of you."

Then, she seated herself beside Shannon, her eyes alight with curiosity and an expression so friendly, Shannon decided she must have imagined the undercurrents of the last few minutes.

"So, now we have the chance to become better acquainted." She hesitated, frowning in concern. "Lady Rohese, you appear so wan; does your ankle hurt you much?"

Shannon nodded. The short hobble to the garden, until Adam had swept her off her feet, had been far more painful than she had expected, and now it ached so much, she felt a little nauseous. "It does, actually, Lady Isabella."

Isabella placed one hand on her arm. "Need we be so formal? We seem to be of an age, please, call me Isabella."

"And I'm just Rohese."

They looked at each other, and Isabella's face lit up again. That's when Shannon realised who she reminded her of. She had the same colouring and face shape as Chloe. *And that's so weird, that I'm sitting here with my great, great, loads of greats, grandmother, and we're the same age.*

Isabella cut in on her thoughts. "Rohese, should you like me to fetch you something from the infirmary? I'm sure Sister Ursel has something to dull your pain; a poppy syrup, mayhap, or some willow bark infusion?"

Yuck! Opium or willow bark? She shuddered. *No thanks.* She would rather have ibuprofen. She hadn't had much wine; surely, it would be okay. "I have an opiate from Bolohovenia in my chamber which I would prefer, but I can't face walking just now. If I sit here for a while, I'm sure it will ease. It doesn't hurt nearly so much when I talk – I suppose it stops me dwelling on it."

"Then, by all means, let us talk. My husband is about his own business, I am alone and it will be pleasant to have your company." Then, glancing shyly at Rohese, she said, "I confess, I am curious that you were on the road unaccompanied. You do not mind me asking why?"

And now, Shannon would find out whether her cover story would stand up to scrutiny. Isabella listened to her tale with eyes like saucers, uttering little squeaks of dismay as Shannon embellished her story, explaining how the messenger from her father had caught up with them half a mile from the abbey with the news that their castle was under siege, and how she, Rohese, had declared her intention to travel the last short distance alone, crossing her fingers that Isabella would believe her. Even to her own ears, it sounded rather thin. Still, fully committed now, she ploughed on.

"And so, I instructed my guards to return and do their duty to my father and his lands." She jutted her chin imperiously, daring Isabella to challenge her. "It's enough that my poor mother and half the household are so ill. My father's need of the men was far greater than mine. The abbey was in sight; I thought to be safe enough." She leaned forward and rubbed her ankle. "I hadn't taken this accident into consideration. You can imagine how glad I was for your help."

That was a much better tale if the look on Isabella's face was anything to go by; plenty of time to update Aunt Hildegarde later. The pilgrimage idea was definitely out, how could she enjoy herself if she was meant to be on pilgrimage?

"But why did you not ride? How came you to be walking?"

Oh. She hadn't thought of that. She cudgelled her brain. "Well, I was travelling in a litter so I had no horse to ride. Anyway, I thought if I walked, it would be like a penance. You know, for being the one who is not ill. I thought God would see it as a prayer for my family." She held her breath. Would

Isabella swallow it? "It's something we do in Bolohovenia." *Maybe that will side-track her.*

It worked.

"Oh, Rohese, is it expected that your family will recover?"

Improvising again, Shannon said, "The messengers from my father said they are weak though likely to survive." She mopped her eyes and sniffed, the better to add colour to the fiction. "He instructed me to remain here for the nonce. Enough that my mother, sister and brothers are ill. He doesn't wish to have me endangered, since, thus far, I have escaped."

"But, Rohese, you did not know we have spotted fever here also?"

"Yes, but not as badly as my poor country, Isabella. There, it scours us like a plague. Thousands have died. Aunt Hildegarde says there are no new cases here at present." And fingers crossed it stayed the same. How ironic it would be if, after all her ingenuity, she fell victim to the very disease she had concocted to explain her presence here.

Still, she reflected, *I'm sure if I did, Auntie Hildegarde would get me home somehow. I expect they can treat it at hospital; it's not as though I'll have to die here.* Surreptitiously, she rapped on the trunk of the tree beside which she sat. *Touch wood.*

Isabella patted her hand. "I will pray your family recovers and your father prevails. It must be such a comfort to have your aunt's prayers and those of the sisters."

Wait a minute. If she appeared too sad, Shannon decided, she wasn't going to get any fun out of this visit. She stopped dabbing at her eyes and raised her head saying with confidence, "Oh yes, indeed. And, to tell truth, I am not at all worried. My father *will* prevail, and I am certain my family will recover. In many ways, I should rather be with them, but they insisted, and since I am here," she paused and allowed herself to smile again, "I wish to enjoy myself. I have never travelled alone before, and it's rather invigorating." *There, that should do it.*

Isabella opened her mouth as though there was something she wanted to ask, then shut it again.

Shannon gave her a quizzical look. "Were you going to say something?"

"I, er, no."

"Yes, you were. What was it?"

"You'll think me rude."

"No, I won't. Go on, say it." Better have it straight out than for Isabella to be speculating.

"Forgive me, I was just wondering – you are not married? You wear no ring on your heart finger. Have you no husband back in Bolo…Bolovenah, no…" She paused, furrowing her brow in concentration before saying with an air of triumph, "Bolohovenia!"

Shannon resisted the temptation to roll her eyes. "No, in my country we do not wed so young as

85

here. It's thought better to allow us time to grow. Sixteen is the earliest we can marry, and my parents wish me to wait a little longer yet." Well, that was true enough.

Isabella leaned forward, hands clasped, eyes filled with longing. "Oh, how I wish I lived there."

Shannon was taken aback. "But you love Sir Giles, don't you?"

Isabella veiled her eyes with her lashes. "Er, yes, of course. He is a good husband to me."

Good? Is that all?

"And, indeed, he is not so difficult to love," she whispered, a flush spreading over her cheeks.

As her meaning sunk in, Shannon felt her own cheeks burning. *Whoa! We're discussing my ancestors' love lives. Too much information!* But Isabella didn't feel like an ancestor, just a friend.

"My first husband, though, was an ill-tempered man." The flush died away; Isabella's eyes hardened and her lips compressed. "I was wed to him at fourteen, and I hated him; when he died, I was glad. And as for that witch of a mother of his, when she had a seizure after his death and died too, I did not mourn her, either. I behaved as though I did, but inside, I was dancing." She stared at Shannon as though challenging her. "And if that is a sin, then I am not sorry for it, for I tell you, I *rejoiced* to be free."

The fire died out of her eyes to be replaced by a look of horror. One hand flew to her lips, as though she couldn't believe what she had said, and she gazed at Shannon with desperation, before glancing around fearfully, clasping both hands before her as though in prayer. "Lady Rohese, please, oh please, forget I said that. Please, don't tell anyone. You see, I was so young, and he was not kind."

Shannon's eyes misted over. *Poor Isabella*. She reached for the hands that were gripping each other convulsively and covered them with both of her own. "Oh, I won't, I won't, I *promise*. Oh, Isabella, don't be so scared. You can trust me." Then she reddened, remembering the lies of just a few moments ago. *But that's different,* she told herself. *I had to do that. And I'd never break Isabella's confidence. It's not the same.*

For a few minutes, they sat there, and Isabella's terrified expression started to fade. Shannon said nothing; she didn't know what to say. She knew about child brides; it still happened in 2012, of course it did, but not in Britain, so she'd never seen the horror first hand. Thinking about it now, she felt sick.

Isabella broke the silence first. She got up, holding her hand out to Shannon. "Forgive me, I forgot myself. Now, is your ankle still hurting? Should you like to return to your chamber and rest, or would you rather stay here? I must go; I have things to attend to. My lord will return soon." She frowned. "At least I think he will, and I must make our chamber ready for him." And it was as though the previous conversation had never happened.

Shannon understood. Isabella wanted to forget again, to shut it away and return to normal. In fact, she also needed a short time to herself to come to terms with what she'd just heard. "No, thank you, I'd like to sit here a while longer. You go."

"Are you sure?"

"Yes, go on. You have things to do. I'll just rest."

Isabella, all smiles again, turned and glided through the gardens back to the guest-house. Shannon watched in admiration; maybe it was a good job she'd hurt her ankle for she could never move so elegantly. At least now no one would expect it of her.

She continued watching until Isabella had turned in to the guest-hall, then gazed unseeingly before her for some moments, jumping as a hand touched her shoulder.

"Your pardon, Mistress, I didn't mean to startle you."

Shannon looked up. Adam was standing over her, his eyes alight with mischief. Shannon was pretty sure he had known she was lost in her thoughts and that he *would* startle her, but he was a welcome distraction. "I'm sure you didn't." Her tone was dry, but she laughed up at him before veiling her expression, not sure whether to invite him to be seated. It didn't seem to matter; he sat anyway and proceeded to beguile her into more laughter.

Shannon was enjoying herself. Adam wasn't exactly flirting with her, nor was he asking awkward questions, and she felt herself beginning to relax in response to his light conversation when he suddenly glanced across the garden – or the garth as he had called it – stiffened and got to his feet.

"Mistress, the time has passed most pleasantly; however, I regret…" He lifted her hand to his lips and, before she could respond, he almost melted away out of sight.

As she sat there, mouth slightly agape, Hildegarde swept into view. "Well, child, how have you been faring? Here, I have the book I promised you."

"Wow, thanks…er…" She'd been caught off guard again. "I mean, thank you, Aunt. How lovely." Oh, she *must* learn to become more prim.

Hildegarde started to frown, then shrugged. "No matter, it will come as you accustom yourself to being Rohese. And how does your ankle?"

She hadn't thought about it; however, now her attention had been drawn to it again, she became aware that it still hurt. "It aches. I sat here to rest."

"Well, now I suggest you rest properly in your chamber for a while, just until supper, which may take in the guest-refectory. After that, I think you ought to retire." She put her head on one side. "Mind you, I shall expect you to accompany me to Compline regularly as soon as it becomes more comfortable. And, I shall expect you to attend Vespers with me also."

Shannon pulled a face. Hildegarde ignored her and continued, "If not, questions might be asked. Besides, you may even find you enjoy it. Come." She held out her arm, and Shannon was glad to lean heavily on it as she limped back, collapsing gratefully onto her bed and propping her ankle on a cushion. The walk back had started it throbbing again, and she was feeling more washed out than she cared to admit.

"Tired?"

"Mmm. More than I expected."

"You've had a long day, and it's wearying living under an assumed persona – I remember. You've had to concentrate almost without a break; it's hardly surprising you feel exhausted. Rest awhile; I'll return later."

CHAPTER EIGHT

Shannon woke with a start to the sound of a distant bell. Automatically, her hand shot out to switch off the alarm before she remembered where she was. Of course, that must be the bell calling the nuns to prayer.

So, what time was it then? The light was quite bright, so, unless she had overslept, it must be, what? Six am? Seven? When did they celebrate Prime? No, it couldn't be that; that was earlier in summer. Terce then? Groping for her watch, she remembered it had been in the bag of things Hildegarde had confiscated. *Bother her! Did she have to be so pernickety? How am I going to manage without that?*

After such an early bedtime, even though the bell had roused her briefly a couple of times during the night, she realised she was wide awake. And with no chattering voices or traffic noise to disturb her here, she had gone to sleep quite quickly, despite the early hour.

After supper yesterday, everything had gone very quiet. She'd tried to speak to Hildegarde before she'd gone to bed, but the Abbess had put her finger to her lips and shaken her head. So what was that, then? Did they have some kind of silence here after Compline?

She lay there considering for a while, then threw back the covers. If it was Terce, she may as well get up. *I don't want them to think I'm lazy. Or a, what was it they call it here? A sluggard?* Swinging her feet to the ground, she winced as she forgot and put her weight on her injured ankle. *Ouch!*

There was a bowl on a small table by the wall, along with a covered jug – ewer? (she must remember the right words) – of water. A dish sat next to it with a lump of something semi-solid on it. Limping slightly as she left her bed, she reached out and put a dollop into her hand, sniffing it. It smelt like some kind of soap. She sniffed again; it was vaguely flowery, really quite nice. There was a wash cloth – she supposed that was what it was, anyway – and a sort of napkin laid next to it. A towel, maybe? Must be.

What she really wanted was a shower, but she must do the best she could with what was available. Now, how to clean her teeth? She found a tissue she'd managed to get past Hildegarde's eagle eyes, twisted the corner into a point and scrubbed at them, then remembered the hazel twig her aunt had given her yesterday. Rubbing her teeth experimentally with it, she found it worked – sort of. Cupping her hands over her face, she breathed out, smelling her breath. Not too bad, but oh, for some toothpaste. At least she could rinse her mouth; Sister Joan, the hospitaller, had left a cup of water last night, and she had a little left. Next to the cup, she found some fennel seeds – what were they for? She chewed one experimentally. Breath fresheners?

Finishing her ablutions, she sighed, wishing she felt cleaner. Still, maybe she'd get the chance to bathe sometime. The nuns would have a bathroom, called the laver she thought, but she supposed she couldn't use that. She'd find out later.

Looking critically at her shift, she discarded it for a fresh one, deciding to keep the first to use as a nightshirt. Then, she pulled a dress off the pole. Sister Joan, small, round and bustling, had taken the deep red one to brush off the mud along with her cloak after she had changed into the pink one for supper yesterday. Today, she chose the yellow gown with blue embroidery she'd bought online; prettier than her mum's old bliaut.

She wriggled into it, smoothing it down around her and was struggling to tie the laces when she heard a knock at the door heralding the arrival of Etheldreda.

"Good day to you, Mistress Rohese. The Abbess sent me to help you. I'll bring you something to break your fast." And she was gone, leaving Shannon frustrated and wishing for someone to chat with. Never mind. After breakfast, she might be able to find Isabella. And, wasn't Hildegarde expecting her to go to the abbey services with her today? Well, that would be boring! If she used her ankle as an excuse, she'd probably be instructed to rest. She limped over to the window and sat in the chair, propping her foot on the stool. Might as well save it now so it wouldn't ache so much later.

She was idly gazing through the window when another knock sounded, and Etheldreda bustled in with a platter of cheese and a chunk of bread. *Is that it?*

Etheldreda set a cup before her, and Shannon sniffed it before taking a tentative sip. *Yuck! Ale? For breakfast?* Still, she was hungry and thirsty, so she tucked in.

As Shannon ate, Etheldreda busied herself tidying the bed. Finished, she sat on the chest and waited for Shannon to complete her meal.

Shannon was finding the bread tasted slightly strange but nicer than she'd thought. *Much tastier than at home. I suppose it's really fresh, though, and the cheese hasn't got that horrible plastic wrapping on it.*

She ate the last morsel then braced herself for another swig of the ale. She guessed she could get used to it, and she must wash her food down with something. Pity it wasn't coffee, though.

Etheldreda took her platter and mug and left, turning at the door with a tentative smile. "Mistress Rohese, I'll be back shortly. The Abbess has asked me to serve you while you are here until she can find you a maidservant, so I will be able to remain with you, except for during the Offices."

What? She smiled back at the nun, but groaned inwardly. How could she have any fun when her companion was a nun? Then she brightened. *There are loads of Offices.*

"However, she says I may miss some while I'm acting as your companion, Mistress."

Shannon felt the smile slipping from her face and turned away quickly, but Etheldreda had already gone.

When the nun returned, she gazed enquiringly at Shannon, saying, "How is your ankle today?"

Shannon considered. It certainly hurt a little less, and she didn't intend to be stuck indoors. "It's a bit better; I think I can walk today as long as I don't overdo it. Can we take a look around the abbey, please? As long as I keep stopping to rest it, I think it'll be ok–" She broke off in confusion, trying to think of a better word.

Etheldreda smiled reassuringly as Shannon tried to gather her wits. "Mistress, you need not be careful of what you say to me when we are alone. I know who you are, for I met your lady mother.

Indeed, I helped to secure her safety." Her eyes shone as though remembering something exciting.

Oh yeah, Shannon remembered now. Her mum had said there was another nun who helped, apart from Hildegarde and Sister Ursel; this must be her. "Mum, er, my lady mother was ill when I left home, so she only told me a little. I'd love to hear what happened."

"For certès, my dear, but it would be best to stay here whilst I tell you." She looked conspiratorial and suddenly younger. Maybe having her around wouldn't be too bad.

Etheldreda would not normally be doing this, but since the young woman had arrived, inexplicably, without a maid, Hildegarde had taken her to one side and explained that Rohese was Marion's daughter. So that was why she had seemed familiar. The nun tilted her head to one side and studied her covertly. Yes, she bore a definite likeness to her mother. *Another one from future times.* She sniffed. *Bolohovenia, indeed!*

Truth to tell, Etheldreda was entranced and also rather honoured to be in Abbess Hildegarde's confidence. She had grown in responsibility since Marion's time here and was now subinfirmaress; also, apart from Ursel and Brother Bernard, she was the only other person who knew the truth about Marion. And Brother Bernard, bless him, would never notice the similarity.

She'd thought there was something familiar about her yesterday, no matter the story the girl had told her about some strange country far from here. She was ingenious, of a surety, but so many lies! Etheldreda tutted to herself. *Although, for certès, she could not tell the truth. And there, I am being uncharitable again, dear Lord. And she's the niece of our dear Abbess. That she trusts me to be a companion to her is an honour indeed.*

While her soul would miss the nourishment of the minor offices, she felt a spring in her step, *For,* she mused, *is not a change good for the spirit?* And it would be interesting to view the abbey through the eyes of another. *I may consider myself blessed indeed for this chance to serve not just my Abbess, but a guest. And is it not said that in serving others, we may be serving angels unawares?* And it was a link to Marion, whom she remembered with fondness. *After all, had it not been for Marion, I should not have seen the power of our Lord to protect when faced by dangers like that evil boar.*

Indeed, the incident with the boar, which happened when she was aiding this girl's mother, had increased her faith and added wings to her praises. So now, she took to her duties with delight as well as humility and again became aware of the extra bounce in her heels, which she tried to quell, as she escorted Mistress Rohese on her tour.

When she had shown her around as much of the abbey as was fitting, she took her out through the courtyard and across the gardens to Hildegarde's private chambers.

Hildegarde arrived at the door as Etheldreda went to knock. "Thank you, Sister, you may leave Rohese with me now."

Etheldreda dipped a curtsy and left. Hildegarde ushered Shannon into her room, closing the door behind her. Indicating a chair to Shannon, she seated herself behind her desk.

"Now, child, how are you feeling today? How is your ankle?"

"It aches a bit, but it's not too bad if I'm careful. Sister Etheldreda took me for a tour of the abbey." As Hildegarde raised her brows, Shannon added hurriedly, "We took it slowly and I kept sitting down so I didn't do myself any more damage. I'll rest all afternoon. It's so beautiful; It's really sad so much of it was destroyed."

"Ah well, for that we may thank Henry." Hildegarde rested her chin on her hand. "And, are you enjoying yourself? Remember, I will help you return at any time, if you wish. If you get bored, maybe?"

"Oh no, I'm fine. I'm enjoying it. I don't want to go home yet."

Hildegarde's smile wavered a little, for she had hoped Shannon would want to go sooner rather than later. Very well, then, she would need to make arrangements. She wondered how long the girl intended to stay. Hildegarde clung to the fast-fading hope that boredom would eventually discourage her, and she was praying devoutly that she would be able to keep her out of trouble in the meantime. *But there! We are in an abbey. What mischief could she possibly get up to in here?*

Unfortunately, however hard she tried to convince herself, she had a nagging suspicion that Shannon would find herself in hot water before long. She swallowed down her doubts and mentally pinned the smile more firmly to her face. Where was her faith?

"Sha…er, Rohese, I've spoken to my nuns, and they will be happy to make you some veils to replace the one you used as a bandage. The ones you brought with you are far too heavy, anyway. We shall make them opaque enough that you are respectable, but sheer enough as befits a young woman of a good family. And they have agreed to make you one more garment."

Agreed? She'd been astonished at their reaction. Ursel had been in the right of it, as usual; even the most sober of her nuns had almost clamoured to be allowed to take part in the venture. *I suppose they have sewn enough altar cloths that the thought of pretty gowns comes as a pleasant change. Maybe none of us are so far out of the world as we think.*

There had been one exception; Sister Aldith had hung back, her face expressionless. There had been trouble enough with her when Marion had been here. *Let us hope she's outgrown her desire to spread rumour and gossip now.*

To be sure, Hildegarde had not had to chastise her for over a year now; however the girl had a judgemental streak in her still. She hid it well, although the Abbess believed she had not yet conquered it. Unfortunately, her expression was permanently pious, her eyes always carefully cast downwards, making her thoughts hard to read.

"Now, while you are with us, you'll be needing a maid. I have assigned Etheldreda to you for the nonce, and you may be easy with her for–"

"Yes, she knows, doesn't she?" Shannon cut in, meeting her eyes guilelessly. "I like her, but, can the maid be closer to my age? I mean, Etheldreda is lovely, but she's as old as my mum, I reckon."

Hildegarde pursed her lips. A maid Shannon's own age? Well, mayhap somewhere between the two ages. She would interview some girls from the village; possibly Magda could recommend some. They must be of suitably modest demeanour to discourage Shannon from any tricks she might get up to.

Shannon was looking at her speculatively. "Do I actually need a maid?"

"For appearance's sake, yes, if you wish people to take you as a young woman of good birth."

"Oh." Shannon pulled her braid forward and fiddled with it.

Hildegarde smiled at her. "Now, I'm spending most of today with you, apart from the Divine Offices, so pray tell me what you wish to do."

"Well, I'd really like to get to know Isabella better."

That might be a good thing. Isabella will be shocked if Shannon starts to get out of hand, and Shannon will be on her best behaviour; it might help to keep her reined in.

Besides, Hildegarde felt sure Isabella was lonely. There was an expression in her eyes that she recognised. Perchance they would make good companions, although she hoped Isabella wouldn't become too attached. Shannon's visit wouldn't be for any longer than she could help.

She rose to her feet, holding out her hand. "A good idea. Come."

CHAPTER NINE

Hildegarde tapped lightly on the door of the chamber, and a plump maid with a cheerful grin opened it. Inside, Giles was lounging on a chest, watching his wife and a chuckling toddler with amusement. Isabella glanced up from where she knelt, eyes alight with laughter, her braids uncovered and in disarray where the child was tugging at them. "My lady Abbess," she greeted Hildegarde distractedly, trying to disengage the chubby fists and rise to her feet, but Hildegarde dropped to her knees beside her.

"Well, and is this my godson? What a fine fellow you are, Dickon. How you've grown since I saw you last."

Dickon, staring at the new arrivals, lost his balance and plumped down on his bottom. His chin puckered, he thrust out his lower lip and began to bawl, but Hildegarde hoisted him in the air, and he was sufficiently distracted to grasp at her pectoral cross.

"No, indeed, you must not play with that. Here, you may have this." She unhooked her paternoster from the girdle at her waist and dangled it before him. He reached for it and immediately put it into his mouth, dribbling as he sucked on the beads.

"Oh, isn't he gorgeous? Is he yours?" Shannon was enchanted.

Isabella nodded, pride glowing like a beacon. Giles rose lazily. "Yes, Mistress Rohese, meet Dickon, my heir."

Shannon knelt down beside Dickon with Isabella and Hildegarde. "Oh, you sweetheart."

Dickon chortled.

"He enjoys an audience." Giles laughed.

"Mayhap he is meant to be a jongleur." Isabella chucked him under the chin which made him giggle and dribble some more. He struggled to get down and then, lunged over to his father, where he made a determined grab for the sword lying on the chest.

"Or, more suitably, a tourney knight," Giles said languidly.

Isabella frowned. "I do not wish to think so far ahead, my lord. The idea of him old enough for that chills me."

"Well, and he will have no need. He will have enough on his trencher as my heir. And it's far enough ahead that you may keep this chick safe in the nest a while longer."

Dickon grabbed again at the sword, and Giles pulled it from his reach. Before the child could start to wail, Giles took a wafer from a dish on the table and held it out to him. Dickon stretched out a pudgy fist and, securing the object of his desire, thrust it into his mouth. A trickle of honey oozed from the wafer and ran down his chin, and he beamed beatifically as Isabella hurried to wipe it.

He waved a sticky hand as he crammed the last of the treat between his lips, and his nurse caught at him, cleaning the mess from him quickly before he could besmirch himself and all around him.

Shannon's face lit with pleasure as she watched. Dickon saw her attention was on him and beamed. Giles and Isabella laughed, delighted to show off their son.

The child kept them entertained until the clamour of yet another bell interrupted them, and Hildegarde straightened, righting her veil and habit. "Sir Giles, Lady Isabella, might I leave Rohese with you?"

"By all means," Isabella said, lifting Dickon. "Here, Jehane, you take him now."

Jehane lifted him from her, tossing the giggling infant high into the air. "Come to Nurse, sweeting."

Isabella stood, then tidied her braids and pinned on her veil. "Come, Rohese, shall we walk?" She turned to Giles. "My lord?"

Giles stretched and looked regretful. "I'm afraid I have things I need to attend to, sweetheart." Isabella made a moue of disappointment, and Giles relented. "Well, mayhap in a while, we might go riding. What say you, Mistress Rohese? Will you join us?"

Riding? She fumbled for something to say. "Er, I'm not a very confident rider, and my ankle is still sore. Also, I don't have a suitable horse."

"You would be welcome to ride one of ours when your ankle is less painful; however, I suppose it would not be such a good idea at the moment, especially if you lack confidence. A pity."

"Er, yes. Thank you; for now, I'd prefer not to." She tried a different tack. "I'd much rather not do too much for a little longer anyway, just until my ankle is better."

Hildegarde had been hovering in the doorway. "I think Rohese would be better not trying to ride or walk too much for a few more days. If you wish to ride, she may come with me."

"Oh no." Isabella held out her hands. "Indeed not. We shall sit outside, and you can tell me more of Bolohovenia. It will be most interesting, for I have never travelled afar."

Giles got to his feet, saying, "I have travelled somewhat, but never to Bolohovenia. Your tales will be of interest, Mistress Rohese. I'm sure you and Isabella will entertain each other well." He kissed his wife on the cheek. "My love, she will blow your mind with her tales of travelling, for certès."

Shannon blinked. *What? He surely didn't just say that?* She must have misheard.

Isabella laughed at her confusion. "Ignore him, Rohese. It's a phrase he likes to use from time to time. I have no idea where he got it from, for I never heard it before I wed him. In truth, it sounds most vulgar. I pray you, do not start using it; your parents will be wroth with us for teaching you."

I bet I know where he got it from, though, Shannon thought. It was Mum's favourite expression, and she'd got it from Gran. *Wait till I get home and tell her.* It sounded so funny coming from a twelfth century knight. No wonder Isabella laughed.

Shannon and Isabella spent a pleasant time seated in one of the garths. It hadn't been too far for Shannon to hobble, supported by her stick and Isabella's arm. Jehane brought Dickon out, and after a while, several nuns clustered around watching him toddle, pulling flowers up and digging with his fingers in the dirt, until an older nun came and chased them back to their duties. As yet another bell rang, Isabella looked up. "Noon already; time to dine. I confess, I am hungered, though I need to wash my hands first." She gazed ruefully at them, streaked as they were with mud and dribble. Come to my chamber. But wait, you don't have your eating knife. Do you wish to fetch it?"

Shannon was just wondering what to do, when Etheldreda came across the garth. "Mistress, you left these behind." She held out a pouch with a loop on it, and fastened it to Shannon's girdle, giving her a wink as she did so. "The Abbess asks if you and Lady Isabella would join her in her chamber for dinner?"

Isabella dimpled; she had a beautiful smile. Shannon nodded. "Lovely, I'll just go to my chamber to, er, wash my hands, too. Shall I meet you there?"

Isabella shook her head. "No Rohese, it will be a shorter walk for you to come with me, and you may lean on me. Come." She held her arm out, and Etheldreda took Shannon's other arm. Between them, they helped her hobble to Isabella's chamber where they sluiced their hands in a laver. Giles returned in time to join them as they went to Hildegarde's chamber.

Etheldreda and Ursel also dined with the Abbess. Pottage was served with crusty bread, then trout with almonds and spices followed by a frumenty and some small honey cakes.

Shannon was surprised at how good everything was. The fare was not sumptuous but still tasty and satisfying.

It was all washed down with the inevitable wine or ale although, to Shannon's relief, Hildegarde also offered water, fresh and icy cold, from the abbey well. In response to her slightly worried glance, Hildegarde assured her the water was safe to drink.

"We've had some problems with the water in Bolohovenia," Shannon explained to Isabella, who appeared a little startled. "It was thought, at one time, our wells were the source of disease." She ignored the bland expression on Hildegarde's face, guessing the Abbess might be a bit shocked by her lies. *And anyway, they aren't really lies. I'd never drink anything apart from tap or bottled water back home.*

When they finished eating, Shannon discovered the nuns were expected to rest on their beds for an hour. Invited to do likewise, she shook her head emphatically. *A midday nap? No way!*

She and Isabella, who seemed no more inclined to rest than did Shannon, went back outside, without Dickon this time, as Jehane had borne him off, grizzling, to set him in his truckle bed for a while.

They sat in the herb garden quietly chatting. Then, Isabella stood, dusting her skirts. "I beg your pardon, Rohese. I think it time I took myself back to my chamber. Giles may return shortly, and I must needs speak with him. Will you stay here? Or shall I help you back?"

Shannon shook her head. "No, I think I'll remain a while longer."

Left alone, she sat in silent contemplation watching the butterflies flit in and out of the herbs and flowers.

The breeze caught at some blossoms and scattered petals across the garden like confetti. Shannon was lost in her thoughts when a shadow was suddenly cast over her. Looking up, she saw a pair of green eyes laughing down at her. Adam! Her heart beat a little faster, and she was sure she blushed.

"May I?" He glanced at the space beside her.

"Please do." Now, she knew she was blushing; her cheeks felt as though they were on fire. She looked down but not before she had seen him quirk his lips as though he was aware of her discomfort.

"I wondered what had happened to you. You sort of vanished yesterday, almost like a ghost," she said, and the laugh died out of his eyes.

"Indeed, Mistress, I apologise. I try to avoid the Lady Isabella; she has no liking for me. She would be angered if she saw me talking with you, and that would make my life difficult." He was sober now. "She has something against me, and, besides that, she is a most stiff-necked woman."

"Really?" Shannon would have said she was anything but.

"Indeed, yes; however, it's naught for you to be concerned about. Merely, it's more pleasant for me if we do not cross paths. Better, too, if she does not see me speaking with you, for she'll tell Sir Giles to forbid it. And that would be a shame, would it not?" His mouth curved upwards again, and Shannon looked at him doubtfully.

"Fear not, Mistress. I will be very circumspect. I confess, I find it most agreeable to spend time with you. You do not mind?"

"Er, no, I suppose not." She was having trouble thinking straight; those eyes did something very strange to her. Anyway, he was fun. And, for goodness sake, they were in a public place. And an abbey. She pushed her doubts aside as he pulled a blossom from the late-blooming apple tree and presented it to her. "A fair flower for a fair demoiselle." Shannon felt herself blushing again but took it from him, laughing.

"So, tell me about yourself," he said.

Shannon smiled. "Only if you tell me about yourself first."

"There is naught to tell."

She let her disbelief show. "I'm sure there is, and I won't go first."

He grinned ruefully. "Very well, if you must. I am my father's youngest son; however, our estates are large, and thus I'm well provided for. I'm in Sir Giles' employ until I come into my inheritance, so for now, I must abide with him."

"And do you like working for him? Have you squires? Does he have many knights?" If she could keep him talking, there'd be less time for him to question her about anything. Besides, she was fascinated.

He held up his hands as though to fend her off. "Mistress, so many questions. Sir Giles is my liege lord for now. He has not many knights, but his brother's wife is my sister. He is Count John's man, so my father wished me to be esquired to him, and he it is who sponsored my knighthood. He's a fair man," he paused, "when he does not listen to that wife of his. Indeed, I know not why she dislikes me. I fear she poisons his mind against me."

Shannon kept a smile on her face and decided she'd make her own mind up about Isabella. Perhaps it was just a personality clash; maybe Isabella and Adam were each jealous of the other's influence on Giles.

"Were you with Sir Giles long before he married?"

"Indeed I was. I have been with him since my twelfth year. Now, I have my own squire – young Thomas. He's a good lad," he paused, giving a wry grin. "Well, most of the time."

"And does Sir Giles have other knights?"

"He has three others. All older than I and, if I tell truth, I call them all tutmouthed. They don't laugh much, and I like to laugh. Still, it's not a bad life. In another year I shall return to my father." His brow darkened a little. "And then, of course, marriage."

Oh, so he's not free. But I won't be here then, so why should I care? Anyway, Chloe would tell her there was nothing wrong with flirting, just as long as she didn't let it get serious. It was just a bit of fun; she tossed her head defiantly.

"Marriage?"

"Aye. I'm promised to Alys, yet the lass was only twelve at our betrothal. We will be wed when she reaches her fifteenth year. Even then," he sighed, "she'll be but a stranger to me, and little more than a child. I confess, I should prefer a woman. It will be my job to teach her to be a wife. Or at least, my mother's, for the most part. She's a most well-born young woman; it will be a good match, though it's not one I would have chosen." He looked down, studying his nails, then back up at her. "And you, Mistress? Are you not also betrothed?"

Taken aback, Shannon jerked upright. "No, I... Well, I was; er, he betrayed me."

He took her hand. "Demoiselle, he must have been out of his senses. Why would a man turn elsewhere when he had a betrothed so fair?"

Shannon blushed again. Never having been much inclined to flirt before, she was recovering from her initial discomfort and found herself to be enjoying it. It *was* fun; in fact, she was discovering it was quite heady.

"Ah, you must not be embarrassed by my forwardness. I am but a mortal man. I confess, my own senses are in a way to becoming disordered when I look at you." He let go of her hand and reached to stroke her face, then tweaked her braid from beneath her veil, before dropping it and placing his hand on his heart. Then he stood, kissed her hand and vanished silently again. Shannon was left sitting there, confused and disorientated – though not for long. Hildegarde came walking from the direction of the cloisters, heading towards her. How the heck had Adam known she was there? No wonder he had melted away so quietly.

"Rohese?" Hildegarde smiled, as Shannon raised her head; the girl appeared to be daydreaming. No matter that she was alone then; she seemed happy enough, and at least she wasn't getting into mischief. Hildegarde was relieved; when she had seen Isabella in the guest-hall with Sir Giles, she had come hurrying to make sure Shannon was keeping out of trouble.

Her nuns were clamouring to get started on Shannon's gown and veils. A new dress would also keep her occupied. "Come with me, child. We need to measure you, and my sisters are most anxious to start their needlework."

"Really?" Shannon beamed sunnily back at Hildegarde. "That's so kind. I didn't know nuns did things like that."

"Indeed they don't, but they are accomplished seamstresses; their embroidery is exquisite. Truth to tell, they are looking forward to a change of industry very much." She laughed inwardly at the memory. "So keen, in fact, I almost had to fight them off. I had more volunteers than you could possibly need for one gown. For certès, I may have difficulty restraining them from making more. When they heard how you had been unable to bring your coffers, they were most eager to offer their services." She looped her arm beneath Shannon's, handing her the walking stick. "How fares your ankle? You haven't walked too far today, have you?"

"Only when Sister Etheldreda showed me around. I've mostly been sitting since then, firstly with Isabella and then..." She tailed off as Hildegarde eyed her suspiciously. "Er, and then, just sitting thinking. The garden is lovely."

"Yes, I like it too. I find it a place where I can sense God's presence most easily."

"Mmm."

She doesn't have a clue what I'm talking about. Hildegarde resolved to leave something of God, a seed, if you like, in Shannon's soul before she returned to her own time. *I wonder if Marion has any faith.*

"Well, come with me now, and my sisters will measure you. You will forgive them if they are too garrulous." Which was likely. They were fluttering around the fabrics Magda had bought like moths around a flame, fingering the silks, exclaiming over the fine wools and linens. *If I could only hear and not see them, I should never guess they were nuns. They will struggle with the Great Silence tonight.* Still, it was seldom they got to work with anything but altar cloths or habits. Hildegarde couldn't begrudge them a little fun; they were taking such vicarious pleasure in Shannon's new garments.

Indeed, several of the nuns who were not involved in the sewing had been tiptoeing into the room, creeping like timid mice, wanting to share in the excitement. Hildegarde had beckoned them in; after all, why should they not partake of such a rare treat? Even Aldith, with her mouth less prim than usual, had undertaken to sew a veil, embroidering sweet violets along the edges with a flourish.

When Hildegarde ushered Shannon into the room, they almost smothered her, exclaiming, measuring, twittering at her. Hildegarde had to clap her hands to make herself heard.

"Sisters, calm yourselves, please."

When Hildegarde called a halt a couple of hours later, Shannon looked quite wilted. Hildegarde guessed she'd found the nuns more exhausting than she had expected. Indeed, they had been sweetness itself but had behaved like a gaggle of doting aunties, despite many of them being little older than Shannon.

"Now, do you wish to eat supper in the refectory, Rohese? Or are you quite worn out?"

Hildegarde's eyes were twinkling; for her, the afternoon had been most exhilarating.

"Oh no, I'm fine. It'll be nice to eat with the others. Will you be joining me there? Or are you eating with the other nuns?"

"I think, for today, I had better eat with the sisters." They would need her steadying influence if they were to go to Vespers in the right frame of mind. "I will send Etheldreda to bring you to Vespers." She held up her hand as Shannon started to look doubtful. "No, do not argue. You need to be seen attending, and it will do you no harm. You may sit at the back and follow the responses. If you've ever been to evensong, you may find it not quite so unfamiliar as you expect – except, of course, it will be in Latin.

"Etheldreda will go through the order with you before you attend and accompany you there. Until she comes to you, you are free to pursue your own amusements, although personally, I would suggest you rest.

"Supper will be served shortly after Vespers is ended, and again, after that, you will be free, although the abbey and most of the rooms are locked immediately after Vespers, and you'll find many folk retire." She grinned suddenly. "If we did not lock the gates then, I suspect some of our guests would retire in a different direction – to the village alehouse – and poor Sister Porteress would be hard put to keep her temper with them when they returned the worse for wear. This way, neither her temper nor our peace is strained beyond limits.

"After Compline, please try to remember not to speak to the sisters. We are bound by the Great Silence then. Bedtime follows almost immediately. Etheldreda will light your lantern for you before she retires."

As they walked, Shannon suddenly realised they were crossing the gardens which led to the guest-chambers. The crafty abbess! She'd virtually seen her to her room before Shannon had realised it. Still, she had to admit, she was weary. Seated on the chair by the window with her foot up, her elbow on the sill, chin on her hand, she watched the comings and goings idly through the window.

The sun was still bright, but Shannon reckoned it must have been just after seven when Etheldreda scratched lightly at the door before entering.

Having tutored her charge in the ways of the Office, she lent Shannon her support to the abbey and deposited her on a long stone bench fixed to the wall before taking her place with the other nuns. There were no other seats of any description in the main body of the church save one stool which was occupied by a glum-faced Ursel.

Once seated, despite her initial reluctance, Shannon was entranced, barely noticing the hard stone beneath her.

The windows blazed with light, those of stained glass throwing multi-coloured flashes along the nave and over the nuns in the choir, reflecting on the tall columns. The other, plainer windows had glass in fragments of different shades, apparently the closest they came to clear glass here.

Some of the small panes in those were almost clear; others were in shades of pale yellow, still more in a light green, almost like the colours of the ocean. The light from them pierced the gloom which puddled between the windows and around the pillars, and the darker recesses glowed dimly with beeswax candles which smelled of honey. The fragrance of incense drifted in smoky fingers through the air, and through all this, the thin, silvery voices of the nuns rose to the great vaulted ceiling and echoed ethereally round the stone walls.

The hairs on the back of Shannon's neck seemed to stand on end as a sense of holiness settled over her like a cloud. More than that, she could almost feel a divine presence lingering about her, tugging at her heart, coaxing her to relinquish her very soul – almost as though the Spirit of God was actually reaching out to her.

Still lost in wonder when the Office drew to a close, she moved dazedly outside where she sat on a bench quietly, eyes open, but seeing nothing, while she slowly returned to the everyday world.

Hildegarde, glancing over at her, was satisfied Shannon might finally have grasped something of that which she herself knew and was certain she would not have to be coaxed and cajoled to attend Vespers in the future.

She was right. Whatever the girl got up to in the following days, on each of the bright evenings she would file obediently into the abbey and sit quietly, eyes lifted, face lit. Hildegarde hoped the hunger she saw in her would linger when she returned to her own time.

Now, though, she came sweeping across the garth, claiming Shannon and assisting her to the refectory where she kissed her brow and left her. Shannon's heart sank as she spied Father Dominic bearing down on her; then, she felt a hand beneath her elbow. "Shall I save you from being bored to your death?"

"Adam! But can you eat with me?"

"My lord and lady sup in their chamber tonight. And even if it were not so, they would see no harm in my being your table companion for such a short meal. And, since the alternative is our good Father Dominic, they would surely feel I was doing you a service."

"Being my knight in shining armour, in fact?"

"Most assuredly."

Supping with Adam was a very different affair from dining with Father Dominic. However, as the trenchers were being cleared, the mugs drained, yet again, he suddenly rose silently from the table and was gone. Shannon looked around; who had disturbed him this time? Or did he just have very

119

good instincts? No, he must have seen Sister Etheldreda, who had entered and was headed towards her. Oh well, it seemed as though there would be plenty more opportunities to spend time with him. He did seem to have a knack of being around when nobody else was. She sighed. Now she had to learn how to behave in Compline. After that, she allowed Etheldreda to help her back to her room, remembering not to speak, then sat on the bed, lost in thought.

CHAPTER TEN

Over the last few days, Isabella had seen with growing concern how often Adam had been hovering about Rohese. Each time, she had been about to approach when he'd slipped away in that disconcerting manner of his. She had, at first, thought he had noticed her watching, but every time he disappeared, it had been moments before the Abbess had gone across to Rohese. And yet, she thought Hildegarde had not noticed him.

Should she meddle? Rohese, for all her confident ways, was innocent of guile, she felt, and as a virgin, would be less aware of the ways of men like Adam. Mayhap the men of her parents' household were more trustworthy. Of course, they would not dare treat the daughter of the house with less than the utmost respect. Here, though, she was unknown and almost friendless. Here, there were no parents, only an aunt who had other matters which required her attention. Surely Adam would not...

She shook her head. Who knew what he would be capable of? For certès, since she had warned Beatrice, he had no liking for her.

She smoothed out the wrinkle between her eyebrows with her fingers, kneading the band of tension away. What should she do? It would be presumptuous to remind Giles to keep a watch on him again since he'd already promised he would. Could she speak to Rohese? No, she thought not. The girl might resent a warning or see it as a reproof of her conduct.

Should she leave things as they were at present? Yet if she did, Rohese might be hurt. Worse, if she could not fend off his advances, she might be despoiled. If left unchecked, Adam's behaviour would reflect badly on both Giles and herself. Something must be done, and she could ask no one else. It was down to her, and part of her rejoiced that she could address him openly on the subject. He should see she was no timid mouse but mistress of her household. Squaring her shoulders, she set off to track him down, cornering him in the stables. He made her a deep bow. "My lady?"

"Adam, have a care where you flirt, if you please."

Watching her speculatively, he gave her a sidelong glance that shimmered with heat before dropping his gaze, raking it down her body.

Isabella, correctly reading the first part of his thoughts, recoiled as though she'd touched a flame. Lady Mary preserve her; surely, he was not flirting even with her! She straightened her shoulders as he raised his eyes again and gave him stare for stare. "Adam, the Lady Rohese's father is of high rank; would you bring his wrath down upon your own head? Upon all our heads? Have a care," she repeated, "or I shall tell Sir Giles of what I suspect."

He bowed again, though as he dipped his head, she caught the mocking gleam in his eyes which made the respectful gesture naught but an insult. She stood there a moment longer, unable to move, shaken and humiliated, feeling as though even that horse of his was sneering at her. *Oh!*

Finally managing to totter away on trembling legs, she was glad of the cool breeze that fanned her cheeks. *I should have left it to Giles.* In truth, the opportunity to put the swaggering braggart in his place had overwhelmed her natural diffidence. How she had itched to slap that self-satisfied smirk from his face. *And I have my just desserts, for now he thinks I'm hot for him.* The humiliation flushed through her again, burning her like a brand. "And I'd not touch him were he given to me by the King himself," she hissed beneath her breath once out of his hearing.

At dinner, Adam chewed slowly, considering his options. *So, the Lady Rohese is of high rank, is she? And careering about the countryside alone. Mayhap her parents should have more of a care to her.*

Knowing Rohese was of noble birth, far from quelling him, increased his ardour. The game had more spice to it now, and if he laid his plans well, who knew where they would lead him? As for Alys, he mused, well, she was but a chit of a lass. It was unlikely her heart was engaged, and he had no wish for a child as his bride. And once wed and living beneath his father's roof, he'd have to behave with more circumspection.

No, he wanted to taste the pleasures of more willing companions, and while he guessed Rohese was inexperienced, she was older and bolder than Alys, curvaceous and very comely. It would be no hardship to be matched with her, and the promise of wealth and position added to her allure.

He must be cautious though. He was avoiding her during this meal, and he could see from the droop of her lips that she was disappointed to be paired with Guy; in truth, he did not blame her. The other knight was courteous, true, but not, Adam acknowledged with self-satisfaction, as charming a table companion as himself. But then, the disappointment now would make for greater gratitude later. And supper was a safer time for him. His lord and lady were partaking of their supper privately whilst here. It baffled Adam. Had he been wed to Isabella, he would have spent no more than the nights with her; her conversation and company did not appeal, even if her body did. Now Rohese, she had something more about her. Something different. She was as bold sometimes as his other less gently-bred wenches, but still had breeding and discretion, and the air of innocence about her made him want to possess her. Indeed, it would be most pleasant to fritter some hours with her, mayhap even… His thoughts trailed off. He needed to think on this matter.

He watched carefully for the remainder of the day, assessing through half-closed eyelids. So distracted was he that Giles spoke sharply to him on several occasions, which earned Isabella another notch in the tally stick of grievances he had against her.

Mistress Rohese was not always accompanied; could he trust anyone to carry messages? Thomas? Mayhap not. The boy was loyal to him, for certès, but possessed no guile. The other lads? Unlikely. He cast his eyes further afield, watching, assessing. Romance. That would be the key, and…

CHAPTER ELEVEN

Shannon had been waiting for the recreational time the nuns had each day. There were several novices coming into the rose garden with the Novice Mistress. Her ankle was feeling much better, and she had been thinking of asking if she could go for a walk by herself or explore the grounds.

She watched, amused. While the professed nuns reminded her of black doves with their soft voices and gentle movements, the novices were more like a flock of starlings. Gawky and full of chatter in that precious part of time which was their own.

Once the bell sounded for the end of recreation, they would disappear back into their section of the abbey, but for now, they twittered about, awkward in their eagerness.

Apart from the Novice Mistress, none of the older nuns were about, except one, who was headed in her direction. Shannon looked up smiling until she realised it was Sister Aldith, the one nun she could not quite take to. There was something about her, with her prim mouth and her pious expression. She seemed so godly, yet Shannon felt judged by her. Why that should be so she did not know, for Sister Aldith barely raised her eyes and never spoke; yet today, her face was flushed as though she was suppressing a delicious secret. It transformed her, and Shannon found herself responding.

"Mistress, please, will you come with me?"

"Is something wrong?"

The nun, shorter than she and very thin, was almost radiant. "Not at all, but we, the sisters and I, have something for you."

And Aldith had been sent to fetch her? How strange. Shannon's curiosity was piqued as she followed her back towards the inner courts.

"Am I walking too swiftly? Is your ankle still troubling you?" She was almost babbling in her eagerness. Whatever had come over her?

"No and no. My ankle is much better." She touched Aldith's arm. "Won't you tell me where we're going?"

The woman's eyes glowed. "You'll see," she promised. "Come, this way."

Aldith led Shannon to, of all places, her own guest-chamber, opening the door and ushering her in as though Shannon herself was the guest. Once inside, Shannon saw a cluster of nuns, including Hildegarde and Etheldreda.

She stopped dead, eyes wide, as she saw what was laid out on the bed. A gown of a shade of deep apricot in soft, fine fabric with green embroidery and an undergown of a yellow-green colour with more embroidery, plus two veils of sheer silk – one in pale cream embroidered with gold thread and the other of palest rose with delicate violets embroidered on it. "Ohhhh," she breathed, "they're *gorgeous.*"

There was a twitter of delight as she picked up the garments. "I can't believe you finished them so quickly. It's so kind of you all. I'm...I...I don't know what to say."

They crowded round her, holding the gown against her, fluttering and exclaiming.

Shannon could see the longing in their faces. "Would you like me to try them on?"

Several pairs of hands clapped.

"Would you like us to help you?" That was Aldith.

"Sisters, give her room to move. Off with you now, and once she is dressed, you may come back in." Hildegarde's voice rose above the others, and gently quelled them as she shepherded them out.

As they filed out reluctantly, Shannon realised there was a girl in the room who was not a nun. A rosy-cheeked girl in russet and grey with a white veil covering blonde braids which snaked past her waist. As she studied her, the girl lowered her eyes and dropped a curtsy.

"Rohese, this is Amice. I have engaged her to be your maid," Hildegarde said.

"My maid?" Shannon's voice was almost squeaky with shock. She had just got used to the idea of having Etheldreda as her companion, but this girl was much more her own age, probably a little younger; she was finding it hard to judge age here.

"Yes, for good Sister Etheldreda has her own duties to attend. Amice will see to your needs and be a companion to you." Hildegarde's brow creased slightly. "In truth, she is considerably more youthful than I had in mind, although I daresay you will enjoy her company."

"Oh." Shannon couldn't think of much to say. How on earth did you talk to a maid? What was she supposed to do? She took another glance at Amice who was peeping up at her, blue eyes sparkling. Well, she looked as though she might be fun.

"Now, come. Amice will help you out of your gown and into these. My nuns have put much work into them, and I'm sure you noticed their eagerness to see you displaying their handiwork. Amice, if you will?"

Amice dipped down in another curtsy, then helped Shannon out of the gown she was wearing, nimble fingers untying the laces and undressing her to Shannon's embarrassment. As she stood there bare but for a short chemise, she noticed two more fine linen shifts on the bed. Oh, that would be so much better. She had begun to feel the need for a change of clothes, and she had worn both her other dresses already and all her shifts. Yesterday, she'd tried once more to talk Hildegarde into allowing her to wear the silk dress she had brought with her, pouting a little, but Hildegarde had remained unmoved. It was too fine for everyday wear. Now, all disappointment was forgotten.

As Amice helped her into the shift and then the undergown, she ran her hands over the fabric before diving into the apricot gown. Amice pulled it down, smoothing it over her hips, fastening a beautifully embroidered girdle around it, before Hildegarde opened the door and the nuns all swarmed in again, their usual soft murmurings forgotten as they clustered around admiring her, tweaking the gown, asking her to turn this way and that.

"Oh, but you must wear the cream veil." Aldith took off her uncomfortable white veil and fitted the new one over her braids, draping it and pinning it up. Then she stood back, admiring the effect. "My lady, you look very lovely. Do you like it? I embroidered them both."

It felt wonderful – like gossamer. Immediately, Shannon felt much freer. The white one had been stiff and thick of fabric, much like the one Amice was wearing. It obscured her vision slightly and made her head feel itchy. This was so much nicer to wear.

"Oh, they're so beautiful. Sisters, I'm lost for words, but thank you, *thank* you."

Glowing eyes and delighted faces rewarded her, and Shannon hugged each one of them, even Aldith. "How kind you all are."

"And now, Sisters, you have admired your handiwork quite long enough. Off with you." Hildegarde clapped her hands and shooed them out, one or two casting lingering glances over their shoulders as they left.

"Oh Auntie." Shannon was almost breathless with delight. "How lovely of you all. Thank you."

"Not at all, child. They were delighted to have a change from their usual tasks. In fact, they are now so excited, I shall have difficulty bringing them back down to earth. You've given them more excitement in a few days than they normally get in a year." She laughed. "I shan't be able to get any sense out of them for a week. And indeed, I…" She looked down, reddening slightly as she muttered something, and Shannon thought she caught the words 'silk' and 'over-indulgent aunt' before she raised her head again, saying, "Now, I shall leave you to become acquainted with Amice. Amice, I trust you to take good care of your mistress."

The maid curtsied again. "Oh, yes, my lady." And Hildegarde left the room.

Shannon and Amice, left alone, stared at each other, and Shannon felt suddenly awkward until Amice bobbed yet another curtsy.

"Um, Amice?"

And another curtsy. "Yes, my lady?"

"Could you, er, would you mind not doing that all the time? You're beginning to make me dizzy."

The maid giggled. "Sorry, Mistress. I haven't done this before. My ma said I must be sure to behave and curtsy often."

"I don't think she meant all the time. And you don't have to call me Mistress. Just Rohese will do."

"Oh no, Mistress, it wouldn't be proper. The Abbess might send me away."

"And you really want to be a maid, do you?"

"Oh yes, Mistress, it will be so much better than working for Dame Agatha in the dairy, and I'll earn much more. It'll buy me some fine clothes for my wedding."

"Well, call me Mistress when there are others around, but when it's just the two of us, you can call me Sh...Rohese."

Amice started to dip down in another curtsy, remembered, and bounced back up again. "Yes, Shrohese."

Shannon started. "What did you call me?"

"Shrohese, just as you said."

Shannon grimaced. *Oh, I must be more careful.* "Amice, that was a slip of my tongue. Sometimes, I'm afraid I stutter. Just Rohese will be fine."

"Yes, Just Rohese."

What? Shannon looked hard at Amice. The girl grinned. "Sorry, Mistress, I couldn't resist." She gave another infectious giggle, and both girls started laughing.

Yes, Amice would be much more fun than a nun. Etheldreda was very nice, but she had that sort of serious air to her. Now, Shannon could be more herself – well, almost herself.

"So, Amice, what shall we do with ourselves?"

"Could we see the stables, please? I'm ever so fond of horses. Sister Aldith told me there are some wonderful beasts here at present. More exciting than old Horace."

Oh, thanks Aldith! Shannon was not very keen on horses; they didn't have brakes, and they did have teeth and hooves. Still, it might be a good idea to get used to them a bit; if she wanted to go anywhere, she'd have to sit up behind someone. Someone like Adam. The thought gave her a frisson of delight.

Amice seemed to be familiar with the abbey grounds. She led the way confidently, chattering as she did so. Shannon learned that she was fifteen and betrothed to the miller's son, whom she would marry in a year or two. She learned, also, that

Amice loved her parents and her five brothers and sisters and, though she was looking forward to being married, she also quite fancied the sons of the smith, the alewife and several others. "But don't tell. And Ulfgar will make me a good husband; I shall be happy with him. Only until then..." she shrugged. "Well, I may as well enjoy a handsome face. As long as my da' doesn't catch me." She covered her mouth to hide the giggle Shannon was sure was about to burst from her.

She talked all the way to the stables, and Shannon was relieved not to have to go over her story again. Better a maid wrapped up in her own life than one who asked awkward questions.

Once they reached the stables, Amice exclaimed in delight, clapping her hands. There were so many, she exclaimed. Fine beasts, all of them. And what of that one? The roan with the white flash along its face.

As she spoke, a figure detached itself from the shadows, and Shannon's heart skipped a beat. Adam!

He came to her, holding his hands out. "Mistress Rohese. Have you come to make acquaintance with Blaze here? Oh, but he will be pleased. He has an eye for a pretty face, that horse. Come." He tucked her hand in his arm and drew her to the roan. Blaze snorted and tossed his head, and Shannon tried to back away.

"Ah, don't be nervous, Mistress. If you walk away now, you will break his heart. Here, give him this." He reached into his tunic and held out an apple. She took it and gingerly held it out between her fingers, but Adam took her hand again, uncurled her fingers and spread them, placing the apple in the flattened palm of her hand, his own beneath it. "No, sweeting, like this. Ah, you're trembling. Don't be afraid, see, I'll keep my hand here. He'll not bite you, I vouch for that. One apple, and he'll be your slave for life."

He looked into her eyes. "For me, it takes less. One sweet smile from you, and I'll be your slave too."

Shannon dropped her gaze, embarrassed, and he said no more, just held her hand out to Blaze, who snuffled his whiskery lips softly into her palm, curled his tongue around her offering and caught it up, crunching it between large teeth.

"There, Mistress, that wasn't so bad, now, was it? You see, you needn't be afraid of him; he is as smitten with you as is his master." Adam retained her hand, stroking her palm with his thumb. "Now, try touching him. Like all good fellows, this one enjoys being caressed. Here, like this."

Still holding her hand, he turned it so the back of it pressed against his palm again and swept it down Blaze's nose. He stood close behind her, and she felt his breath on her cheek.

"See? He likes you." Stepping back, he released her hand, and hers felt cold as the warmth from his faded. "As do I," he murmured, moving to face her, standing close.

A cheerful whistle sounded, and the spell between them was broken as one of the stable-hands clattered into the yard. Adam stepped back. "And now, sweet Rohese, you had best return, 'ere you're missed. Mayhap later?" He tilted his head, winked and sauntered off.

Amice, who had been giggling with a stable-boy, noticed and rejoined her, sighing. "He is such a handsome knight, isn't he? Oh, Rohese, if I were a lady, I would find him hard to resist."

Shannon was finding the same. Thoughts of Jackson had been completely eclipsed. Yes, she thought in satisfaction as she and Amice wandered back, this holiday was just what she needed.

CHAPTER TWELVE

Shannon was seated on a rough wooden bench beside the small tributary that had been dug from the river. It flowed in, around and back out of the abbey, returning to its source. She crumbled bread and threw it to the fish, laughing as they fought over the scraps, water boiling as they surged. A drake dabbling downstream fixed her with a beady eye and waddled over as fast as his short legs would allow, quacking his indignation that she was not throwing her offering to him. As she turned and tossed him the last of her bread, a hand covered hers. Adam.

This was happening more and more often. She'd come to expect him to turn up whenever she was alone. Their times together were always short, which just added to the intensity of them. Shannon was beginning to feel something much deeper than flirtation, and so, it seemed, was Adam.

She glanced around, fearful they'd be seen together. Thus far, he'd been more secretive. She need not have worried; not a soul was about. The nuns were all in Divine Service; Isabella must be with Giles, and she had left Amice fretting over a small tear in one of her shifts. Of the others, there was no sign.

Taking her other hand in his too, he drew her to her feet, standing so close, she could feel the warmth of him.

"Such cool hands." He held them to his chest. "Let me warm them."

She laughed. "In Bolohovenia we say, 'Cold hands, warm heart.'"

He smiled down at her. "Then I hope, with all my soul, it's true. Is your heart warm for me, love?"

Shannon felt as though she was in a romantic novel, and it was beautiful. Slightly unreal, but still, it stirred her. After all, just now, she wasn't steady, sensible Shannon. She'd let herself be drawn into a life that had nothing to do with Shannon; Rohese she was, and the twenty-first century was so far away, she was almost forgetting what it felt like to be a modern woman.

"Where are you, Rohese? You look at me as though your thoughts are elsewhere." Her hands were still held to his heart; she could feel it beating through his tunic. If Jackson had treated her like this...

"I think you must be hypno...er bedazzling me, Adam. I don't know whether I'm on my head or my heels."

"As to bedazzling, sweeting, I think it's you who does that. It's your eyes; I can never decide what colour they are."

Shannon wished she could believe him – her eyes were a drab hazel rimmed with grey. If only they were a true colour, not a mix of such dull shades. Pulling a face, she said, "Murky is the description I'd use."

"Not so, they are captivating; a man could drown in them." He stroked her cheek. "When you're troubled, as you are now, I think, they are like the sea in winter, but when your mood is light, I would swear they were dark amber jewels set in pewter. Your eyes bewitch me, Rohese." He touched her face again, his own eyes gazing earnestly into hers.

Shannon caught her breath as his fingers moved to trace her lips. Never before had she felt so precious. As she put her hand up to push back a lock of hair which had fallen across his brow, he moved closer, bent his head, and his lips touched hers. Not quite a kiss; the pressure on them was the merest whisper, more like a caress. Perhaps the promise of a kiss. He raised his head and cupped her face in his hands. "Rohese, you touch my very soul. I–"

Suddenly, he dropped his hands and backed off, his head tilted to one side. "My lady Rohese, how does your ankle?"

Lost in the past few moments, Shannon gaped at him, confused by his change of attitude. Her whole world was still spinning. "What?"

"Your ankle, my lady. How does it now? Does it still pain you? Do you wish for my aid?"

As he spoke, Isabella came into view. How had Adam heard her approach? He must have the hearing of a bat, or maybe, and the thought nudged at her like a threat, he had practice at clandestine meetings.

Isabella smiled at Rohese and gave Adam a look that was hard to define. "Adam, my husband is seeking you. Rohese, do you wish to walk awhile? The day is so lovely."

Adam may have recovered himself in an instant, but Shannon was still slightly dazed. She gawped at Isabella blankly before managing to focus on her words.

"Or if your ankle is still paining you, mayhap we could sit on that bench beneath the apple tree." She indicated the same bench they had sat on previously across the other side of the garth. "Adam, lend the Lady Rohese your arm, if you please; then, you must go to Sir Giles. You will find him in the forecourt."

Adam extended his arm to Shannon, and she laid her hand lightly on his, feeling as though the touch of his skin to hers would burst into flame.

140

Thoroughly disconcerted, she let him escort her to the bench and seat her; then, Isabella dismissed him with a careless wave of her hand, wrinkling her nose as he walked away.

"Giles says he is inclined to neglect his duties sometimes. And in truth, he was ever a man with a weakness for a fair face." She glanced at Shannon speculatively through her lashes. "He is a born courtier, do you not think? Quite dazzling when he chooses to be."

"I, er, yes. I suppose."

"Enough of Adam." She drew her arm through Shannon's. "I would learn more of you, Rohese. I have not many friends of an age with me. Have you heard from your family? Do you think you will stay long with your aunt?"

"Er, I don't know. My father will send word when all danger is past. And it is good to spend time with my aunt, for I never met her before." She was uncomfortably aware that she sounded very stilted, but so did Isabella, so maybe she would think Shannon's awkward speech was because of her embarrassment at being caught alone with Adam.

"And you, Isabella? Do you visit for long?"

Isabella sighed. "I wish I were not here at all," she said, then raised rueful eyes to Shannon's shocked face. "No, not at the abbey. I would be happy to stay here for as long as my husband wishes. We are on our way to court." Her face clouded. "I hate it there. I would be happy never to go there again. We were to meet with Giles' brother and his wife, then go on our way together with them; now, that plan is spoiled, and I will not have their support."

"Why are you going if you hate it so much?"

Isabella paused; hesitated. "I've said too much. And I do not even know if I can..." She paused again, hand to her mouth.

Shannon watched her. "Is something troubling you, Isabella?" The brown eyes looking back at her clouded, and Isabella turned her head, her focus fixing on the grass at their feet. Shannon impulsively reached for her hand. "Would it make you feel better to tell me? You can trust me. I don't even know anyone to gossip with, and I wouldn't do that anyway."

Isabella looked up again, her eyelids flickering, then said in low tones, "I believe you. I know not why, but I feel I can speak openly with you. And already I have confided in you, told you one of my secrets. I suppose..." She nodded as if making a decision. "Yes, it will help to speak of it.

"Giles has to meet with John. I *loathe* him; however, Giles insisted I come." She frowned. "I would rather be at our manor with my son; the air at court is poisonous, and I'll spend my time avoiding being seen by John and avoiding the gossip that festers like rotting flesh." Pausing again as though lost in thought, she sighed heavily before raising tremulous eyes to Shannon. "Can we speak of something else? I do not wish to even think on it.

Tell me about your home? Are the customs different there?"

"Er, a little. My mother hoped I would learn many of the ways here from my visit to my aunt."

"Might you ever consider taking the veil?"

"Not likely! I mean, no. But my mother hasn't seen my aunt for many years. In truth, she is really my cousin, in fact my grandmother's cousin, though it seems more polite to call her aunt. My mother only met her once. It seemed a shame to always be so far apart, and in addition to their need for me to be safe from the fever, I've been sad at home. It was thought the time spent with her would cheer me."

"I understand how worried you must be for your family, but why sad?"

Shannon could see things being no better here than back in 2012 if she didn't nip this in the bud right now. She didn't want the same sympathetic glances in 1197, it was why she had got away, for goodness sake. "Sorry, Isabella, like you, it's something I'd rather not dwell on."

"Then let us think of something else before we both end up in tears. Do you play chess?"

"Not very well."

"Merels?"

"Sorry."

Isabella got up, dusted her skirts and held her arm out to Shannon. "I'll teach you. Can you walk back to the guest-chambers, or shall I summon help?"

"I can manage. My ankle is much better now." She took Isabella's arm, and they wandered back to the rooms, where Isabella opened a chest and brought out a board and counters. "Giles prefers chess, but I find merels more light-hearted. See. We put these here and then…"

When Giles returned, he found his wife and Rohese laughing over the merels board. As he entered the room, Isabella looked up, her face alight with humour. "Husband, Rohese has never played before. At last, I have someone I can beat."

Giles chuckled. "You do my wife a great service, Demoiselle, for she doesn't often get the chance to win." As he spoke, he started to remove his hauberk, and a young squire darted forward to help him. At the same time, a knock on the door heralded two lay brothers carrying a tub and some of Giles' servants bearing buckets of hot water. They shut the door, and Giles removed his shirt as they started to fill the tub. Shannon suddenly remembered, to her horror, that in medieval times men thought nothing about disrobing before everyone. Not sure whether Giles would retreat behind a screen, she panicked and jumped up, knocking the merels board to the ground. Isabella stared, and Giles grinned. "That's one way of not losing, lass."

"Er, yes, sorry. Isabella, I must go. I need to, er, speak to my aunt." She dashed for the door before Giles could remove any more clothing and closed it behind her. Leaning on it in relief, she heard them laugh, and a hot wave of embarrassment coursed through her.

She cringed all the way back to her chamber. Amice was sitting on the chest darning a hole in her hose and glanced up as she entered. "Mistress? I mean, Rohese?"

"It's nothing, Amice, I just need to be by myself a moment. Do you want to go for a walk or something?"

While it was nice having a maid and Amice was good company, even though it had only been for a few days, Shannon was feeling a bit crowded. There wasn't much privacy unless she found errands for her. It was certainly pleasant not to have to do her own mending and such, and she'd got over the awkwardness of having someone do things for her, but Amice was almost constantly with her. Even at night, she slept on a pallet at the foot of the bed. She helped her dress and undress, did mending and tidying, brought water for her to bathe, which was nice; then, though, she wanted to help her in and out of the tub, clucking in disbelief when Shannon told her she bathed alone in Bolohovenia. She would consent to go for a walk while Shannon bathed but returned all too quickly.

When Shannon had finally recovered from her embarrassment at her awkward exit from Isabella's chamber, her mind wandered to Adam. *Heaven knows how I'm able to spend so much time with him.*

Their brief meetings were charged with intensity, and how they managed them at all, Shannon had no idea. Somehow, Adam always came to her, found her when she was alone. She contrived for that as often as possible, though he didn't always appear. When he did, he materialised as silently and suddenly as any ghost, vanishing the same way the instant someone else came on the scene.

She ached to spend more time with him. *I think I'm falling in love, proper love this time. Nothing like the way I felt for Jackson.* She held her hands to her face to cool her burning cheeks. *But it can't come to anything, can it? He's betrothed, and this isn't my world; there's no way we can be together, is there?*

Whether or not there was a future for them – and how could there be? – she couldn't stop herself falling deeper in love with him. It was crazy. Stupid! Yet there was something about him that just drew her. *I'm sure it's not only a holiday romance. It feels so real. I shouldn't have come, but I did, so maybe that means I'm meant to be with him.*

People talked about how fate brought lovers together; maybe she and Adam were meant to meet, to fall in love. He was only betrothed, not married, and his wife-to-be was so young, she probably didn't even want to marry him. From what he'd told her in their snatched moments, she sounded like a haughty little miss. Adam wasn't in love with the girl; he'd said so. When she'd asked him if they should be seeing each other, he'd given her a mysterious smile, saying, "Trust me to work it out, sweeting. If this is meant to be, I'll find a way." But how could he?

On the other hand, he's managed to work it out so far. Maybe he has a plan. Maybe it could happen.

Mum would be upset, and how Dad would feel when he knew what had happened and realised where she would be was anyone's guess. *But if I'd fallen in love with an American or an Australian, I'd still be miles away. I can go home for visits, so it's almost the same thing. I wonder if Dad and Chloe can come here? Mum can. Anyway, I can go home sometimes; I'll have to go back once a year to get my EpiPens. If Adam loves me, he'll understand.*

After all, Mum had needed to tell Giles, and that worked out okay. *And she'd had to tell me, too. And I believed her.* She stopped worrying and gave herself up to the dream. It would all come together. It had to.

There was another problem though. Giles and Isabella would be leaving for court in a few days, taking Adam with them. How could she bear him to leave? She'd once read that the way to tell if it was true love or not was not how you felt when you were with someone but whether you could live without them, and she knew without him, her life would be empty. Still, he'd said to trust him, hadn't he? He'd sort it. It was his world; he knew what he was doing.

Meantime, had Shannon known it, Isabella was fretting about going to court without Maude. "For she'll not be able to leave while her parents are there, will she? Giles, you promised I'd have her to bear me company. And I don't want Jehane to come with me, for I do not wish for Dickon to be exposed to that poisonous atmosphere. Nor do I wish John to remember you have a son." She gave him a beseeching look. "Could I not just await your return here?"

Relaxed from his tub, now clad only in his braies and shirt, Giles felt his own heart sink. He could not even explain to himself why it was so important to him that she came. "You will still have Mahelt with you. She'll be able to give an eye to you."

Isabella shook her head resolutely. "You know she will not. No, Giles, a maid will not answer. I need a companion of my own standing. Unless," her eyes glimmered with sudden hope, "my lord, might we ask Rohese if she would accompany us? And Abbess Hildegarde?"

She clenched her hands convulsively by her sides, he noted, wanting to ease her distress. And mayhap this was the solution. Certainly, the Lady Rohese was a comfortable companion for her. He was watching his wife blossom as she enjoyed her new-found friendship; her confidence was growing too. "I'll ask the Abbess."

Isabella almost sagged; relief, he guessed. Her hands reached for his. "Thank you, Giles, *thank you.*"

Taking advantage of the moment and the fact that her women and his men were all occupied elsewhere, he bolted the door and, turning to her, kissed her gently, then again, more deeply. "Suppose we discuss how you can show your gratitude?"

She dimpled back up at him. "Now you've relieved my fears, I think that might be arranged. After all, should I not be a dutiful wife to my lord?"

He growled at her. "And your lord is such a hard taskmaster, is he not?"

Giving a squeak of merriment, she said, "Oh, indeed he is, my lord. I would not dare displease him." And toppled, laughing, onto the bed.

CHAPTER THIRTEEN

Shannon couldn't believe it. *I'm going to court. I'm going to court. I'll be with Adam.* She wanted to dance, shout, jump up and down screaming, but it would startle Amice, and anyway, the Abbess was regarding her soberly. "Oh, yes *please!*"

"Well, I hope this is a wise decision, Rohese, for I found it difficult to think of any reason I could give Sir Giles and Lady Isabella for you not to attend. Indeed, I did try; however, they would have none of it. It seems," and she quirked her mouth a little, "I'm to be her guard dog as well as your own, the poor child. She is most uneasy, which I do understand, although I'm sure her fears will come to naught. I confess, I am still not easy in my mind about the venture, though."

"Oh, Aunt, please. It would be fantastic. And," Shannon coaxed, "it would mean I didn't waste my money buying that silk gown. It cost too much to never wear it.

"I'll be really careful. I've done well so far, haven't I? I'm sure no one thinks I'm odd or out of place. I bet Amice would enjoy it, too, wouldn't you, Amice?" In her excitement, the veneer of medieval speech had slipped, she realised guiltily, glancing at the maid.

Amice, however, didn't seem to have noticed. She was wringing the skirt of her gown between her hands, her face crumpled with distress. "Oh, my lady, I should, I really should, but my da' will never let me. It's one thing me working at the abbey, but he don't trust those nobles at court one bit. He'll never let me. I'm that sorrowful." In her misery at being denied this treat, her speech, too, had altered – now she sounded more like maid than friend. Shannon felt for her. She knew how disappointed she'd be, and, like her, Amice might never get the chance again; however, she could do nothing except hope the lack of a maid wouldn't dissuade the Abbess.

Shannon watched Hildegarde's face as she considered the options; it gave nothing away. After what seemed an age, Hildegarde spoke again.

"Very well, I think it need not present a problem. I will be accompanying you, and Isabella will doubtless bring her own maid." She turned to Amice whose downturned mouth left no one in doubt about her disappointment.

"Well, Amice, I will speak with your father. If his mind is not to be turned, mayhap you would like to remain here. You may serve with the lay sisters until we return, if you wish."

The maid whisked a tear from her cheek, and her lips wobbled upwards again. "Oh yes, my lady. Thank you."

"And we'll have need of you to help pack Mistress Rohese's coffer, will we not? Now, we leave on the morrow after Prime, so you may start your preparations immediately, and I will excuse you from Vespers today; however, I expect you to accompany me to Compline. I'll not be able to say it then, so I shall say now, sleep well tonight. You'll be surprised how tiring travel is here, my dear."

"That's a strange thing to say." Amice spoke the instant the door was closed behind the nun. "For you travelled from Bolo...Boho...Bo...oh, wherever it is! And that must have been ever so many more miles."

"I expect my aunt forgot that. And, then, much of it was–"

"On a boat? That must have been so exciting. No one in my village wants to travel, except me." Her face fell again. "An' now, I likely never will. Still, you c'n tell me all about your journeying; then, at least I'll be able to see it in my head." She plumped down on the bed, looking at Shannon expectantly, which left her no choice but to paint a highly inaccurate picture of medieval travel. Amice, with no experience to draw on, was entranced, making little sounds of alarm as Shannon spoke of the waves which threatened to swamp her imaginary ship, the threat of pirates, the mal de mer which her companions had suffered, and the death of one who had been blown over the sides in a gale.

"And all that way with no serving women, my la...Rohese. It must have been such a hardship for you. How terrible to lose your maid overboard, especially when your ladies were too unwell to come with you." Her eyes were as wide as saucers, and Shannon felt exhausted but triumphant when she reached the end of her far-fetched adventures.

"Yes, terrible. Still, now I have you, and I'm glad."

The little maid grinned. "And if they'd been with you, I'd never have had the chance. I'd still have been with Dame Agatha. She's such a misery. 'Fetch this, bring that, work faster on that churn, girl, don't daydream.' It's so much nicer serving you, Rohese. I wish I could be your maid forever."

What could Shannon say? "But, you know, I must return home before too long. Unless..." She paused and Amice jumped in.

"Unless Sir Adam...well, you never know. I think he's smitten with you, Mistress."

Shannon grinned. "Well, if that should happen, if you wanted, you could come with me, I expect. Won't your young man have something to say, though?"

"Oh!" Amice tossed her head. "Well, he can say what he likes. If I had to, I'd run away. I c'n always find another man, but I'll never get another chance to travel! And once we're gone, how is he supposed to get me back? It's different for you, Rohese. Your parents could send men to fetch you."

Not that easily, thought Shannon.

"My da' can't, not if I'm in your employ and you're wed to Sir Adam. My da' would choke on his own spleen; he wouldn't dare do aught about it, though."

Shannon wasn't at all sure Hildegarde would appreciate this conversation. Still, if and when, it could all be sorted out. She jumped off the bed and clapped her hands. "Anyway, come on, Amice, you can show me how best to pack. Which goes on top and which beneath?"

In that she was mistaken though, for Amice, never having worked for a lady before and never having travelled, had never had to pack before she came to the abbey. The gowns were difficult to stow without creasing, but by trial and error, the job was done. At least Amice had the foresight to add some herbs to the coffers; 'To make the garments smell sweet,' she said. Shannon stored that trick away in her mind for future reference.

As she obediently made her way to Compline, she wondered how she would ever manage to stay still for the short office. However, once she entered the abbey, the peace seeped into her soul, steadying her, and, for a while, at least, her excitement stilled.

Not for long, though. As she headed back to her chamber, the fizz she thought had been calmed started to bubble up inside her again. She managed to walk decorously until she closed the door to her chamber but then, whirled silently around the room to Amice's wide-eyed astonishment, until she subsided in a heap on the bed, smothering her face in the pillow.

Shannon, still overexcited, had lain awake for ages before finally nodding off into a deep sleep from which she was dragged by Amice's insistent voice in her ear. "Rohese! Rohese! Oh, wake up, Mistress, please do! The bell for Prime has already sounded. Rohese!"

As she struggled to wakefulness, she felt rain on her face. *What?* She managed to force her eyes open to see Amice sprinkling water from the ewer over her. "Mistress Rohese! *WAKE UP!*"

Wide awake at last, she automatically glanced at her wrist for the watch that wasn't there. Then, urged by Amice, she almost leaped out of bed to wash.

Amice had laid out her thickest veil and the despised itchy wimple. "Better to travel decent," she assured her.

After the fine clothes she had been wearing, Shannon felt more like a peasant, though Amice was convinced this was the best thing for the journey. Shannon hoped she was right; she didn't want to look like the maid of Isabella's maid.

Amice went off to find a lay brother to drag out the coffer as Hildegarde presented herself at the door.

The courtyard was bustling. Horses and men milled about; the young squires carried things to and fro, piling them into the baggage wain, and a sudden thought occurred to Shannon. How would she travel? Would it be too obvious to ride pillion with Adam? Could she sit on the cart? With all those chests, would there be room?

Amice stood watching, her eyes filled with yearning. Shannon felt sorry for her, but since her father had refused his permission, there was nothing to be done.

Isabella was already mounted on Merlin, whose red leather harness tinkled with small bells. She walked the horse over to Shannon. "Rohese, how will you travel? Do you wish to try riding Kestrel? I know you are not confident, but she's very gentle and can be led." She indicated a sturdy bay mare which, although not particularly large, looked big enough to the inexperienced Shannon.

"Um, I don't think–"

Before she'd finished speaking, Adam was there, holding Blaze's reins, one hand stretched to her, Eustace by his side. "If it pleases you, my lady, Mistress Rohese may ride behind me. Blaze is a most comfortable ride."

It clearly didn't please Isabella, who opened her mouth to protest; however, before she could utter any comment, Adam had swung into the saddle,

156

Eustace had lifted Shannon up behind him, and Isabella was left with nothing to do but frown.

Shannon felt a frisson of delight as she clung to Adam a little more tightly than necessary, since Blaze had not even started moving yet. This was going to be heaven.

Adam placed one hand over her own as she clutched his waist, and they waited for the command to depart. At last, the gates were swung open; Giles and Isabella took their place at the front, and they moved out.

The rhythm of hooves, the jingle of harness, the creak of the baggage wain all added to the romance for Shannon.

She saw nothing of the countryside they rode through, her thoughts too full of Adam to notice anything else, but when they stopped to dine and he helped her down, his hands firm around her waist, she felt stiff and sore. Her back and arms ached, and she wished she could stretch to ease them, but it didn't seem very ladylike. As for her bum!

While the squires and Mahelt, Isabella's maid, were setting out a cloth and food, Shannon wandered behind a bush to massage her buttocks.

She jumped and let her skirts fall as a hand touched her shoulder, twisting round indignantly to see who had caught her in such an embarrassing position, relieved when she realised it was only Hildegarde.

"Are you sore, child?" Shannon nodded. "Yes, I thought that might be the case." Hildegarde grinned conspiratorially. "As, indeed, are parts of me." She had been riding Horace, the abbey nag. Giles had offered her a more spirited, comely mount which Hildegarde had gracefully refused, saying she was familiar with Horace's ways.

"Fortunately, Sister Ursel had foreseen the complication and gave me this." She held out a jar of what looked suspiciously like goose fat. Shannon wrinkled her nose. "Would you rather break out in blisters? No, I thought not. Then, you must learn to accept the remedies of the day; you'd be surprised how many of them have some efficacy."

She proffered the open jar again and Shannon took it reluctantly, dipping her fingers in and sniffing them. To her surprise, the grease smelt of roses and lilies.

"You'll find it will ease your discomfort, and even your unaccustomed nose should be able to find no fault with the fragrance. Sister Ursel, thankfully, believes no remedy should be entirely cheerless. Indeed, if you wish, you may keep this and use some as perfume; I have a spare. Come, smooth some on your skin now while everyone is preoccupied. I'll stand watch over you, and you may do the same for me, for I confess, I will be as grateful as you for Sister Ursel's care."

Shannon found the salve very soothing; the soreness eased almost instantly. Making the most of the cover of the bushes, she stretched her arms luxuriously and shook out her shoulders which helped loosen her up. Then she and Hildegarde wandered back to the main party.

Shannon had tucked the small pot Hildegarde had given her into the pouch which hung at her belt, having also rubbed some onto her neck beneath its covering of fabric. The potion smelt gorgeous. She hadn't thought about it before, but Isabella must use something as fragrance; she always smelt of spices – maybe cinnamon or cloves?

Realising how hungry she felt, she was delighted to discover Isabella had laid out pasties, pieces of cooked meats and crusty bread, followed by small tarts filled with figs and wafers which tasted of almonds and honey. Were they from the abbey?

The repast over, she leaned against a tree, watching idly as Isabella supervised the repacking of cloths and dishes. Adam was lounging at her shoulder, one arm around her waist, as though he had cast caution to the winds. Although, he would probably disappear again the instant everyone stopped being too busy to notice him.

He sniffed her neck appreciatively; she laughed. "Adam, you look just like a dog smelling a roast chicken."

"Well, indeed, you are as delicious as a chicken, little bird, although you smell of a far sweeter fragrance than that. You'll make my senses swim when you ride with me." She felt his lips touch her cheek for a second. "Although, I confess, I like not this wimple and veil, for I cannot kiss your neck."

She turned to smile at him, but he had moved away. Still, at least she would be up behind him again soon. She couldn't wait.

Isabella, finished with her repacking, came over. Bearing in mind her earlier stiffness, Shannon asked, "Do we have far to go?"

"Would you rather ride on the baggage wain with Leofwine?"

From the expression on Isabella's face, this was an idea she had jumped on. What was the matter with her? Did she really hate Adam? Or maybe she was jealous. What had she said about him being dazzling?

Well, she isn't going to spoil things for me, that's for sure, Shannon thought, saying, "No, thank you. I'm quite content to ride behind Adam. I just wondered how far it was, that's all."

"As you wish." Isabella sounded rather cool but thawed again as she said, "It's about the same as the distance we have already covered. Indeed, we ate a little early. Giles was quite importunate. He says riding makes him hungry; I think it's more that he knew we had pasties." She laughed. "He can never resist a pasty." Then the smile dropped from her face. "I shall miss your company when you return to your home."

If Shannon had been unconvinced of Isabella's motives before, the expression on her face now reassured her. *I expect she's just worried I'll get hurt;*

she's too nice to be jealous. I'll have to watch myself.
Jackson cheating with Sienna has made me suspicious of
everyone. I don't want to be like that.

"Never mind, we can stay in touch." Oops, that
was a bit of a faux pas. Isabella was gazing at her
rather blankly. "I mean, we can always write to
each other," she amended, realising as she said it
that, if she did return home, they couldn't. But if
she stayed...

"I know, but you'll be so far away, and it will
take so long for messages to pass between us. Still."
Isabella tweaked her lips back up again, "we have
the now, and who knows the future?"

Shannon's eyes danced. *You never spoke a truer*
word, Izzy. Who knows?

Isabella continued. "And, for the nonce, I
suppose we had better continue on our way." Her
mouth turned down. "I do not look forward to this;
however, at least I will have you to bear me
company."

She really did seem stressed. Could it be that
bad? Shannon, for her part, was looking forward to
it, but then, apart from Isabella, who wouldn't?

They wandered back to the horses, Isabella's
steps dragging a little. Shannon was eager for
someone to help her mount. She, at least, was
happy, although she suspected she'd be as stiff as a
board by the time they reached their destination.
She hoped that salve was good for aching muscles,
too.

Adam held her close for a moment before he lifted her up onto Blaze, murmuring, "Hold tight, sweeting."

Hold tight? Well, she didn't really need to. She had her balance now, and the pace was not fast, but the opportunity to lean close against him, her cheek pressing into his back, was too pleasurable to resist, although after a while, she did spare a glance for the area they were riding through. They were surrounded by hills. The Chilterns? They must be, but everything looked so different in this century. Unable to get her bearings, she wrapped her arms a little tighter around Adam and leaned her head close again, the better to enjoy the rest of the ride. Nevertheless, she found she was grateful when they neared the castle; her behind was beginning to feel quite numb.

As they approached the court, Shannon tried once more to work out where she was. Berkhamsted, maybe? She knew there had been a castle there. Wherever it was, they'd passed through a small but busy town first and Shannon had leaned even closer to Adam as the horses picked their way through the throng of people. She'd wrinkled her nose as various smells drifted up and winced as children with open sores ran alongside the horses, relieved when they left the town behind them.

She found it was no quieter here; the place swarmed with people. Ladies on high-stepping palfreys, maids going hither and thither, farriers and armourers, smiths hammering, knights practising with swords, and some very dubious-looking women in garish clothing, worn far tighter than seemed decent. Tripods with cooking pots were set over fires, cook-stall owners called their wares, women scrubbed at laundry in great tubs. Dogs and children swarmed everywhere. As Shannon stared, taking everything in, a man emerged from a tent adjusting his clothing, and a woman dressed in a gaudy gown blew him a kiss before counting coins in her hand as she walked away, her head bare, hair rippling down her back, tousled and greasy.

Tents – pavilions, Adam had called them – were everywhere, smallish, dull-coloured ones at first, but as they got nearer the castle, they became larger and more brightly coloured, in multi-hued stripes, pennants fluttering outside. At last, they drew to a halt by a pavilion with bright brown and yellow stripes. Giles dismounted and held out his arms to Isabella. Adam did the same for Shannon, hands lingering about her waist, his lips brushing her forehead lightly before he let go. Hildegarde accepted Miles' offer of help, and the horses were led away.

As they dismounted, a youngster watched them – a slight girl with light brown hair and grey eyes, nearly as tall as Shannon but several years her junior. Her face had lit up when she saw them arrive, and now she rushed over to them, laughing, and dropped Isabella and Giles a curtsy. "Sir Giles, and oh, Lady Isabella, how lovely! I've not seen you here for such an age."

Shannon watched with interest as the girl drew Isabella aside and plied her with questions which Shannon could not quite hear. She stood observing, charmed by her obvious delight, until the girl was called away by an older woman. Not as finely dressed as the girl, so perhaps maid to her? Unlikely to be her mother, for the girl was clearly of good birth.

As the men went off about their business, the women were ready to enter the tent when a priest spied Hildegarde and came hurrying up. The Abbess seemed to be remonstrating with him. He waved his hands about until she nodded, then he bowed, strutting away again, full of importance.

Hildegarde turned and spoke to Isabella who made little sounds of dismay, her hands clasped against her breast. The colour drained out of her face. Shannon, perturbed, hurried to her side.

Hildegarde took Isabella's hand and led her into the tent, which had been erected by the men Sir Giles had sent ahead of them. The Abbess drew her gently to a stool and sat her down, still holding her hand.

"I'm so sorry, Lady Isabella. I'm afraid there is no choice, but don't be fearful, for I will not leave you at any other time. I'll remain with you, as will Rohese. If Sir Giles can escort you to and from the pavilion and stay by your side until he has brought you to us, I promise to safeguard you. Don't fret,

John will not intimidate me; I promise you, I am more than a measure for him."

Shannon looked from one to the other. "What's happened?"

Isabella turned; her face was blank. It was Hildegarde who enlightened Shannon. "As soon as the chaplain saw my badge of office, he was determined I should have a small private chamber allocated to me in the castle."

"Well, that's all right. I can stay with Isabella. And you'll have Giles and his men." She gave Isabella an encouraging nod. "They'll keep you safe."

Isabella raised her eyes, looking hopeful, but Hildegarde shook her head. "Unfortunately, when I refused the chaplain because I was travelling with my niece, he said he would ensure we had a chamber large enough for both of us."

Shannon was gutted. No Isabella meant no Adam, but she put that thought to one side in the face of Isabella's distress, putting her arm round the shaking shoulders. Why was she so afraid?

"Isabella, I'm sure you'll be all right. My aunt and I will only leave you when Sir Giles is by your side. And what can John do to you?"

Isabella managed a wobbly smile. "I'm being foolish, and mayhap I am nervous over nothing, for I'm sure John has other fish to fry, but oh, Rohese! He makes my skin crawl, and he knows it. If he sees me, he'll not be able to resist baiting me."

"Well, I think you're worrying over nothing. I'm sure he has plenty of other people to upset. How long is it since he saw you? He might not even remember you; he must meet loads of people. You stay with us, and we'll take care of you, won't we Aunt?"

"Indeed, and I think Rohese is right. Look around outside. The hall will be packed with many people clamouring for his attention. Come, let me get someone to brew you a tisane. It will calm you." She disengaged her hands gently, and left Isabella to Shannon, going first to her bags, then over to the maid, Mahelt, who nodded and went off, coming back a short while later with a cup of something.

"One of Sister Ursel's calming remedies stirred into hot wine," Hildegarde murmured to Shannon. "Not enough to make her drowsy, yet enough, I hope, to take the edge off her fears. It may not be the tea or coffee you are used to, however, I find a hot drink of any description always soothes, and Ursel's remedies are most effective."

It did seem to work. Shannon remembered how her mum had said she was given a drink which helped calm her, and she watched as the colour returned to Isabella's face. She was still subdued, but that might have been the dose. At least she'd stopped shaking and seemed better able to cope.

"Do you think she'll be all right?" Shannon muttered to Hildegarde, who nodded.

"Yes, I think it was just the shock. The poor girl thought she had arranged matters, and then, the chaplain undid all her plans. When she has had a chance to readjust, I think she'll be able to cope. And we need only use the chamber for sleeping. At all other times, when we are not in the great hall, we can remain here. I doubt Sir Giles will want to stay more than a couple of days anyway. He is not overly happy at court himself."

Shannon nodded, then, since no one else was near, said under her breath, "Aunt, which castle is this anyway? I've been trying to work it out. Is it Berkhamsted?"

Hildegarde smiled. "Well done, Rohese. It is indeed. I believe, in your time, there is only a vague idea of what this looked like, and that may be wrong, so you will find it all the more interesting."

Wow! She certainly would. She had visited and seen the plans of what they thought it had looked like in the twelfth century. Now she was here, she knew they weren't quite right. She'd have to make a mental note of it, and when she got back – *if* she went back, she corrected herself – she'd try and sketch it out, make a return visit to the ruins and compare it what she had seen on their information board.

CHAPTER FOURTEEN

They remained in Giles' pavilion until it was time to eat. The company and the dose Hildegarde had given Isabella seemed to revive her, for she slowly lost the pinched expression she had been wearing. When she started chivvying the squires to set the stools, coffers, trestles and pallets here not there and directing Mahelt hither and yon, Hildegarde and Shannon exchanged relieved glances.

By the time Giles returned, she had almost recovered herself and told him of the change of plans with relative equanimity. "However, it's of no matter, my husband, for Abbess Hildegarde and Rohese have promised to bear me company at all times except when they sleep, and then, I shall have you near me. And indeed, I am likely being foolish, for doubtless, John has long since forgotten me."

Her tone was light, but there were still small lines of strain about her eyes; Giles responded in kind, privately vowing to keep as close to her as he was able. For John to overset all he had worked for now would be insupportable. His jaw tightened. If John were not brother to the King, Giles doubted he would still live. He had made enemies of too many who would otherwise have served him with their hearts, not just their hands. For certès, he had not the gift of winning men, and for that he was to be pitied. Yet since Isabella was doing her best to maintain a cheerful disposition, Giles determined to do likewise.

They stayed for a while, waiting for Giles' men to join them. Shannon was changing the heavy veil and wimple she'd worn during the journey for her silk veil, wishing she had a better mirror than the polished metal disc she had borrowed from Isabella. She'd propped it on a chest and was doing her best to view herself in it when Isabella gave a sudden cry as she caught at Shannon's right hand. "Why, how strange! That ring you wear. Look! It's twin to my own. My lord gave it to me on our betrothal, but my fingers are too slender. In truth, even to keep it on my thumb, I've wound thread around it on the palm side. See?" She held her own hand out next to Shannon's. It was smaller than Shannon's, with narrower fingers. Shannon's hands were square and sturdy, like Marion's.

Shannon was dismayed. It had been a mistake to wear it. She hadn't stopped to think, just pushed it onto her index finger when her mum gave it to her and forgotten to take it off. She gave a tight smile.

"I had believed it to be unique," Isabella said thoughtfully. "Giles' father commissioned it made for him when he was knighted. Still, it is not beyond the realms of possibility, I suppose, that someone else should have made a similar one. How came you by yours?"

Shannon opened her mouth, but before she could speak, to her relief, Giles, who had not been attending, turned to them.

"Come then, Wife. Ladies?" He nodded to the other two, bowed, and offered a courtly arm to Isabella and the Abbess. Adam did likewise with Shannon, and they strolled through the pavilions towards the castle and up the steep stone steps that lead through to the antechamber. It was an outwardly merry group who entered the great hall. If Giles could feel a tensing in the muscles of the arm laid along his and hear a tremor in the light laugh Isabella gave as she responded to a sally he made, it was doubtful anyone else would have noticed.

Shannon was to be disappointed though. She expected, since Adam had taken her arm to lead her to the hall, that he would be her partner. Instead, he disengaged himself from her and strolled over to a group of his contemporaries. So many people milled around, she lost sight of him and had no choice but to suffer Guy as her companion.

The food was delicious; roasted meats, spiced stews, even a peacock complete with feathered skin put back after cooking, honeyed, spiced fruits, nuts and a subtlety shaped like a unicorn. Although Guy attended diligently to her needs, he had little to say. Indeed, as soon as the trestles were cleared, he excused himself, leaving her and joining a group of men at the edge of the hall. Isabella was claimed by a lady who drew her into a corner and started an earnest conversation, and Hildegarde was much in demand also.

Shannon was left on her own, watching the crowd and feeling like an outsider when she became aware of someone approaching her.

"Hello."

She raised her head to see the same youngster who had pounced on Isabella earlier standing before her with a tentative smile on her face. She was wearing a light veil now, her braids falling in two thick ropes down to her waist with a silver fillet embellishing each.

Shannon grinned back; the child had such an open, guileless look, she couldn't resist her.

Encouraged, the girl moved closer, saying frankly, "I haven't seen you here before. Did you come with Sir Giles and Lady Isabella?"

"I did, and with my aunt, the Abbess of Sparnstow. My name's Rohese. What's yours?"

"I'm Alys. That's my mother, over there with Lady Isabella. I was eating with my betrothed, but now the tables are cleared, he's gone off and left me. He always does that. It's because I'm still young, I suppose."

It didn't seem to bother her overly, for all she wrinkled her pert little nose. "I saw you seated with Sir Guy. Is he your husband?" She stopped and clapped a hand to her mouth, the colour rising in a tide over her neck and up her cheeks as though she realised she was being impertinent. "I'm sorry, I shouldn't have asked. My father says I talk too much, though truly, how am I to learn if I do not ask?"

"How indeed?" Shannon was finding her quite irresistible, and now she had someone to talk to, even if it was only this child, she felt much less of a wallflower. "You must always ask, for, as you said, how else will you learn?" She was enchanting. She seemed very young, even though Shannon would guess she was about fourteen. Just an inch or so shorter than she, but very skinny. "Yes, I supped with Sir Guy, and no, he is not my husband. I don't have one."

"Really?" Alys' eyes were round with surprise.

I must seem too old to be single. "Well, I was betrothed." *At least, I thought Jackson was serious*, she excused herself silently. "However," she let her lower lip droop, "he betrayed me."

Alys opened her eyes even wider. "Oh, Rohese, how awful for you. How did you bear such shame? Was your father very angry? Mine would have been furious. Oh, I think if I had been played false like that, my heart would have broken."

She plunked herself down next to Shannon on the bench, big tears of sympathy welling up. "How tragic, Lady Rohese. Are you not heartbroken?"

"Well, I was at first. Although, Alys, you know, sometimes these things do happen for the best. Imagine how unhappy I would have been had we wed and I then discovered his perfidy." She found the style of speech coming quite easily now; she was even beginning to think in medieval terms.

Alys chewed on her thumbnail before pulling it away and examining it with a disgusted air. "I must learn not to bite my nails."

Shannon hid a smirk; things weren't always so different here. Alys looked at her, a dubious expression on her face. "I suppose it was better for you so, though many men do stray once they are wed. My grandmother says it's to be expected. I am lucky, my betrothed loves me; he would never betray me. My mother and father chose him well." She grinned expansively. "He's very handsome. My parents say they will not allow us to wed until I reach my fifteenth year, but I would marry him tomorrow if they would let us. He agrees with them though. He says it's better for a woman to be a little older if she's to be a good wife." She heaved a gusty sigh. "And I suppose he is right." Then brightened, saying, "And once I am his wife, he will spend more time with me."

Then, the mobile little face fell again. "Although, I do not like his parents. But neither does he so, mayhap, we will not spend too much time with them. He has his own manor, even though he is not his father's heir. We might spend our time there for, once we're wed, he will not need to be a hearth knight."

Shannon wasn't so sure. Didn't brides as young as this learn the ropes with their in-laws? Still, she supposed Alys knew more than she did, and maybe it was the heir whose wife learned from his parents, although the kid was obviously an optimist, looking at life through rosy spectacles. She hoped she wouldn't be disappointed. Shannon couldn't begin to imagine her running a household. "Aren't you a little young for that responsibility?"

Alys put her chin in the air, and, suddenly, the idea of her giving orders didn't seem quite so strange. "My mother has taught me well; she says she has no expectations of me disappointing her. Besides, we'll have a steward and others to serve us, so it won't be difficult. And in another year, I'll have grown in stature."

She leaned forward, left elbow on her knees, elfin chin resting on her hand, then stood and pointed. "See, Rohese, it's the Queen's favourite jongleur. I heard he has written a new lay for her."

The Queen? Eleanor or Berengueria? Shannon looked, but there were too many bodies between her and the dais, and she couldn't get a clear view. She craned her neck and found she could just see a group of musicians tuning up their instruments – none of which she recognised. A lean man with curly hair and bright clothing was down on one knee before the dais, but she still couldn't see who he was bowing to. Getting up, he strolled over to the other players, picked up something a bit like a small harp, and the hall grew quiet. Running his thumb across it, he hummed a few notes; then, his song rang out. He had a voice like brown velvet, and Shannon shivered with delight as his honeyed tones caressed each word, strumming the strings of his instrument until they almost wept with intensity.

"You blazed like a comet
through England and France,
leading both of your kings
in a wild, moonstruck dance.
No puppet, no damsel
no douce little queen,
the beautiful Eleanor,
bold Melusine.

Wife of two kings
and of kings, a mother,
All men have desired
Eleanor for their lover.
All other beauties
are cast in the shade;
when Eleanor smiles,
others wither and fade.

In the light of her laughter
our strong men grow weak,
beguiled and bedazed,
be they never so meek.
Other realms ache with envy,
their eyes lose their sheen,
for there's no one to match
England's dazzling Queen."

There were a few other verses; she couldn't catch all the words. Rather extravagant – Eleanor must be knocking on a bit now. She supposed it never hurt to flatter a queen though. At any rate, the crowd roared its approval, though one man, who looked to be in his early thirties, stood back, leaning against a pillar, one eyebrow raised, giving him a sardonic expression. As Shannon watched him, he caught her eye and bowed, blowing her a kiss. Embarrassed, she turned away but not before she saw the curious expression on his face.

She could see the ladies on the dais now; there were several of them, all applauding, and an older one was on her feet, beckoning him. The jongleur came to her, bowed down again, and she gave him her hand to kiss. Shannon was in awe. This must be Eleanor of Aquitaine. And she was actually seeing her. Not that she could see much; the lady was soon obscured by bodies again.

Shannon was captivated. She'd really seen Eleanor, was in the same hall! Not that she could ever tell anyone in her own time, but she hugged the knowledge to herself. What a privilege.

Then, she noticed the man who had blown her a kiss earlier was still staring in her direction. She gave a half smile and turned away, but she felt as though he was still watching her. The sensation was so strong, she almost fancied he was burning a hole in her spine. But she was just imagining it, wasn't she?

She shifted position slightly so she could take a surreptitious glance out of the corner of her eye. *Blast!* He was not only still looking, he'd seen her peeking at him. Now, she was feeling more than uncomfortable. The look on his face was strange, and he wasn't even hiding the fact he was watching her – staring quite openly.

She resolutely dragged her gaze away and began to talk to Alys, whose small face was glowing, but all the time, she could feel those eyes watching her. Who was he? And why was he so interested in her? Had she slipped up somehow? Could he tell she wasn't like the others? She peeked again. Still that narrow-eyed catlike stare. He was almost licking his lips. *Oh, yuck! What a perv!* She took another quick glimpse. *Hell!* He seemed to have moved a bit closer, or was that her imagination? He'd be a bit less menacing if he wasn't half in the shadows.

So distracted was she, she hadn't been paying attention to Alys until the girl gave an excited squeak and grabbed her hand.

"Rohese, look!"

Shannon followed the direction of her finger which was pointed at a group of knights clustered on the far side of the hall.

"That one," Alys whispered proudly, "is my betrothed. The one with the chestnut hair. And, Rohese, you can't tell from here, but he has the most beguiling eyes."

Shannon recoiled in shock. *This child-woman was betrothed to Adam?* The blood drained from her face.

Alys didn't notice. She was still gazing at Adam. "Is he not handsome, Rohese? Oh, I am so blessed." She sat smiling at her secret thoughts.

Shannon turned blindly and groped for her goblet, sending a splash of wine down her skirts. Alys turned in horror and began mopping at it. "Your gown! Come, let me take you to the bedchamber. We must deal with it quickly else it will be spoilt." She seized her hand and pulled her, unprotesting and white to the lips, from the hall. "My maid will deal with it. How fortunate you are not much taller than I. You may borrow one of my gowns while yours dries."

Still numb with shock, Shannon allowed Alys to lead her from the hall and out across the bailey to a wooden building. Opening the door, she dragged Shannon in behind her. Then, she opened another door which led into a small chamber. "My father had been going to bring our pavilion," Alys prattled on, "however, so many have come, it was decided to turn some of the outbuildings into guest-quarters."

There was only one bed in the room – a large one, heavily canopied. "Yours?" Shannon asked.

Alys giggled. "My parents sleep there. Here is my niche." She drew Shannon to a small curtained corner where there was a chest and a pallet and no room for anything else. "Sit you down whilst I fetch Tilda."

Shannon sat obediently, biting her lip and trying hard to stop the tears falling from her eyes. When Adam said he was betrothed, she had not imagined this engaging child. How could he? How could *they* betray Alys like this? How could they bring pain and shame to this sweet imp?

Lost in misery, she never heard anything until the curtain was pulled back with a rattle. She turned, shocked to see the man who had blown her a kiss earlier eyeing her in a manner which made her feel horribly exposed.

He came and stood just in front of her. Way too close for comfort. She wanted to shudder but didn't dare. She had a nasty feeling he might have enjoyed that. She'd have to brazen it out. Lifting her chin, she gave him stare for stare. His lips twitched into a smile. *Damn!* He seemed to like her direct approach. She felt sick. How could she get rid of him?

He held his hand out to her. "A new face to court, I see, sweeting. What is your name?"

Obviously wealthy, the hand held out to her wore lavish rings. His face was handsome, yet there was something about him which repelled her. She started to rise without his assistance, but he gave her an imperious look, and she allowed him to help her. His hard fingers squeezed her hand unpleasantly. "Your name, my lady?" He repeated.

"Er...Rohese...er, my lord." She had a feeling the 'my lord' was expected of her.

"Sweet Rohese. What a delightful name. And what a delightful gown." He frowned. "I see you've spilled something down it. Allow me to assist you. You must needs remove it before it stains."

Shannon froze with horror. "My lord?"

"Come now, you mustn't be shy with me." His tones were silky. He still had hold of her hand, pulling her closer to him. What should she do? What *could* she do? This couldn't be happening.

She was about to protest when the chamber door opened again. The man dropped her hand instantly and turned, an urbane expression on his face. "Alys, you've been remiss, puss. This demoiselle has need of assistance. Indeed, I thought I should have to help her myself."

Alys stopped dead, faced her uncertainly then turned back to the man, dipping into a low curtsy. "My lord, I've brought Tilda to help."

"As well for you, child. It does not do to neglect so charming a lady. How terrible it would be if something should befall her." He gave Shannon a mocking glance, turned on his heel and stalked to the door, glancing over his shoulder as he left the room. "Until we meet again, Demoiselle. I assure you, I look forward to that with the greatest pleasure."

Shannon dropped back onto the pallet – her legs would hold her up no longer. Alys was white as chalk, her hand to her mouth. "Oh, Rohese, I'm so sorry. I would never have left you if I'd known Lord John had followed us."

"Lord John?"

"The King's brother. Did you not know?" Her eyes were huge, her lips trembled. "Never, ever allow him to catch you on your own. It's not safe."

Tilda put her hand on her young mistress's shoulder. "There, sweeting. No harm done. Sit you down next to Mistress Rohese. I will fetch you both wine."

Alys clutched her hand. "No. Please stay."

Tilda freed herself. "Mistress, there's wine in the chamber. I shan't leave you, child, but the pair of you are as pale as new cheese. One moment." She whisked from the alcove, returning with two cups.

Shannon almost snatched one from her and took a gulp. Her heart was hammering so hard, she was sure they could hear it. She took another large swallow.

"Now, Mistress, be calm. Naught happened, did it?" She eyed Shannon closely. Shannon shook her head. "Well then, all's well. Come, let me see your gown." She pulled at it, tutting over the stain. "Mistress Alys, this should have been put to soak at once. Yet, mayhap it's as well you had not already removed it. Quickly, slip it off, and I'll deal with it." She lifted the lid of the coffer and pulled out a gown of soft green linen. "Here. This will look well on you."

Hildegarde had just extricated herself from the company of a garrulous countess who was eager to impress her with the gifts her husband had presented to an abbot for whom Hildegarde had great disdain, knowing him to be no man of God but a hard-hearted political aspirant. She searched around her but could find no sign of Shannon. Drat her. Did she not realise the danger here? Taking care of an entire convent of sisters was as nothing beside watching this headstrong girl didn't get herself into trouble.

A worried frown puckered her brow, and she half rose when she saw Shannon enter the hall accompanied by the young Lady Alys. Sweet Mary, what had happened? The pair of them were the colour of putty, and Shannon looked as though she might vomit. And that was not the gown she had been wearing earlier. That one had been the peacock silk; this was a soft green.

Hildegarde's hand flew to her throat, horrified, as she realised that, in these colours, Shannon bore a remarkable resemblance to Marion on her first appearance at the abbey.

From the other side of the hall, she could see Prince John was also observing them through narrowed eyes, one hand stroking his beard as though he racked his brain to think who she reminded him of. As Hildegarde reached Shannon, he blinked and stared harder.

Hildegarde put one arm around Shannon and with the other, steered Alys in the direction of her mother. "Child, I need to speak with Rohese privately. Attend upon your lady mother." Then, with the other arm still around Shannon's trembling shoulders, she propelled her to the back of the hall and up the steeply-winding stairs leading to the gallery, beyond which was the small private chamber they had been given in deference to her rank. Shutting the door firmly behind her, she opened the coffer and pulled out the second of the gowns Shannon had brought with her, the apricot one the nuns had sewn.

"Quickly, Shannon, remove that gown. You must not – you simply *must not* – be seen in those colours. Here, put this on. Then, tell me what happened. But we mustn't tarry here overlong. We need to be in the safety of the hall."

As she sat on the bench with her back against one of the tapestries which decorated the walls, Shannon's head was swimming. Still upset about Adam and edgy from her royal encounter, she'd definitely had too much wine, and the smoke from the torches around the hall was making her eyes smart. She turned to speak to Hildegarde; however, that lady's attention was claimed by a matron to her left, wearing a gown in a violent shade of puce, which clashed horribly with her flushed face.

Shannon stifled a giggle and rubbed her sore eyes. She needed some fresh air; her head was muzzy, and she felt queasy. Where was Alys? No, she wouldn't go to her. She was with her parents and Adam, and not for worlds would Shannon draw his attention. She tried to find Isabella amongst the crowds of gaily-clad women, but she was nowhere to be seen. Surely, oh surely, it couldn't hurt. She'd just go outside for a few moments.

While she was still thinking about it, she was surprised to see a large cage full of finches being brought in. The cage was taken to a trestle in the centre of the hall and opened, leaving Shannon entranced as the birds flew out, fluttering overhead.

She watched them in delight until several men brought in falcons and, to her horror, released them. All around her, bets were being taken as the falcons swooped on the small birds, killing them, to the raucous amusement of the guests. Shannon gasped in dismay, sickened, tears filling her eyes as she sprang to her feet, determined now to leave the hall.

Keeping a watch on John, who was lounging in a corner, flirting with a woman in a very tightly-laced dress, which revealed much more than Shannon thought was decent in this era, she slipped through the noisy throng to the door, tiptoeing into the antechamber. After a quick glance over her shoulder, she sped across the room to the open archway and slipped out. Leaning against the rough stone, she took deep gulps of fresh air. The coolness cleared her head and soothed her aching eyes as she strove to erase from her mind the images of the massacre she'd witnessed.

A couple of men-at-arms jostled past her, then turned to stare, one saying something in an undertone to the other, who laughed and made a lewd gesture. In a panic, Shannon darted back inside, out of their view; however, as she turned towards the door leading back into the hall, it opened, and John stood there, talking to someone she couldn't see. He had his back to her – he wouldn't have noticed her.

She stood frozen to the spot for a moment, then spied a narrow stair and fled up it as fast as she dared, holding her gown in one hand and clinging to the stone walls with the other. The steps narrowed towards the centre of the spiral and had dips worn in the middle; the soles of Shannon's shoes were thin, the leather slippery, and her heart was in her mouth as she tried to hurry yet not misstep. If she fell on these, she would break bones at the very least. Probably her neck.

Heart thumping, almost dizzy with fright, she trod carefully on the widest part of each step. If only there was more light.

She gasped as one foot slid from beneath her, wobbling precariously until, by some miracle, she managed to regain her balance. It was no good. She'd have to slow down. She pressed tighter to the wall, trying to gain support from the stone.

After a few more nightmarish moments, she reached the top and paused, not knowing where she was. Then, she heard soft footfalls behind her and, without looking round, turned right, hoping to find somewhere she could hide.

The torches blazed up here as well, but their flickering flames threw dark shadows along the hallway. Shannon hurried as best she could along the short corridor trying to find another stair back to the hall. She rounded a corner and came to a dead end. Panting and disorientated, she turned back the way she'd come, to see John padding towards her, a smile on his face like that of a hunter who'd spied his quarry.

"Sweetheart, who is it you seek?" His expression grew lascivious as he stared at her, his gaze lingering on her body, raking her up and down. "Might I hope you are desirous of renewing our acquaintance?"

He advanced on her, flames from the wall sconces reflected in his eyes. Shannon started and moved backwards. "Mistress, be not so shy. Do you seek refuge from the hubbub below?" She nodded mutely, and his tongue flickered over his lips. "Then, let us seek sanctuary together."

Shannon took another step backwards and then another, unable to look away from his hypnotic gaze. She felt like a rabbit before a snake. Each step she took backwards, John mirrored with a forward one, until she suddenly felt a door at her back and could retreat no further. The cold metal studs on the door she pressed against were not responsible for the tremor that ran through her.

John put his hands lightly on her waist, and she tried to urge her frozen brain to work. A knee to the royal groin, although it appealed to her just now, was probably not the safest way to rebuff a prince. How might a medieval woman get herself out of this predicament?

As John moved one hand to cup her face, tilting it upwards ready for his kiss, his other hand sliding down to her hips, she looked him full in the eyes. This had to work. "My lord, I'm aware of the honour you do me, truly I am." She searched his face for a sign of compassion and found none. "But I pray you, do not do this. Do not make me imperil my soul."

Giving a snort of laughter, he asked, "Why should I not, when my own is so often imperilled? Is your soul of so much more value than mine? Come, sweetheart, let us enjoy the fruits of the flesh tonight, and tomorrow confess and be cleansed. And," he continued silkily, "is it a greater sin than displeasing your future king? The one who can imperil your body, if not your soul?"

Shannon said nothing, but her horrified gaze was fixed on him. She felt like a deer who could see the headlights of the car; she could not move to save herself. She had never fainted in her life, but now, black specks filled her vision; her legs felt weak.

John swore and rolled his eyes as her knees buckled. He let go of her chin and caught her around the shoulders as she began to sink to the floor. Sweeping her off her feet, he kicked open the door behind her, carried her into the chamber and deposited her upon a padded chest.

As Shannon lolled against him, she was dimly aware of the fragrance of cinnamon, cloves and bay overlaid by a faint smell of sweat before he thrust her head down towards the floor. She struggled, then relaxed as he said with a wry laugh, "Do not fear, sweeting, I have no demands on your virtue at this precise moment, I assure you. I'm merely trying to restore you to your senses. I may have varied tastes, but a fainting woman holds little appeal."

She sat there, his hand pressed to her shoulders, her head hanging over her knees until the faintness receded. When, at last, she eased herself upright, and he slid his arm around her, she found herself too grateful for the support to worry about anything else.

As she began to recover, however, the wine she had drunk earlier started to roil in her stomach, and she gave a hiccup. Before she could gag, John had her on her feet and was propelling her inexorably towards a curtain, which he pulled aside, revealing a garderobe. Holding her veil and her hair back from her face, he pushed her to her knees, and she put both arms thankfully on the smooth wood surrounding the hole. The evil smells which came from the latrine shaft put paid to her last shred of self-restraint, and she lost her supper, retching uncontrollably.

Finally, her eyes streaming, she sat weakly back on her haunches, and through the blur of tears, she saw that they hadn't been quite quick enough. John was gingerly wiping a splash of vomit from his elegant shoes.

"Finished?"

She nodded. "I think so."

He gave her a crooked grin. "I confess, that was not quite what I had in mind for the evening's amusement. Come."

He raised her to her feet and steered her carefully back to a chair in the corner of the room then, fetching a laver of water and some napkins, he wiped her face gently.

"Lass, I find you've quite despoiled my appetite for the delicacy tonight, to say nothing of my shoes." He moistened another napkin and mopped her mouth and her still-streaming eyes. Then, with a barely disguised twinkle, he said, "I think we'll blame the wine. In truth, I found it somewhat over-spiced myself." He patted her hand. "Rest you here awhile, sweetheart, and I'll send someone to attend you. It's to be hoped our next encounter will be memorable in pleasanter ways than this one."

As the lady beside her prattled on, Hildegarde was becoming increasingly aware that Rohese was nowhere to be seen again. She sought Alys and spotted her standing with her parents and a knight from Giles' household whose name she did not know. An uneasy feeling began to creep over her, not improved when one of the stewards came to her and cut in abruptly on the lady Richildis' conversation. Richildis' already florid complexion darkened in offence as the steward waved an airy hand at her and, taking Hildegarde's arm, drew her towards the door.

Hildegarde paused, pulling back slightly, and the steward turned, an enquiry in his eyes. "Young man, have the goodness to tell me where you are taking me." Her tone was frosty. The steward looked back with total unconcern, which further aggravated Hildegarde's worries.

"My lady Abbess, my lord has need of speech with you concerning your niece."

Hildegarde's knees felt suddenly weak. Drat that girl! What danger had she got herself into this time? She was further discomfited by John's knowledge that Shannon was her 'niece'. She knew he had been watching her. Had he also been making enquiries? *Sweet Mary, protect us. And a curse...* No, that was not seemly. Pulling herself together, she followed him to the alcove beyond the door of the great hall.

John appeared in front of her, a little older now than when she had last seen him. She curtsied deeply and then raised her head. "My lord?"

He offered his hand and assisted her to rise, saying, "My lady Abbess, pray do not be alarmed."

Well to expect her not to be alarmed with an opener like that. Did he have to be so theatrical?

"Should I be, my lord?" She kept her tone low, even managing to raise a smile. Heaven forfend he should think she had aught over which to be concerned.

"In truth, I think not. However, the lady Rohese has been taken unwell."

If you've touched her... "My lord?" Still that carefully even tone.

"I came across her in the corridor. She seemed to be ailing."

She is likely indeed to be ailing if you have touched her, you...you...

She allowed her brow to furrow a little, gazing at him quizzically, and wished she had not when she saw the mischief on his face.

"I had the pleasure of being able to aid her. I'm afraid she'd partaken a little too liberally of the spiced wine." He gave her a confiding look. "She seems to have evaded your careful watch. I feel sure, had you noticed, you would have prevented her 'ere it came to this."

Hildegarde clenched her fists under the sleeves of her habit, then forced herself to relax again, hiding her mortification behind a blank expression. He was blaming it on her, and to a degree, he was correct. Then again, it had been hard to concentrate on Rohese once Lady Richildis had claimed her. "It seems I have cause to thank you for your care of her, my lord. If you would allow your steward to take me to her, I will see what may be done."

John's lips curved upwards. Why was it his smile made her trust him less than his wolfish expression?

"I assure you, it is no great matter for me to take you myself. Hugh, you may resume your duties." He waved the steward away and took her arm. Even wearing her habit and at her age, Hildegarde felt unpleasantly vulnerable to his predatory nature. Swallowing her bile, she gave him a gracious nod and allowed him to lead her from the hall, trying to remember the route they took.

He paused at a twisting stone stair, released her arm and gestured ahead of him. "My lady."

She felt no better when he let go, for it seemed almost as though his eyes were burning into her spine as she trod cautiously up the steps. How she hated castle stairs. In the abbey, she'd had guard rails added to prevent accidents, but there was no such luxury here.

The darkness of the poorly-lit stair, the sense of John's presence, the dampness of the stone all served to increase Hildegarde's unease. As she ascended, her foot slipped on a worn step, and she felt herself start to topple backwards. Before she could regain her balance, John's hands came around her waist to steady her.

"Have a care, my lady Abbess. I would not wish men to say you met your death at my hands."

Hildegarde felt suddenly sick. It would be so easy, wouldn't it? She took a deep breath and trod with more precision.

As the stair twisted one more time, she glimpsed the top and almost sagged with relief before she straightened her back and resumed her customary poise.

"There, Mother Abbess." His eyes were mocking her, green glints lurking in the depths. "Never let it be said I have failed the Church. Do you wish to recover your breath before we proceed?"

He leaned against the wall in the full light of the torch sconce, a slight smirk tweaking at the corners of those mobile lips.

"My lord, I am a long way from being decrepit." How she itched to slap his face; John did not bring out the best in her, she would have to pray about that later. "Please, do lead on." Thinking, *I would so much rather follow you than walk beside you.*

She was out of luck. He took her arm again and led her down the short corridor to a dead end. The door which blocked the way was suspiciously ornate, and Hildegarde felt as though her worst suspicions were about to be realised, when, to her surprise, John paused and looked hesitant before he raised the large lion-headed latch and ushered her inside.

The chamber was large and richly furnished. Bright tapestries hung from walls, light flooded in from the expensive glass windows, and on a bed covered with silks and furs, the hangings drawn back, Rohese lay asleep, her head pillowed on her hand. As Hildegarde, stunned, took in the scene, a woman, older than herself but just as ramrod straight, dressed in a brocade gown embroidered thickly with gold thread and scattered with pearls, emerged from a shadowy corner. Her face was stony, her lips pressed tightly together; a gleam of something very unsettling flickered in her catlike eyes.

"John? What does this mean? Explain yourself, if you please."

John detached himself from Hildegarde's arm and went towards her, holding both hands out. "Ma mère, I see, once again, you've exercised that uncanny ability of yours."

Hildegarde quailed. *Ma mère?* Unsure of the protocol of the situation, she forced her slightly creaky knees into as deep a curtsy as they would allow. "Your Grace," she murmured.

The Queen ignored her and ignored the hands John held out to her. "Well, John? What folly induced you to bring your latest leman here? To use my own apartments?" Her eyes blazed, but her voice was cold as ice. Hildegarde felt as though her throat was closing and fought to stay in control. She could not afford to make a slip here. Standing upright, she braced herself, praying she would not err.

John seemed unmoved by his mother's fury. "Ma mère, you do me great injustice," he protested, that irritating, hateful smile of his lurking.

A smile? He was smiling even now? What arrogance! It was as much as Hildegarde could do to stop her legs trembling, and she was not a woman who gave way to fear easily.

The Queen's eyes narrowed further until they were mere slits. "How so?"

"Believe me, ma mère, had she been my bawd, the last place I would have brought her would be your own apartments. I came upon her taken ill in the passage and thought the best way to keep her reputation intact would be to bring her here. Even the most slanderous of my enemies would not suspect me of ravishing her on your bed, Madame. Although, it would seem you are all too ready to believe the worst of me." The smirk on his lips twisted downward in a sudden pout. "Sadly, as always, you credit me with that which even they would not."

As she stood there, an expression of disbelief on her face, he took her hands and raised them to his mouth, pressing a kiss onto each of them. Her eyes widened, her tight lips bent into a reluctant smile. She inclined her head. "Very well, John, I will believe you. Although, in truth, you try my trust so often, I fear it becomes difficult." She turned in Hildegarde's direction, "And indeed, it is unlike even you to bring an abbess into your amorous activities."

"Ma mère, this is the Abbess Hildegarde of Sparnstow Abbey. The lady Rohese is her niece, so I understand. I thought to fetch her myself." Hildegarde dipped another rusty curtsy and watched the Queen. Almost, she could see the cogs turning in her head.

"My lady Abbess, welcome. I have you to thank for my son's life, I believe."

When Eleanor looked like that, no one could withstand her. Hildegarde felt the warmth come back into her frozen face, and her legs ceased their ridiculous wobbling. Eleanor held her hand out for Hildegarde to kiss and indicated that she should rise and seat herself.

"My sisters and I are always at your service, Your Grace. Yet, I promise you, we did very little. And your gift was so generous, so beautiful..." Hildegarde was genuinely lost for words. She was used to ruling in her own little community, completely confident and able to outface most men, whatever their rank, but she had never before met Eleanor. And indeed, the illuminated book which had been sent to the abbey as a token of gratitude was more beautiful than anything Hildegarde had ever seen. Words failed her. Her confusion was not missed by the Queen who inclined her head graciously.

"It was nothing, Abbess Hildegarde. I assure you, I was most grateful for your loyalty and the care you gave my son. However, I was at a loss to know why he had also brought you here." She paused and turned her head. "I confess, the workings of your mind, John, are beyond even my ability to fathom."

"That must be both a blessing and a curse to you, ma mère." He stalked to the door, turned and, outrageously, thought Hildgarde, blew his mother a kiss. "I leave her in your oh-so-capable hands, Mother."

Eleanor raised her slender shoulders ever so slightly. "The more sons a woman has, the more she must be driven to distraction." She gave Hildegarde a disarming smile. "And now, what must be done with this niece of yours? I think you may have to watch her more closely in the future. We cannot have her coming to harm with any of the rogues and churls who call themselves knights."

Hildegarde kept her tongue still with difficulty. The most likely person to cause Rohese harm was the hellspawn whom Eleanor called son.

A noise from the bed caused them both to turn round. Shannon was sitting up, a slightly green tinge to her face, veil askew, one hand to her lips, her eyes wide with alarm.

"Child, where are your manners?" the Abbess scolded. "Do you know where you are?"

Shannon flinched and scrambled inelegantly off the bed, performing a deep and very wobbly curtsy. "Your Majesty, I'm so...so..." Sorry was somewhat inadequate, Hildegarde supposed. And how would she have greeted royalty had it been her in such an awkward position?

Shannon stood up, appalled. What should she do? She glanced at the creases and folds she had made on the bed and – *oh no!* Was that a small patch of drool? She looked up again. The Queen was regarding her with a straight face, but Shannon thought she detected a slight tremor at the side of her mouth. With a bit of luck, she was finding the predicament amusing.

She curtsied deeply again, keeping her balance a little better this time by bracing herself against the side of the bed and pushing against it to help her rise. "Your Majesty, I am so..." and her voice trailed off. *So what? So sorry to have been sprawling and drooling all over your royal bed? So sorry to have been sick in your toilet?* She took a deep breath and tried again. "Your Grace." How did one address Eleanor of Aquitaine? That was something she hadn't checked. She forced her trembling legs into another deep curtsy, this time remaining in it. "Madame, I'm sorry, I can't find the words. I never...I didn't...I felt so ill, you see. I didn't know where I was. I'm so, so sorry."

"I see." Eleanor's lips had stopped twitching, although Shannon thought she could see a glimpse of humour in those green eyes. "And my son came upon you in your distress?"

Er, your son caused my distress!

Eleanor, unable to read her thoughts, continued, "And he brought you here, did he? I trust he was gentle with you."

"My lady, he was very," Shannon paused; those eyes watched her intently, "very kind to me, once he realised I was ill."

Well, that was true. Once he realised she was going to be sick, he was kindness itself. She blushed, remembering the vomit on his shoes.

"And I am pleased to see you are recovering. My child," the Queen came to her and placed one finger under her chin, tilting her head up, looking into her eyes, "be aware that not everyone will be so kind to a young woman alone and in distress. Some might even be the cause of that distress."

Shannon accurately read the message Eleanor conveyed. *She knows.*

"Allow an old woman to offer you some advice. Make sure you do not stray so far from the care of your aunt in the future. You cannot always be sure of being rescued by my son, although it does seem," she paused, head on one side, "yes, it does seem he has had a care to your welfare. This time."

Only because I was sick on him. Shannon bit her lip to make sure she didn't utter her thoughts.

CHAPTER FIFTEEN

Shannon shifted restlessly on her narrow pallet at the foot of Hildegarde's bed. She couldn't get comfortable. The mattress was lumpy, stuffed with straw, and there was no pillow. It was pitch dark; the stone walls of the small, cramped chamber they had been allocated smelt dank and musty even with the shutter open, and the occasional owl-like shriek from outside made her jump.

Hildegarde lay still, making no sound except for her quiet breathing. Lack of a pillow didn't seem to worry her.

Shannon fidgeted again. Her mind was sifting through the events of the day, and she wept silently, trying not to hiccup, scrubbing at her eyes and nose with some squares of linen she had found in her coffer.

Were they all like that? She would never trust another man as long as she lived. They were all hateful; how could she ever believe a word any bloke said ever again? She wished Chloe was here. She'd always thought her sister flighty but...she sniffed...maybe *she* was the flighty one.

Three men taking her for an idiot, one after the other. Chloe didn't get herself into situations like this; she wasn't so gullible. Shannon hiccuped again. And she still felt sick. She'd drunk far too much of that spiced wine.

Suddenly, she stiffened. What was that scrabbling in the rushes? Surely not...not mice?

Round and round her thoughts went, as she tossed again with a little too much fervour, and the pallet wobbled dangerously. She clutched the sides. She must lay still or she'd never get to sleep. And she didn't even want to tell Hildegarde about Adam; she'd be disgusted with her. *I'm such a fool. If my eyes are all red in the morning, I'll have to let her think I'm still upset over John. Oh, Adam! I really believed in you.*

Love and hate warred within her, along with anger that they'd treated the kid so badly. So what if he didn't want to marry Alys? *Get over it!* she chided him mentally. He must know Alys adored him – there was no mistaking it. *He should have been straight with me. At least he could have warned me Alys was here.*

She hadn't considered she was doing any harm, hadn't thought they were hurting anyone. *And now, I'm as bad as Sienna – mind, I suppose I wasn't engaged to Jackson. I'm not as bad as her – I'm worse! Did Adam really love me? If he did, he'd have prepared me.* She threshed about again and Hildegarde's breathing paused briefly as though disturbed by her movements.

When she finally drifted off, muddled images and confused snatches of the day chased each other through her mind: Alys pointing proudly to her betrothed, her face bright with joy; mice nibbling Shannon's toes as she lay there in the dark; bizarrely, Jackson kissing Sienna, leaning against the battlements on the wall walk. What were *they* doing here?

The dreams grew darker. Adam was laughing as he told Alys he was going to wed Rohese. Alys, a tragic expression on her face, was crying, saying she thought Rohese was her friend, ripping off her veil and running away from them. Hildegarde comforting Marion when Shannon told her she wasn't coming home. John pawing at her. Shannon herself running blindly through a maze of stone corridors, always with footsteps chasing after her. In her dream, she threw herself desperately from the castle walls trying to escape John and woke to find she was lying on the floor, morning light filtering through the small window arch, the pallet upturned beside her, and Hildegarde watching her with concern.

"Child, did you hurt yourself?"

She moved her arms and legs gingerly. "No, I don't think so. I moved too much and turned the stupid thing over."

"Did your dreams trouble you?"

"I dreamt of John. I was running and running, and he was always there." She gave a reluctant grin. "I dreamt I'd thrown myself off the wall. Looks like I nearly did."

"Poor Shannon."

She got up, set the pallet to rights and sat on it as Hildegarde got out of bed and poured water from the ewer into a basin.

"Aunt, will we be here long? I mean, some of it was fun, but," she stifled a retch, "I don't think…" Putting a hand to her mouth, she rushed to the tiny privy set in a corner of the wall. Not again; she'd been sick enough yesterday.

Hildegarde watched her, an amused smile on her face. "Feel better now, Shannon?"

"I don't think I can face any more wine today. Is there some water anywhere? As for dinner!" She put her hand to her mouth again. "I certainly don't want that. I don't want to face John again, either, if I can help it." She pulled a face. "He's vile."

"I'm sorry, Shannon. Your introduction to court hasn't been what I'd hoped for. I'm afraid life amongst the nobles is not as courtly as one might wish; there are always undercurrents. Isabella has not had pleasant experiences either, which is why she was so reluctant to come. I expect she told you.

"If I could have kept you from it, I would have. However, I suppose it's been an experience for you, at the very least, and as for vomiting over John," she paused, chuckling. "I shall amuse myself for long imagining that. It must have been a very effective rebuttal."

Shannon grinned back despite her nausea, as she splashed the lukewarm water on her face.

"As for water, they have a very good well here. We'll go down to the kitchens on the way to the pavilion. And have your coffer ready to go. As soon as Sir Giles has concluded his business with John, I think he and Isabella will be quite as anxious as you to leave." She paused. "I think, Shannon, if I were you, I wouldn't mention your encounters to Isabella. She's quite nervous enough of him as it is. You need never face him again, but she may well have to."

"Okay."

"Good girl. Now, have you finished washing?" Shannon nodded. "Come, we'll get some water for you to drink and then, take refuge in the pavilion. I confess, I had worries enough trying to keep track of you yesterday without enduring more today. I enjoyed my meeting with John little more than you did your own."

CHAPTER SIXTEEN

The weather had held. It was a pleasant day for travelling, and the memories of John faded as the distance from the castle increased. This time, Shannon chose to sit on the baggage wain, which was more loaded than previously since the pavilion had been taken down and piled onto it.

Adam had not been amused at her flat refusal to ride behind him, but she kept seeing the look of pride on Alys' sweet face, and she knew she couldn't be the one to wipe it away. The wain rumbled along, and Shannon gazed unseeingly at her surroundings.

Hildegarde watched her from the corner of her eye. If she wasn't much mistaken, the glamour the girl had thought to find here was irretrievably tarnished. Mayhap, she would soon feel the urge to return home. It would be no small relief to her; in truth, being Rohese's watchdog was every bit as difficult as she had anticipated. A smile tugged at the corner of her mouth. For all that, she had come to love her, and what an unlooked-for blessing to reconnect with her family. She had best enjoy the time they had left; it was unlikely to happen again, unless... She shook her head. Please God, no, that would never do.

Shannon glared as Adam, with brows tightly drawn together and lips set in a thin line, moved to ride alongside. He caught her eyes upon him and quirked his lips back upwards. "Sweet, come, do not look at me so. I did not wish to neglect you." He gave her a look of such melting sweetness, she was nearly won over; then, he wrecked it as he rolled his eyes. "Believe me, Alys' mother has eyes like a gyrfalcon."

Shannon flicked a glance sideways at Leofwine who had schooled his features to bovine stupidity and was doing an excellent impression of deafness. He hunched over the reins, head down. Even so, she lowered her voice though still it throbbed with rage. "And just when, pray, were you going to tell them you will not wed Alys?"

"My love, believe me, this bond can be broken at any time. I have but to speak with my father."

Shannon's lip curled. "Oh, it's that easy, is it? And what of Alys?"

"Trust me, she'll be happier wed elsewhere."

"And is it the custom then, in England, that you wed for love? That's not what I've heard."

"You know it isn't. Nevertheless, custom can be overturned if the will is there."

She tossed her head, then wished she hadn't as she nearly lost her balance. Adam smirked and reached out a hand to steady her. She shook him off resolutely saying, "Adam, I find I do not believe you. I think it's time we faced the facts. You may love me, or you may not – I honestly don't know – but the courses of our lives are already mapped out. You must marry Alys, and I must marry a man from my own land."

Adam recoiled as though she had slapped him. "But, you said…"

"I know what I said. And I did think I loved you. Maybe I still do, I don't know. I thought I was ready to spend my life with you. But, Adam," she paused and gave him a long, steady stare, "you lied to me."

Shannon closed her eyes for a moment, painfully aware of her conflicting emotions. She'd spent so long agonising over him last night and was beginning to realise Adam might not be the man she'd thought him to be. If he could treat Alys like that, if he could lie to both of them, could she even trust him? And she was angry. Angry he'd put her in that situation. Angry he dismissed Alys so casually.

"You know this isn't going to happen whatever we might want. I don't even know if you really love me. And, if truth be told, I'll likely have to return to my kin soon. I'm just waiting to hear word from them that it's safe. Once they send for me, we both know I cannot stay."

He looked hurt and opened his mouth to respond, when Isabella, who had also been keeping a surreptitious watch on Shannon, moved from riding next to Giles, manoeuvring Merlin between the baggage wain and Adam. Just before she came between them, he muttered, "Rohese, this isn't over."

Isabella inclined her head to Adam as she edged alongside, forcing him to drop back, waiting until he was behind them to say, "Rohese, I think you do not wish Adam to accompany you? If I ride alongside, it will discourage him."

Shannon bit her lip.

Isabella continued, "But are you sure you wish to ride on that awful wain? If you do not want to ride behind Adam, you could sit pillion with Fulke, or Miles, or Guy. It's of no great matter, and it would be more pleasant for you."

"Truly, Isabella, it doesn't matter, I'm quite happy here." She paused, thinking, *At least, I would be, if I could only get Adam out of my heart,* before continuing, "I haven't actually ridden on a wain before. It's quite fun."

Isabella quirked one eyebrow at her.

"Really. I'm quite hungry though. Will we be stopping to eat?" The meagre fare she had eaten at the castle before leaving had not sustained her for long, and the fresh air had cleared her nausea. "My stomach thinks my throat has been cut."

Isabella laughed. "I'll speak to Giles. We have ale, cheese and bread; poor fare, though if I know the right of it, he will be glad to stop for food. He'll likely have no complaints from his men, either." She urged Merlin into a trot and caught up with Giles again. Adam did not return, keeping behind Shannon, who was uncomfortably aware that he watched her with reproach.

After another half hour or so, Shannon was ravenous. She was relieved when, ahead of her, Giles turned off into a copse, reined in and swung off his horse. His squires also dismounted, and Leofwine halted the wain. To her dismay, Adam, dismounting quickly, ran over to her. Deliberately ignoring his outstretched arms, she turned instead to Leofwine, who had climbed down and now hovered uncertainly. "Leofwine," she said, giving him such a glittering smile, he looked as though he had been blinded, "pray, assist me. I do not wish to bother Sir Adam."

Her lips tightened, and she fumed silently when Adam dismissed the man with a nod. "It's no trouble, my lady. Come." He held out his hands.

With no other option, she allowed him to grasp her and lift her to the ground. He did not immediately let go but stood there for a few seconds, his hands still on her waist, his eyes gazing deep into hers. She lowered her head but felt as though his gaze scorched her.

He released her waist with one hand and tilted her chin up; she kept her eyes lowered. "Rohese, why will you not look at me?"

She gritted her teeth. "You know why." She did look up now, glowering at him. "In a word, Alys."

He was wounded. "Sweeting, I told you. She means nothing to me. The betrothal can be annulled."

"Maybe so, but you mean all to her."

"She's just a child. She knows naught of love between a man and a woman."

He let go of her waist, then caught at her hand, his fingers closing tightly, possessively. There was an ardent glow on his face, and Shannon was beginning to feel uncomfortable. She tried to catch Isabella's notice, but Isabella was engaged in supervising the squires. Adam tugged at her with one hand, leading his horse with the other. "Come, walk with me. Let me explain. We can find a way; we can make a way. If you truly love me, this is not insurmountable."

Shannon unwillingly allowed herself to be pulled along a few more steps. She glanced around for Hildegarde, but the Abbess was speaking with Giles. The only way to catch her attention would be to shout. She tried reasoning with him again. "Adam, let me go, please. It's over."

"Sweetheart, listen to me. The plight troth can be annulled. Alys is related to me; it would be a sin for us to marry."

She looked at him sceptically. "And how long have your families known of this?" He had the grace to flush slightly but didn't answer. She glared. "Well?" To her annoyance, he still didn't answer. They were getting further away from the group now, and no one seemed to have noticed. "It's all very convenient, Adam, but get this through your head. I am *not* interested in marrying you. In fact, I'm beginning to think I don't even like you very much."

He tilted his head to one side, still drawing her further away from the others. "Now, sweetheart, be reasonable." Green sparks glinted in his eyes. "Do I detect a hint of jealousy?" He laughed smugly. "This thing between us, this feeling, this passion, is beyond the ordinary. You bewitch me. Would you have me marry Alys and leave both her and me unloved and unloving? I swear to you, you are my heart, my soul. Alys will be glad, you'll see. She does not love me; it's just a child's fancy." He tugged at her again. "Come, love, I know you want me."

Shannon wasn't just uncomfortable now, she was beginning to feel alarmed. There was a strange expression on his face, and a determined smile played around his mouth. She turned her head, and her free hand flew to her lips. The others were out of sight. He had succeeded in getting her well away, and they were, to her horror, deep into the woods. She stood stock-still, and he tugged at her again. She tried to pull away from him, but he caught her round the waist and pressed her to him, his lips to hers. Not soft and warm as they had been when he had kissed her before – this time they were hard and bruising. She held herself rigid, unresponsive, and he broke the kiss, gazing at her passionately. "My love, you will break my heart. Come," he coaxed, "be not so unkind. I want you and only you. You feel the same, I know it."

He sounded ridiculous, like a ham in a melodrama – as though he had learned the words and was quoting them badly.

When he gave her that coaxing look again, Shannon's self-control broke. She lifted her hand and swung as hard as she could. The smack as her palm connected with his face was shocking, and he recoiled, letting her go, his head snapping to one side.

Adam steadied himself, and for a moment they just stared at each other, his face reddening where she had hit him, the palm of her hand stinging. Then, he caught his lower lip between his teeth before saying, "Well, if you want to play this the hard way, sweeting."

Shannon gathered her skirts and turned to run, but he caught her around the waist and with a smooth move, hoisted her up onto his horse's withers, swinging himself up behind her and holding her tightly against him. She tried to scream, but he had her face pressed too closely to his chest, his mantle wrapped about her.

He was galloping now, the sound of Blaze's hooves echoing in her head. She couldn't breathe. She was choking. He laughed. "Sweeting, did I muffle you too tight? No matter. If you pass out, I'll release my grip a little. Love, forgive me, for I *must* have you. Truly, I'll make you happy. Once the deed is done, I promise you, you'll not be sorry."

The sound of the hooves in her head got louder and louder, and she struggled to draw breath. She was going to suffocate. He was going to kill her, and he didn't even realise it. As her head swam, she forced herself to stop struggling and relax against his grip. Stars were dancing in her eyes; the blackness in her head was threatening to overcome her. She had to breathe – she *had* to. She made herself sag a little as though she had fainted. He must have noticed as he loosened his grip, allowing her face to come free from the muffling folds of his cloak. She took a despairing gasp and revived a little as the air flooded her lungs. There was no escape. She would just have to hope someone had noticed she was missing and raise the alarm. Until then, she must let Adam play out this game. Only, it didn't feel like a game now.

The ride went on and on. Even if she continued to struggle, what if he lost his grip on her? The ground seemed very far away, and the thought of falling from this height, at this speed, terrified her.

Shannon's head was pounding, and the motion of the horse made her feel ill. Her body ached from the awkward angle he held her at. Worse, it felt as though she was slipping slightly. However much she wanted to be free, to fall now would break bones.

She forced herself to stop thinking about what would happen when they reached wherever he was taking her to. Should she pray? But she didn't know how. What had Hildegarde said? Prayer was just talking to God? Things were so far out of her hands now, there was nothing else she could do. In desperation, she closed her eyes, then opened them again when she realised it made her feel even more nauseous. Fixing her gaze on the sky, she clung on to Adam for dear life and prayed Giles, Isabella or Hildegarde would have noticed she had gone – although they surely would by now. But how would they know which way? That's what she must pray, that they ride in the right direction.

God, sorry, I don't really know how to talk to You, but please, if You're there, make them find me. Please, oh please, make them find me. The tears, which had been kept at bay by terror, now started to seep from her eyes. If she could have fought him, she would. The time for that would come later.

The horse was slowing; was it tiring? She felt Adam spur it on. After another brief bout of speed, it slowed again. Adam cursed, but allowed the change of pace.

Did she dare jump? No, even without the horse, he would be able to outrun her; this long gown she wore would hamper her, but at least now, she could use the slower speed to slacken her grip around him and ease her aching arms.

"Tired, sweetheart?" His voice was tender.

Oh God, he's going to be nice now. What do I do? Try to fool him and make a break for it later? Show me what to do.

Suddenly, his arm tightened around her again, and she braced herself for another stomach-churning gallop. Instead, Blaze came to a halt.

What now? Help me, please.

Adam kept his grip on her and whispered, "Rohese, hold tight to me. I have to let go of you, but you must hold me; don't lose your grip. Don't be afraid. Just trust me. I'm going to let you go now. Hold me round the waist, but keep clear of my arms and stay very still. If you can get my shield, do so, but go slowly now, very slowly."

What? Shannon got her face completely clear of his cloak and looked about her. The track they had taken through the trees had narrowed at this point, and their way was blocked by an overturned cart.

Spaced around them were four men; two armed with cudgels, one with a wickedly large knife and one with a spear. They weren't moving, watching Adam with narrowed eyes, braced, tense, ready to fight.

Adam let go of her and, infinitesimally slowly, she could feel him reaching for his sword. If she could grasp the shield which she knew would be slung over his back, she could use it to protect them. "That's right, sweeting," he breathed into her ear. "Gently now, and when I say so, bring it round to cover yourself in front. Can you undo the buckle?"

"I think so." Her fingers groped blindly for the buckle which held it. Without appearing to move, she managed to undo it and grip the strap. "Done it."

"Then, NOW!" he roared, swinging his sword free. She held tight with her left hand and pulled the shield round to protect the front. Adam slashed at the nearest man, but he ducked and came up beneath it, brandishing his knife.

Shannon felt Adam jolt as the knife gashed him; then, he swung his arm in a backward arc and slashed at their attacker's neck. As if in some terrible nightmare, she watched his eyes glaze and his knees buckle as he dropped to the ground, blood spurting from a gaping wound in his throat. Before she had time to avert her gaze, one of the men with cudgels rushed at them, and she almost felt the crunch as it connected with Adam's thigh. He raised it again and smashed it against Adam's ribs, narrowly missing Shannon's fingers.

Adam sagged for a moment, then he rallied. Grunting, he hefted his sword again. Shannon turned her head away and saw, to her horror, the man with the spear had moved closer. He came at Blaze, which proved to be his undoing. The horse reared and Shannon lost her grip, crashing to the ground. She dimly heard Adam yell, "Roll, Rohese, roll away from Blaze."

Pain shot through her newly healed ankle; she ignored it. She needed to get away from those pounding hooves. She rolled frantically until she had put safe distance between them, then gasped in horror as Blaze's flailing front hooves caught the third man in the chest, dashing him to the ground.

Unable to watch, she covered her head with her arms, but she couldn't shut out the noise of the fight. Blaze stamped the ground too close to her, and she rolled further away, where she lay frozen with fear until everything went quiet bar the sound of laboured breathing.

Cautiously, she moved her arms, peering through half-closed eyes. There was no sign of the fourth man – he must have run.

Blaze was trembling and snorting. At least now, mercifully, he had stopped rearing. But what of Adam? She looked up. He was slumped over the saddle, blood welling from his thigh and arm. As she watched, he slipped from Blaze and hit the ground with a dull thud, one foot still caught in the stirrup. Blaze calmed and stood patiently, sides heaving, blowing through his nostrils.

Shannon tried to stand, wincing as what felt like a white-hot flame shot through her ankle and up her leg. She tried to force herself to stay upright and stumbled – the pain was too great. But she had to get to Adam. For all he had abducted her, she must help him; she couldn't let him die.

She gritted her teeth. There was no time to strap her injured ankle. Adam was bleeding copiously and was unconscious; she didn't know whether from blood loss or if he had hit his head as he fell. Slowly, painfully, on her hands and knees, she inched her way across to him, trying to ignore the agony that seared more sharply through her each time she moved.

He moaned. Thank goodness he was alive. As she reached him, he opened his eyes. "Rohese, I'm sorry. I never meant this to happen. I…" His voice trailed weakly away, and his eyes closed again.

Biting her cheek, trying to ignore her own pain, she gently eased his foot from the stirrup – Blaze was docile now, there was no danger from him – and tried to assess the damage. There was a graze on Adam's cheek, though she didn't think he'd hit his head. The blood seemed to be coming not from his leg, which lay at an awkward angle – *broken?* – but his arm. The sleeve of his tunic was sodden with blood. She tried to rip the fabric so she could take a better look, but it wouldn't tear.

There was a dagger at his side. She grabbed it and ripped into his sleeve, tearing at it frantically. The blood was coming from a wound below his elbow. For a moment, she felt dizzy at the sight of it. *There's so much blood.* She applied pressure, but it continued to bleed. What should she do now? She wished she'd done a first aid course. Racking her brains, she tried not to panic as the blood continued to flow from his arm.

She needed to bandage it. Was it okay to use a tourniquet? She had a feeling it wasn't. Forcing down the panic she could feel rising, she tugged her veil free. Pulling off her wimple, she folded it into a pad, covering the wound before using Adam's knife to slash her veil in two, using half as a bandage. Still, the blood oozed through.

Shannon struggled to think. What else could she do? She used the second half of the veil to make another bandage – tighter this time. Blood smeared her hands, and, as she brushed her loosened hair from her eyes, she streaked her face with red. His arm still bled but much more slowly, and she thought it might stop soon. If not, it would have to be a tourniquet.

She was about to raise his arm, to see if that would help, when she made the mistake of turning her head and caught sight of the three dead men.

Bile rose in her throat. She crawled a few feet away from Adam and was violently sick.

She retched uncontrollably. Finally, her throat raw, she dragged herself away from where she had vomited and flopped forward onto the ground, shivering, her fingers clutching a tuft of grass as though she might find comfort from it, the pain from her ankle throbbing through her. Why was she so cold? The sun was bright and warm on the side of her face, but her body felt frozen. And no one knew where they were; she would die here with Adam.

Her last thoughts before blackness filled her vision, were prayers. *Oh God, please, just help us.*

CHAPTER SEVENTEEN

Hildegarde finished her conversation with Giles and looked around for Shannon. Where had that girl gone now? Where was Isabella? Maybe they were together.

Isabella was supervising the squires as they pulled out food from a hamper. She turned, and Hildegarde caught her attention, beckoning her. Isabella stood up, dusted down her gown and headed over, eyes questioning. "Abbess?"

"Lady Isabella, do you know where Rohese is?"

She shook her head. "No, Abbess. Eudo?" The older serjeant turned in her direction. "Have you seen Mistress Rohese?"

"Aye, my lady, I think she was with Adam."

"Then where is Adam?"

Hildegarde stared around the grove. The squires were still busy at their labours. Two of the knights were coming out of the bushes, adjusting their clothing. Isabella's maid, Mahelt, was talking to Miles, but of Adam and Rohese, there was no sign. Hildegarde felt a pang of anxiety but stilled it. Well, and if the girl had strolled out of sight with Adam, no real harm would be done. She doubted she would lose her head, and even though her reputation might suffer here, once in her own world it would be of no consequence.

Hildegarde took a deep breath and steadied herself, hoping to loosen the knot of worry she suddenly felt in her stomach. He had surely only walked a little way with her, mayhap to show her something. With a prayer in her heart, trying not to fret, she asked, "Eudo, did you see in which direction they went?"

He pushed up his cap and scratched his head, then gazed around dumbly as he gathered his thoughts, and Hildegarde itched with impatience. Just as she was beginning to feel the urge to slap him, he said, "Aye, I think it was that way." He pointed to a track through the trees.

Hildegarde turned and strode off; there was no time to waste. What was Shannon thinking? New to this world she might be, but surely she knew better than this.

She went part-way down the track; they were not in sight, and she was brought up short as another alarming thought struck her, making her feel slightly sick. Turning back the way she had just

223

come, she caught Giles by the elbow, interrupting him as he was speaking to the older of his knights, Guy.

"Sir Giles, I beg your pardon, do you see Adam's horse at all? I'm not sure I recall which one it was."

He turned, smiling. "Why, the roan one with the white streak down its face. Blaze. Over there…" his voice tailed off even as he pointed, for Blaze was not with the other horses.

"Sir Giles, I believe, I am not entirely sure, however I believe Adam may have wandered off with my niece."

His eyes hardened, and Hildegarde's heart almost missed a beat at what she read in them. "My lord, you surely do not think he means ill to Rohese. Do you?" For a moment, he said nothing but it was enough. "Then, my lord, please, make haste to pursue him. They are both missing, and I know not how long ago they went." She could feel the colour draining from her face. *Stupid! Stupid!* How could she have been so lax? "Eudo thinks he went in that direction."

Giles looked steadily at her – she knew her face to be white and strained and wished she didn't appear so anxious. It would only make things worse, but what could she do?

Isabella came up beside him and laid her hand lightly on his arm. "My lord husband, I had warned him to stay away from Rohese." Isabella seemed no less worried than Hildegarde felt.

Giles put his arm around her, kissing her briefly before swinging up onto Troubadour, shouting, "Miles, Fulke, Guy, to me. Eudo, you and the others stay here with the women. We'll spread out, see if we can discover which way they went." The last words were flung over his shoulder as he turned Troubadour and started along the track.

The sun burned brightly overhead; it must be noon. A mound of freshly deposited dung steamed just in front of him; he was in the right direction then. As his shout rang out, the other men hurried to join him, and he took off at a gallop.

Mistress Rohese was of their party, and she was under his protection, as was the Abbess, until they were safely back at Sparnstow. How dared Adam? Why hadn't Isabella told him? But then, she may not have had much to go on other than vague suspicion, and had he not promised to keep an eye to Adam himself? Although he had thought the lad was above meddling with one of Rohese's station. He had thought only that Adam was trying his luck with maids and servants and under his own roof.

He cursed; he should have known. His father was of the same ilk and blood breeds true, but Adam had seemed more likeable, more malleable.

And indeed, he'd wanted to give the lad a chance to escape, to teach him how a man should behave.

He swore again and urged Troubadour to greater speed, hoping this was the right direction.

Behind him, Isabella and Hildegarde watched in dismay along with Mahelt and the squires. Eudo stood a little apart from them, hand to the hilt of his sword, face grim.

Hildegarde, not content with waiting, went to mount Horace. If Giles caught up with them in this frame of mind, she felt certain there would be bloodshed. She never travelled without some basic supplies in one of her saddlebags, and she feared the contents would be needed.

As she asked Alan, another of the squires, to assist her, Isabella led the bay rouncey over. "Take Kestrel, Abbess. She will be better able to catch Giles. Alan, you will accompany the Abbess."

"I thank you." As she spoke, Hildegarde was unfastening her bag with nimble fingers, throwing it over her shoulder

Isabella steadied Horace and called Leofwine. "We will ready the wain. With Giles in this mood, we may need it for Adam."

Hildegarde thanked God they had taken the wain instead of the usual pack-ponies she would have expected. It would be easier, should there be casualties. She did not know what Giles might be capable of when his temper ran thus; God grant he did not kill Adam.

Alan helped her mount. She wasted no time. A competent, if somewhat out-of-practise rider, she urged Kestrel into a gallop, following the direction Giles had taken.

How she would have enjoyed the ride had she not been so concerned. The little mare would have been a delight in any other circumstance, but for now, veil streaming behind her, eyes watering but focussed, head down to avoid any low-hanging branches, she could think of nothing except for what lay ahead. Her heart pounded in time with Kestrel's hooves, and her head took up the rhythm as she prayed. *Let them be all right. Let Shannon be safe, and, dear God, let there be no murder done this day.*

After what felt far too long, she caught sight of Giles and his men through the trees. There were bodies sprawled around Adam's horse, and two of the men were bent over something on the ground. A flutter of fabric lay across the track, and her heart seemed to almost stop beating. Shannon!

As she slowed the mare and slid from the saddle with more urgency than grace, she saw Giles standing over another prone figure, presumably Adam. To her horror, Giles was about to kick him. He swung his leg, and she flew at him, tugging his arm, distracting him so he staggered and missed the body at his feet, calling, "My lord!" His face was suffused with fury, glaring at Adam, ignoring her. She raised her voice, "SIR GILES!"

This time, he responded to her interruption. He seemed to pause for reflection, and she continued quickly, "My lord, you cannot do this. The man is badly injured. Do you wish to cause his death?"

Giles spat. "If he dies, so be it. He is nothing to me. Look instead to your niece, my lady Abbess, instead of this…this…" The expression on her face made him swallow whatever foul epithet he had been about to use.

Thus recalled to Shannon's state, Hildegarde turned, but hesitated, laying her hand on Sir Giles' arm. "Patience, my lord. Let me see them both." Then, she knelt beside Shannon. Her own heart felt as though it pattered erratically, for the girl was covered with blood, and seemed to be unconscious.

For a moment, Hildegarde was too aghast to say anything, then her common sense came into play. Shannon was not dead, and the blood didn't seem to be hers. She touched her face, saying, "Rohese! Rohese, my dear, can you speak?"

To her relief, the girl's eyelids fluttered open, and she shuddered convulsively. Hildegarde held her hand out. "A cloak, if you please." Someone thrust a mantle into her grasp. She tucked it around Shannon tenderly, then gave her a brief going-over. Yes, the blood on her hands and gown was not hers; she had obviously administered first aid to Adam, Hildegarde decided.

So was she just shocked? Or was she also injured? And if so, where? Raising Shannon's gown slightly, she discovered her ankle was bruised and badly swollen. Shannon's hand came out from beneath the mantle and clasped hers. Hildegarde stroked her brow. "Where are you hurt, child? Did you hit your head?"

"No, just my leg, and my ribs are sore too. They hit him, caught me a little. I think I'm just bruised, but my ankle," she bit down hard on her lower lip, "that really hurts."

Shannon's face crumpled, and her mouth trembled. "Please, Auntie, I'm fine. Adam–" She broke off and dashed a hand over her eyes. "I don't even know if he's still alive. I think he's broken his leg, and his arm was bleeding so much. I did try to stop it; I hope what I did was right." She clutched Hildegarde's arm. "Please, go and help him."

Hildegarde rose to her feet. Giles was still standing over Adam, a thunderous expression on his face, though at least he wasn't kicking him. Hildegarde hurried across and bent to examine him; he was in a far worse state than Shannon.

Giles touched her shoulder. "How does your niece?"

"She is in some pain; it's nothing that will not mend. As for this one, he is in bad straits."

Giles face was flushed, his brows down, lips thinned to a tight line. "Faugh! If he were not already, he would have been when I caught him up. How dared he? Abbess, if it were not for Maude, I would leave him here as carrion."

Hildegarde gave him stare for stare. "Well, I would not. How about the others? Are they dead?"

"They appear to be. Certainly, he is." He indicated one body with a gaping wound in the throat. "Are the others also dead, Miles?"

"Yes, my lord."

"Well, since Adam is not, what can be done?" The worst of his ire fading, he squatted on his heels beside Hildegarde.

She examined Adam carefully. A broken leg; please God it would knit well. And a gash to his arm. She loosened Shannon's bandage cautiously and eased it off. Fortunately, although the bleeding had stopped, it hadn't had long enough to dry and stick. Not an artery, but still a deep wound. It would need stitching. She could not do that here, but it could be cleansed and bandaged at least. She pulled out a wine costrel from her bag.

Adam groaned. His eyes were sunken pools of agony when he opened them. "My lord, I beg…" He paused, his breath catching in his throat. "I beg…forgiveness." His voice was hoarse and his words faltering. Giles glared at him, and he moved his sound arm feebly.

Hildegarde took a small vial from her bag and unstoppered it, pouring him a measure of the opiate it contained. Raising him as he drank, choking slightly, she waited for it to take effect. He would need to be unconscious. His pain was already severe, and what she had to do next, he would not bear. She hoped they would be able to get the wain here. The ground was not too unsteady, the passage between the trees not too narrow, the wain not excessively wide. For certès, it would be better than conveying him by litter.

As Adam's head lolled, she drenched the wound with wine, flushing it thoroughly, praying as she did so. Then, binding it tightly, she turned her attention to his leg. It would need splinting. She raised her head, looking for anything she could use, and found Giles had pre-empted her. He held out a piece of wood. It was not ideal, but would do for now. Removing her patient's boot, she felt for a pulse in his ankle. To her relief, it throbbed steadily beneath her fingers. She gently probed along his leg where she could feel the break; it seemed a simple enough one.

"Do you need help?"

"Please. If you can hold him steady, thus..."

She realigned the bone, wrapping it tightly and bracing it with the wood. "Can you find another such? Two would be even better." At least her temporary efforts would be enough to get him back to the abbey, where Ursel could deal with his hurts more thoroughly.

Giles got up and returned to the upturned cart, kicking and tearing at it until more wood broke away, coming back with another piece of similar size.

"And now, Sir Giles, we need to warm him. Your mantle, please."

He hesitated, an inscrutable expression on his face, then unclasped it and handed it over, saying, "For Maude's sake, if not his own."

Done, at least for the present, Hildegarde returned to Shannon who was a little less drawn now, though she still looked strained. Her earlier shivering had more or less subsided, although the odd tremor still ran through her. She watched Hildegarde with anxious eyes.

"Adam will be well," Hildegarde reassured her, praying she did not lie.

Shannon nodded, and a little of the tension left her face until Hildegarde touched her ankle. She gave a muffled yelp and bit down hard on her lip again, enduring Hildegarde's ministrations with a set face.

Hildegarde was relieved to find the ankle was not broken, just badly sprained. She bound it as gently as she could, but Shannon was pale as bleached linen by the time she had finished.

"Good girl. Here." Hildegarde had pulled out another small costrel, and was pouring some of the contents into a cup. "Drink this."

Wan as she was, Shannon still screwed up her face when she sniffed at it. Hildegarde smiled sympathetically. "Yes, I'm afraid it will taste as bad as it smells; however, it will ease the pain, I promise.

Shannon shrugged, then tilted the cup and swallowed, shuddering as the noxious mixture went down. Her already pale face took on a slight tinge of green, and Hildegarde hastily pulled out a honey wafer which she had discovered residing stickily at the bottom of her bag.

Shannon regarded it suspiciously and licked it with caution. As she realised it would rid her mouth of the vile taste, she ate with more enthusiasm, then gazed up at Hildegarde, a tear trembling on her lashes. "Will he truly be okay?"

Hildegarde gave what she hoped was a reassuring nod, and a little colour came back into Shannon's face. "I know he was kidnapping me, but even so..." She trailed off.

"I know. You would not wish him to come to harm. Well, I make no promises, but plenty have survived worse wounds."

As she spoke, the baggage wain came rumbling down the track, along with Isabella and the rest of the mesnie. Good. They would all be needed.

Loading Adam onto the space which had been cleared proved to be an exacting task. He was, for the most part, insensible, and Shannon watched them, whimpering each time he moaned, her hand to her mouth as though his agony was hers.

Isabella had placed cloaks beneath him, yet for all that, the cushioning effect was negligible.

Hildegarde looked at Shannon. "Do you wish to ride with him?"

Shannon nodded, and Giles lifted her carefully, setting her next to Adam. She raised his head onto her lap, stroking his face.

Hildegarde kissed her lightly upon the brow, saying, "Not long now. When we reach the abbey, we can make him more comfortable."

In truth, the journey would take at least a couple of hours, probably more if they were to go gently; however, there was no help for it. Sparnstow was less than six miles hence, and Hildegarde, for once, found herself frustrated at the slowness of travel in this century. Oh, for her trusty car! She mentally shook herself. It did no good thinking about it. Straightening up, she went to the other bodies. Although Giles' men had claimed they were dead, she needed to know for herself.

They had spoken the truth. One had his chest crushed – Blaze had done that. Of the other two, one had his throat cut, the other had dashed his head against a rock, spilling his brains. Giles came over to her, taking her arm. "Abbess, I'll send a man to notify the sheriff. These were outlaws, you can see that."

Hildegarde opted to ride alongside the wain, with Isabella on the other side, and she watched Shannon with concern. The mantle had been well wrapped around her, and over that, Isabella had tucked her own cloak, lined with coney fur. She was still very pale and trying not to cry, if Hildegarde was any judge.

"Rohese, what were you doing? Why did you go with Adam?" Isabella asked what Hildegarde had been about to. What had she been thinking? Or hadn't she? In Shannon's world, it would not have been strange.

Shannon's eyes flashed indignantly. "I didn't go off with him! I wouldn't! He kidnapped me," she hissed vehemently. Then, as the cart jolted again, and Adam moaned, she studied him worriedly before leaning back against the cart, gritting her teeth. "He said he wanted to marry me. I told him I wouldn't marry him if he was the last man on earth." She gulped. "I don't know what he was going to do, but then we saw the outlaws. They'd blocked the trail. They hurt us. He killed them, and now, he's hurt and I can't hate him like I want to." She gave another gulp and buried her head in her shaking hands.

Hildegarde intervened. "Enough, Rohese. We can discuss this later. Rest now, please." The girl had gone through enough for one day. For certès, she didn't know whether it was better they had been stopped by outlaws than Shannon being abducted or worse. It was almost certain Giles would have apprehended them before harm had come to Shannon, and the outlaws had probably saved Adam's life, for had he not already been injured when Giles had reached him, Hildegarde was not sure he would be alive now.

On the other side of the cart, Isabella still appeared shocked. With a click of her tongue, she urged Merlin forward to join Giles, saying in low tones, "I do not think it was any fault of Rohese, but Giles, how could Adam have done this?"

His face set in hard lines, he said, "The fool! I imagine he had fancies of flying high in the service of her father. More likely, he would not have lived long enough to do so. I had thought him to have more sense if not more honour." He snapped his mouth shut and said no more.

It was a subdued party which clattered through the abbey gatehouse some hours later.

CHAPTER EIGHTEEN

When they arrived at the abbey, the outer courtyard was empty save for Berthe at the gatehouse who stared askance at the sorry group. Isabella organised a litter for Adam, carried by Fulke and Miles. He was swiftly despatched to the infirmary where he was left in Ursel's care, his injuries being deemed far too severe for the ministrations of Brother Anselm, the infirmerer for lay brothers and male guests. In more serious cases, Anselm always deferred to Sister Ursel's superior knowledge and skills.

Giles took care of Shannon himself, gently carrying her to her chamber where Amice leapt to her feet, wringing her hands when she saw her mistress being laid tenderly on the bed.

Hildegarde sent her rushing for a cup of hot water. "And mind you put a little milk and honey in it. Add this, and bring it straight back here." She handed over a scoop of her precious tea-leaves. "In fact, bring back two cups. This is a special herb from Bolohovenia," she added, as the maid viewed it doubtfully. *A cup of tea – just what this doctor ordered.* The sweet tea would help revive Shannon, and she rather felt the need for a good, strong cup herself. Oh, bless Marion, if only she knew how much Hildegarde looked forward to her yearly supply. She gave Amice another scoop of leaves.

As she sat by Shannon's bed, the girl gave a sudden wail and hid her face in her hands, weeping. Hildegarde held her until the storm had passed, and Shannon drew away still gulping and shuddering as Amice came back with the cups.

"I never smelled anything like that," she exclaimed as she put them down on the small table beside the Abbess. "They have strange herbs over there."

Hildegarde smiled vaguely and motioned her to leave. Her stint as a maid would likely be over soon unless she wished to work here. That could be dealt with later.

Although Shannon had stopped crying, she was still woebegone. Hildegarde took a napkin and bathed her swollen eyes with cool water, then passed her the tea. Sniffing, she sipped at it before asking, "How about Adam? Will he survive? Can't we take him–?"

The Abbess interrupted before she could finish. "No, child, I do not think it would be wise to take Adam into your time."

"I suppose not, but oh, I don't want him to die. I know I hated him for what he did, but I don't want that."

Hildegarde took Shannon's face in her hands. "Child, he is not dead yet. Nor will he be if I and my nuns can prevent it."

"You haven't got antibiotics or anything here. You can't even give him a transfusion."

"True, child; however, many others have faced more grievous injuries and survived. Sister Ursel has great skill. Also, we have treatments here that, although they would be laughed at in your time, are, nevertheless, quite effective. And bones will knit straight if set right. You may always pray for him. I and the sisters will certainly do that also. And whatever you may believe, I am convinced that prayer does sometimes change things.

"And now, child, do you think you might be able to rest awhile? I have things which need my attention."

Shannon summoned up a small smile. "I think so. Um, Auntie, I think, when my ankle is better, I'd quite like to go home. I think I've had enough of the twelfth century, and I've definitely had enough of men." She swiped a hand across her eyes, then said wearily, "I don't think I'll ever trust another man as long as I live."

Hildegarde, who had just got up, sat down on the bed and gave her a level look.

"Now, that would indeed be foolish, Shannon. Don't you see? You've had two bad experiences–"

"Three! Don't forget John! He was so...urgh! So vile!"

Hildegarde took her hand. "Child, you cannot judge all men by those experiences."

Shannon's mouth tightened. "Three of them, all toads! Never again."

"And what of your father? Is he a toad?"

"What? No, of course he isn't?"

"And do you think your mother never met any bad apples?" By the expression on her face, she clearly hadn't thought of that. Good. "And what of Giles?"

"I suppose."

"Well – and you may trust me on this – he is not, for if he were, your mother would not have been able to return to you; he would have delivered her to John."

Shannon still seemed a little dubious, though Hildegarde hoped her words were having some effect. "And trust me on this, too; you cannot judge one man by another's sins." She smiled. "If we were to do that, the whole human race would likely die out. I promise you, there are good as well as bad men out there, just as there are good and bad women."

The eyes that gazed back at Hildegarde were shadowed with more than just physical pain, and the Abbess began to feel there may have been more between them than she had suspected. The thought was confirmed when Shannon spoke again.

"I did love him."

"No, you did not." Hildegarde was brisk. Shannon opened her mouth to protest, but Hildegarde continued. "You thought you loved him, but you cannot truly love in such a short time. You fell in love with what you thought you knew, with the image he projected. Of the real man, you knew nothing."

Shannon opened her mouth again, then closed it. Hildegarde continued inexorably. "I repeat myself, I know, but listen well. You were in love with being in love, for you cannot love a man fully until you know him. And do not look at me thus; I have not always been a nun, and even if I had, allow me some knowledge of the human heart."

Shannon appeared abashed for a moment, then gave a sniff and swiped again at her eyes with her sleeve. Hildegarde pressed a scrap of linen into her free hand. "Use this, and Shannon, when next you start to fall in love–"

Shannon shook her head. Unruffled, Hildegarde ignored her. "You will, Shannon, I assure you. When next you start to fall in love, give yourself time to get to know the man before you give your heart."

"There won't be a next time."

"Yes, there will; once you have recovered, I promise you, there will be."

"There wasn't for you. If you never fell in love, neither will I, not ever again."

Hildegarde's mouth quirked. "You think not?" She paused; she had said enough for the nonce, the girl was white to the lips again. Patting the hand that lay in hers, she said, "Rest now, dear, and don't trouble yourself with the future. Remember my words though, and next time you meet someone you like, you might do something for me?"

Shannon nodded, but her eyes were cloudy.

"Will you try prayer? Pray for guidance. Learn to lean on God."

"I'll try."

The voice was little more than a whisper, but Hildegarde was content. She had been able to plant a small seed of faith, and this was like to be her only opportunity; the rest was up to God. She smiled. *And He has never failed me yet.*

"Rest now, Shannon. I'll deal with what needs to be done." She released Shannon's hand to drop a kiss on her brow before nodding to Ursel who had just come in, then watched as Shannon's eyes closed. She could safely be left in Ursel's care.

CHAPTER NINETEEN

Having sent for Sir Giles, Hildegarde waited in her chamber, dreading the interview to come. Would he be wroth she hadn't told him about Shannon earlier? Mayhap she had erred.

A sharp rap on the door heralded his arrival. "Abbess?" He strode into the room, cast one look at her face and sat in the chair opposite, studying her. "Is aught amiss? Well, aught else? The lass hasn't taken a turn for the worse, has she?" His face darkened. "In truth, had Adam not been in the condition he is, I should have beaten him senseless myself. Isabella warned me of his nature, but I had not realised the depth of it."

"Sir Giles, he has done a grievous wrong; however, beating him senseless would answer for nothing."

"In your other world, perhaps not; in this world, it is the way of things, as you well know. And I cannot let it go unpunished. Surely, even in your own world, his action would have consequences."

"Yes, but they would not involve rendering him senseless. Although I agree, my other world is inclined to be too lax with discipline. I do, though, have concerns other than Adam at present. I need to get my niece home to her family."

"You wish me to arrange a guard for her? Is she able to travel? Surely, she should wait until she has recovered. And anyway, how far away is this Bolohovenia?"

Hildegarde steeled herself, then said, "About eight hundred years, Sir Giles." His head jerked upwards. "She's Marion's daughter."

"Marion?" The chair scraped along the floor as he leapt to his feet. "Marion?" he said again, incredulously. "And she's your niece? But I... Abbess, you never said! You are Marion's kin?"

Hildegarde watched him. How much should she divulge? No good had come thus far of hiding the facts; still, maybe he should not know he was also her own ancestor. She took a deep breath. "She is not my niece, yet once she had told you that, what was I to say? Indeed, it took me completely aback when you arrived with her, for I have no niece." That, at least, was true; no need to mention the degree of kinship. She continued, "Until I could spend time alone with her, I did not know who she

244

was. However," she paused, "Sir Giles, you may wish to be seated."

He eyed her narrowly. "I thank you, Abbess, I would rather stand."

Ah yes, he paces when troubled. She inclined her head. "As you wish, my lord. Now, how to begin?"

He gave a short bark of laughter. "I fancy I've heard those words from you before, and the last time you said them, you proceeded to, er, blow my mind, as Marion would have said."

She gave a quirk of her lips. "Then, Sir Giles, I should prepare for your mind to be blown again, if I were you, for Rohese, or Shannon as we would call her in her own time, is your descendant – as is Marion." There, she'd said it.

Giles stopped his pacing and collapsed into the chair again as though his legs would not hold him up. "My what?"

"Your descendant. You are her ancestor."

"And you know this, how?"

"I have known it, or rather suspected it, for some time. You may have observed that Rohese wears a ring?" He nodded. "It's a significantly unusual ring which her mother gave her. But have you not noticed its similarity to the ring you wore when first we met? The ring your wife now wears."

He looked dumbstruck.

"I see you have not." *Men!* And they never did change, this much Hildegarde knew to be true; most of them did not see that which was beneath their noses. "I can assure you, those two rings are identical."

"Impossible! My father commissioned mine for me when I gained my knighthood."

"My point precisely."

He ran his hands through his hair until it stood on end. *Any moment now,* she thought, *and he will leap from that chair again.*

She was right. Getting to his feet, he strode around the chamber like a caged beast, still tugging at his hair until it was in complete disorder.

"My descendant? How is that possible? No, Abbess, you're making assumptions. There is no way we can be sure."

"Mayhap not entirely, although I do know Marion had a grandsire whose surname was Suttoner."

"Well, then!"

"And names did change through the years. De Soutenay would have become more anglicised over time." She could see he was affronted. "I also imagine you have not observed the resemblance Rohese bears to Isabella. They have the same colouring and the same shaped face, although Rohese is more sturdy. And, Marion, too, bears more than a passing resemblance. All that differs slightly is their build and eye colour."

"That is not proof."

"No, it is not. Sir Giles, there are some things you will have to trust me on. I know almost for a certainty that Marion is your descendant. Please, do sit. You are in danger of wearing a groove in my floor, and besides, you are making me feel quite dizzy."

Giles sat, looking mulish.

"And, I have noticed Rohese, when thwarted, has exactly the same expression you now wear."

He glared at her.

"Sir Giles, think on this. How many men have been privileged thus? Not just to know your line will continue for nigh on a thousand years, but to be permitted to know your own descendants? What a wondrous gift our Lord has given to you."

His stunned expression was slowly fading as her words sunk in, only to be replaced by one of fury.

"Sir Giles?"

"And that churl of mine has dared to abscond with my own blood?"

"Sir Giles!" Hildegarde held his gaze. "Pay no mind to that."

"Pay no mind? Are you mad?"

"Sir Giles, the boy has already paid for it, and do not forget, he did save her from the outlaws they encountered."

"Aye, and if it were not for him, she would have met no outlaws!"

"Well, yes, that is true, but swallow your ire, for he is not our immediate concern. That matter may be dealt with later." *When you have calmed down,* she thought. "And only consider the wonder of this.

Your own descendant saved your life and lands, and you have had the miracle – for miracle it is, is it not? – of meeting not just her, but her daughter."

Hildegarde watched while his face softened and lit as the full truth hit him. And how could he not be delighted? In a world where ancestry and descendants meant so much, to know his line would still be unbroken so many centuries on, how could that not bring to him a sense of awe?

"Eight hundred years!" He breathed in deeply. "Yes, Abbess, a miracle indeed. If I did not believe in them before, and I confess, I have had my doubts, how could I not believe now?" A beatific smile spread across his face. "What man could hope to know that? And I? Not only have I seen the future, but…"

Hildegarde gave him a sharp glance. Was there something she did not know?

"Er, yes, Abbess." He looked like a boy caught stealing pies. "I did try; Marion saw me and pushed me back. However, in that brief glimpse, I saw wonders!"

She was glad she hadn't known at the time; it would have been a source of concern for her. However, it might make things easier now.

"Well, Sir Giles, now your descendants need your help, as you needed theirs. Rohese it was who delivered the devices, for Marion has been desperately ill." She was not going to explain a cholecystectomy. It may be routine in her own time; to him, it would sound deathly.

"She's ill? Will she recover?"

"She will, though she was unable to travel, and so Rohese came instead. Girls from her time are considerably more independent, and, despite being told not to, she came through and stayed."

He considered for a moment, then said, "Marion must be out of her mind with worry!"

"The child spun her a tale. In their time, young women travel more widely and alone. Marion believes she is elsewhere, and I wish it could remain that way. Though, now, Rohese wishes to return home but cannot walk. Assuredly, we can help her to reach the tree, but we cannot leave her there. Which brings me to my point. Sir Giles, if she has not recovered sufficiently to walk without pain in a day or so, will you help me take her through?"

"Through?" His hands played with the hilt of his dagger. In the confusion, he had forgotten to disarm. "You mean, enter her world?"

"I do. I cannot deny there may be a risk, and I do not wish you to come all the way through. If you could just help me get her halfway, I will be able to manage."

The grey eyes widened. "Not so, Abbess, I cannot leave that to you. I will come too."

"No! You will not. It's too dangerous. And consider Isabella! What will she do if you do not return? Would you leave her bereft?"

Giles brought his fist down on the desk, making the candle wobble. The flame licked up wildly, and Hildegarde grabbed for it as Giles spoke, for it seemed ominously as though he might suddenly overturn the table.

"Abbess, Rohese is my responsibility! My blood. Already, I have failed her; I've not taken the care of her I should. It is not for you to do. She is mine, and I will return her."

"No, Sir Giles, you will not. If you do not care enough to stay with Isabella, let me ask this of you – if you cannot get back to her, how will your descendants be born? I do not even know if *I* can return, but it is my world at least, and I leave no dependents behind. If this can be managed without you, then it must be."

His anger subsided. *As I knew it would, if I could but make him see sense.*

"I see your reasoning. Very well, let us say, if it can be done without me, then good. However if not, know this, Abbess. Marion risked her life coming back for me, and I will do no less for her daughter."

Hildegarde looked at the set of his mouth and knew that, with this concession, she must be content.

"But, I need to speak to my wife. In case there is risk, I must at least prepare her a little."

Oh! She had hoped to avoid this. *Though I suppose he must.*

CHAPTER TWENTY

Isabella seethed. She had thought Giles to be different to Baldwin, learned to trust him. She had believed he would not dishonour her like this. No matter if he had another woman, then? For sure, he would not be the first. Yet jealousy seared her heart like a flame.

"My lord?" Giles stiffened. Isabella was clearly not pleased. Her face had set into sharp lines. "My lord, why should the Abbess wish you to aid this woman? This Marion, what is she to you?"

Giles knew many husbands would not tolerate this from their wives, would ignore them or beat them; however, he had no wish to rule through fear. How should he deal with her? It had taken long for Isabella to even begin to trust him, though he had made slow yet steady progress. He did not want to see her retreat from him now, but how could he share this with her? Better to stand firm.

"It's naught for you to concern yourself with, Isabella."

It was as though a curtain fell between them. Her eyes flickered briefly, and the light died from them like a snuffed-out candle.

"Bella, it's a long, strange story. If you do not trust me now…" Isabella took a step backwards. "If you do not trust me now, by all the saints, you'll not believe my tale."

Isabella flushed. "My lord husband, did I say I do not trust you? I know full well how blessed I am in having you as my lord. You treat me well, have not given me reason to doubt your word." The words were said docilely enough, though the flash from her eyes before she lowered them and turned again to her embroidery belied her tone which cooled another degree as she added, "I know my place."

Giles caught at her hands, taking the cloth from her. "Indeed you do know your place. And I know you. You will give me no reason for anger. You will be dutiful, obedient – and cold as ice. I would prefer you to warm my bed, not freeze it cold as January snow."

She ignored him, refusing to raise her eyes to his.

"And this chill between us will not be good for the child."

"I assure you, my lord, Dickon will be as warmed by my love as ever."

Giles placed a finger below her chin, forcing her face upwards. "And what of the other child? The one in your womb? Will that one also not feel the chill in your heart?"

Isabella gasped, finally meeting his gaze. "But you…I…"

He pulled her to him, sat her down on the bed beside him. "Think you I had not noticed how greensick you have been in the forenoons? Or a certain fullness here." He stroked her belly. "Or here?"

"Giles! I was going to tell you, but I wanted to be sure first. I did not want to disappoint you in case it wasn't so. And then, the time was never right. How came you to guess?"

Tightening his arm round her, he drew her close, kissing her. "My love, I do know the signs. I'm not so simple as you appear to think. When will the child be born?"

"Dame Margery thinks December." She put her hand to his face, and he felt the thaw in her. Then, tentatively, she asked, "Husband, now you've discovered my secret, will you not tell me yours? I know it isn't my right to be told, nor is it my business. If you don't wish to tell me, I will not tease." She paused. "And Rohese? What has this to do with her? And why must you escort her? Cannot the Abbess send word to her kin? It is not that I do not care for her, Giles, but..." She paused. "Bolohovenia? Why must you needs accompany her there?" She shook her head. "Truly, I do not understand."

Giles tensed. She had softened, was merely puzzled now; how would she react to what he must say next? Her initial response had not been favourable. He braced himself and said gently, cautiously, as though feeling his way like a blind man, "My love, it seems she and I have family connections." He watched as her face closed in again and continued, spilling out the words, trying to convince her. "I swear to you, I had no knowledge of this, no idea. I am as bewildered as you, my heart."

"How, then? She told me Hildegarde was her aunt. Is that truth or fable? Are you also related to the Abbess? I do not understand."

Giles shifted. Isabella stood and stepped away from him, that wooden expression back on her face, and his heart sank.

"Ah, Bella." His voice was sombre now. "She is not Hildegarde's niece. That is a story she told us. I know not for what purpose."

She gazed at him dumbly, then, with a set expression and tightly pursed lips, withdrew a hand's breadth further from him as a cold finger seemed to nudge at her spine. She didn't want to know, yet forced herself to ask, "Who, then?"

He sounded exhausted, as though he bore the weight of worlds, as though his words were torn unwillingly from him. Why had he to tell her? Why now? Just as she thought she had his measure. Her world tilted a little on its axis, and she felt her bright hopes for the future begin to splinter.

Giles reached for her, but she moved further apart, and the gap between them yawned like a chasm. Speaking slowly, as though he weighed each word, he said, "She bears my blood."

The castles Isabella had been building in her head crashed down, and she whimpered slightly, wrapping her arms around her ribs as though to shield herself from a blow. Hot colour came and went in her cheeks as she whispered, "Yours? By this Marion?"

He held his hand out as though he would take hers; she evaded him, slipping from the bed, standing on legs that trembled. Giles rose and in one swift movement rounded the bed, flinging one arm about her, his other hand under her chin, lifting it, compelling her to look up at him. She veiled her expression, refusing to meet his eyes. And all the time, the wall of ice which he had so painstakingly thawed between them this last year or two was rebuilding itself as though by an invisible hand.

"Not just mine, Bella. Ours. Yours as well as mine."

Now her gaze did fly upwards, shock mingling with anger. "So what are you saying? You want to take her in?" He had the effrontery to ask her? "Sweet Mary, Giles, she is almost of an age with me. And what of her mother? Do you wish to house her also?" She shivered in his arms, sick with jealousy that he had a daughter by this, this...what was she? Concubine? Lover? And not so much that, for many men had misbegotten offspring, more that he had not told her. He had promised her there would be no secrets. He'd *promised*. An old lover she could handle if she had but known about her earlier.

"Why now, Giles? Why could you not have told me about her at any time in these years we have been together?"

Gone her bright dreams and gone the flash in her eyes as she retreated back into herself. "She is your daughter, my lord. You must do as you wish."

Giles held her to him. She remained rigid in his arms, and he pushed her down to sit on the bed again, kneeling before her, taking her ice-cold hands in his.

"Bella, sit. You distress yourself unnecessarily. I did not say I wished to take her in, nor her mother. And I only said she was of my blood – she is not my daughter."

The stiffness left her. The relief was so great that, had she not been sitting, she would have fallen. She stared at him, her eyes rimmed with unshed tears, and he wiped them gently with his finger. "Whose, then? Ralph's?"

"Not Ralph's either, my love. Mine, yet not mine. Ours, yours and mine, yet not a daughter." He gave her an odd look, his eyes troubled. "I know not how to explain this to you. Bella, have you noticed a strangeness about her? Different ways to ours? The way her speech differs slightly?"

Isabella was puzzled. "A little. Is that not because she is not from here? Because she comes from Bolohovenia? I had never heard of it before."

He shook his head. "She is not from Bolohovenia; that, too, was a story, a fable to give her a background. She had to come from somewhere, and she could not tell you or anyone else from where." His tone was wry. "No one would have believed her. In truth, she should not even be here. Her parents did not send her."

Isabella regarded him stonily. "A lie! It was all a lie. And I trusted her, for I thought her to be my friend."

"Sweetheart, it is not that she would not tell you; she *could* not. Even had she told you, you would not have believed her, as I did not believe her mother. And her mother was never my lover. Indeed, I thought at one time to kill her."

Her eyes were huge, her mouth worked. He got up and poured her a measure of wine. "You should drink this."

She took the cup mechanically, watching him.

257

"You will not believe me. It's why I did not tell you before. Bella, Marion was never my lover. She was…is…my descendant."

Isabella blinked, took an automatic sip of the wine, swallowed the wrong way and choked. Giles removed the cup from her and set it down, turning back to her, bending over her, saying, "She comes from our future. And if she is my descendant, she is also yours."

"You are crazed!" The words were whispered, her hand covered her lips.

"I know it sounds like madness. I did not believe it either. Yet you need only ask the Abbess to verify the truth of it. It's why I have been able to escape from court, and why I have to return each year around Whitsun."

"John? *This* is what links you to him?"

"And why he hates me. Because he needs me and I know the one vulnerability that no one, *no one,* apart from the Queen, knows. I cannot tell you, for if I did, you might not be safe. And I need to be able to appear before him with a clear conscience, knowing I've kept my own counsel. Marion is the link between us. Marion, who came here once by mischance, twice, and we knew we would never meet again. Her daughter should never have found her way here, but she was headstrong and wilful, and now we need to get her safely back to her own time."

Isabella gazed at him, expressionless. "And you expect me to believe this?"

He stood, running his hands through his hair. "I cannot make you believe me, and I know it sounds as though I have run mad or that I am lying through my teeth, yet I ask you to believe me because of the love you bear me. Ah, Bella," as tears sparkled on her lashes and brimmed over, "trust me, love, for I swear it's the truth."

She lifted her chin, dashing at the tears angrily with her hand. "How can I? You make mockery of me, of us, of our life together."

Giles turned and smashed his fists against the door, then came back and, grasping her wrist, pulled her to her feet. She resisted at first, but his grip tightened, bruising her, and she cried out.

"Bella, I don't wish to hurt you, but you must believe me, and I know of only one way to convince you. If you do not come willingly…" He shook his head. "Ah, I will not drag you." He let go of her abruptly, slamming out of the chamber.

Isabella fell back onto the bed, sitting there alone, shocked, motionless, numb as she heard his footsteps fade. Her thoughts, which had tumbled over each other at first, seemed to have left her. Her head felt as though it was stuffed with rags.

She did not know how much time had passed before footsteps sounded again outside and the latch was lifted. Hildegarde stood in the doorway. Isabella looked up at her and broke.

As she choked with sobs, Hildegarde embraced her. "My dear, I know, I know." The Abbess rocked her against her breast as though she had been a child, until she shuddered convulsively and pulled away, searching for a scrap of linen to wipe her face.

Isabella had, at last, been calmed, and Hildegarde had settled her onto the bed, propped up by cushions and sipping at a steaming cup of one of Ursel's remedies.

At first, she had been so overset, her teeth chattering so much, she was unable to drink. Hildegarde had removed the cup from her and soothed her again, and as Isabella had started to accept the tale, her trembling had subsided although her eyes were still puffy and red, and she scrubbed at them with the edge of the sheet.

"I suppose, if you say it's true, then I must believe it." She eyed Hildegarde doubtfully.

"My child, it was as much a shock to your husband when Rohese's mother came through the tree. Indeed, had I not been there, I think he would have killed her, for he took her to be a demon."

"As would I. But, Abbess, how came you to accept this thing with such equanimity? Did you not think her to be a demon also?"

Hildegarde pondered how to answer. To tell Isabella that she, too, had come from Rohese's time, would, she thought, be too much. And, since she hoped to live the remainder of her life here, the fewer who shared her secret, the better. She made a mental note to ensure Giles kept silent.

"Lady Isabella, I've come across many strange things in my life, yet with prayer, it is possible to discern truth from lies." That would have to do. Her brain had been so cudgelled today, to explain further was quite beyond her.

A tap at the door heralded Giles. He came in warily. *As well he might,* thought Hildegarde. Evidently, he was reluctant to cope if his wife was still hysterical. Isabella smiled tremulously up at him, and his hunched shoulders came down from his ears as he covered the space from door to bed.

"How is she?"

Typical man! "Your wife is perfectly capable of speaking for herself, Sir Giles." She sounded waspish even to herself and took a deep breath. It had been a long day already, and there was so much more to come. It would not do to be short-tempered now, however glad she would be when the next few days were over, and life at Sparnstow was returned to its usual serenity.

Isabella held a hand out to him, and he took it, turning it and dropping a kiss on the palm, folding her fingers over, saying gently, "Shall we cry peace, love?"

She nodded.

"I know you've had much to take in. I will tell you the whole tale later, but for now, the Abbess tells me we need to plan Rohese's return to her own time."

Isabella pressed his hand to her face. "Only promise me you will not go to this future time too."

He nodded. Hildegarde forbore to say more; she trusted they could do this without his leaving their century, and to suggest the possibility would do Isabella no good. All she could do was pray this thing could be done safely.

"Then go, love. But mind you keep your promise." He nodded again, and as he turned to go, Isabella called him back. "Wait. If this is true, if Rohese is truly my, er—"

"Shall we say granddaughter, to eliminate confusion?"

This time, she gave a small laugh. "Very well, my granddaughter, Giles. That seems so strange; a granddaughter of an age with myself. Is it possible I might see her before she leaves?"

Hildegarde quailed. It would be all too easy for them to speak heedlessly and be overheard. Bad enough the story had come out, let alone taking more risks. Still, she would not, could not forbid them.

She opened her mouth to speak, closing it again as Isabella continued. "Yet, she is in pain and overwrought, I know. I suppose it would be better to allow her to rest today. But I look forward to seeing her on the morrow. And I should like to give her something – a keepsake, if you will. Would you pass me that?"

She gestured to the casket where she kept her embroidery silks and, when Giles gave it to her, rummaged inside, pulling out a small silver thimble. "It was my mother's. She gave it to me before she died." She held it up. "Do you think she would like it?"

"She will treasure it, my lady."

Isabella smiled. "At least, then, she will have something to remember me by. I shall give it to her when she feels well enough for me to go to her. Please, tell her I look forward to seeing her when she is a little stronger.

"And Abbess, please call me Isabella. 'My lady' sounds too formal when I have just soaked you with tears. Besides, you cannot call me 'child' in one breath and 'my lady' in the next."

Giles laughed. "She's right, Abbess, and by the same token, Giles is sufficient for me."

Hildegarde cast up her hands. "Very well, my children. And now," her voice became serious again, "Giles, we need to make plans. Rest now, Isabella."

Isabella's face shadowed again, and Giles bent, kissing her brow. "Come, sweeting, trust me to come through this."

She flung her arms around his neck briefly, whispering words Hildegarde could not hear. Giles returned her embrace, then he followed Hildegarde from the room, and Isabella was left alone with none but her prayers for company.

As Giles closed the door behind himself, he looked at Hildegarde. "So, how is this to be done?

"That is what we need to think on."

CHAPTER TWENTY-ONE

A short while before Vespers, Sister Berthe sat on a bench outside her gatehouse, reading from a book on the life of Alban, her favourite saint.

So engrossed was she, the faint scratching on the gate went unnoticed. A more peremptory banging made her jump, nearly losing her grip on the precious volume.

Grumbling under her breath, she laid it to one side, rose stiffly to her feet and unbarred the gate to see a lone pilgrim standing before her, the badges on his hat proclaiming his wanderings had led him to such exalted shrines as Walsingham, Rome and Santiago de Compostela.

He enquired humbly of the porteress whether there might be room enough in the guest-hall for a night or two and, before she could answer, slid inside the gates like a snake slithering over a stone.

Sister Berthe shut them behind him and shivered as though the day had suddenly grown cold, for about this pilgrim was an aura of evil despite his meek tones.

Those eyes! Berthe, not normally an imaginative woman, shuddered and crossed herself, muttering a prayer whilst inwardly chiding herself for such foolishness.

Father Dominic, wandering through the guest-hall, greeted a familiar face here and there. Some tradesmen, some poor travellers, a merchant. Sir Giles and his wife were not there, he noticed regretfully, but his men were and her maids.

Spying a new pilgrim, his round face creased into a smile of delight when he noticed the badges on his hat before freezing into a rictus grimace as he saw the face beneath. He turned swiftly and secreted his portly frame behind a pillar. Keeping to the shadows, he peered out, head dipped to obscure his face. Taking another swift glance at the man, whose gaze was darting hither and thither, he withdrew again, breathing shallowly. That was no pilgrim. Father Dominic had seen him before although never spoken to him. Hamo Bardolf, these days one of John's creatures, more wolf than man; lean, hard and finding pleasure in the kill.

Father Dominic had not exaggerated when he told Shannon he was much travelled. A few years before coming to Sparnstow, he had served a great lord, going to many places. He had seen Hamo but thrice, and each time, where Bardolf had been, trouble followed.

Deeply alarmed, the priest attended Vespers with only half a mind, escaping immediately afterwards and retreating to his small lodging at the side of the abbey where he sat at his table, eyes unfocussed, long-forgotten images flitting across his mind like small torments. Recalled to his surroundings by the sudden chatter of a magpie outside his window, he heaved himself to his feet and set off towards the cloisters determined to find the Abbess. If Hamo was here, the Abbess needed to be told.

His brow wrinkled as he puzzled over the problem. What was Bardolf after? He hadn't seen the Abbess, though he knew she'd returned, and they'd been gone a bare two days. Bardolf's quarry could not be Hildegarde, therefore it must be de Soutenay.

Dominic liked the knight; there was a wholesomeness about him. Should he go to him first? No, the Abbess was his immediate priority. He quickened his pace, keeping a wary eye out for Hamo as he walked.

The Abbess proved elusive, but as Father Dominic trotted along as fast as his stubby legs would allow, he finally spied her exiting a chamber in what could only be described as a furtive manner, followed by de Soutenay. The priest put on a spurt, wheezing slightly as he came to a halt before them, barring their way.

Giles regarded him coldly. Much as he liked the little priest, he could talk the ears off a mule, and now was not the time. He nodded tersely and moved to pass him. To his astonishment, Father Dominic grasped his arm. Affronted, he glared; the priest gazed at him earnestly before turning to the Abbess, gasping, "Abbess, my lord, a word please. It is urgent."

Hildegarde eyed him with an expression which spoke volumes; however, he was not to be deterred. "It is most urgent," he repeated, tugging at Giles sleeve. Giles was about to protest when Father Dominic's desperate expression gave him pause, and the priest appeared to sag with relief as Hildegarde indicated a door just a little further down. He stepped back to allow them entry, then almost tumbled in after them, leaning against the door for a moment before moving as far from it as possible.

The room, a storeroom of sorts, was barely more than a cell. He looked around, glancing up at the high, narrow window above his head, then explained as briefly as possible in low tones that Giles had to strain to hear.

Hildegarde listened without speaking, her face drawn, then said, "Thank you, Father."

That was all, yet the priest nodded, satisfied, and had turned to leave when she spoke again.

"And, Father, if you might manage to keep his attention for a candle-notch or two?"

He nodded again, a smile flitting briefly across his face. "I shall recall my many wondrous journeys and then insist on him describing his own. Do not fear, Abbess. I will keep him occupied."

"And he will," she said, as he quit the room, a twinkle briefly lighting her eye. "He can be most tedious on the subject of his travels, as I know to my cost." The gravity returned to her face. "I think we must change our plans somewhat." She hesitated. "Originally, I was not going to tell you this, for I didn't wish to give you reason to hate John more than you already do. Now, however, I think it necessary.

"Shannon had spilled some wine on her gown. I did not notice, and Alys took her to her parents' chamber. John saw them, although I don't believe he thought aught of it beyond the usual." Giles face tightened, and she hurried to reassure him. "Do not fear, Sir Giles, no harm was done, although the encounter was not pleasant. Unfortunately, Alys saw fit to lend her a green gown, and in it, Shannon resembled her mother considerably. I realised it immediately they returned and swept her off to change into something less memorable.

"John noticed; he seemed as though he was cudgelling his brain. I do not think he realised who she reminded him of; it was, after all, some years ago. Now, I believe her likeness, coupled with my presence, may have roused his curiosity."

She looked stricken. "Sir Giles, it's my fault. I should have had a greater care for her. I fear my attention had been distracted; I didn't see the danger until it was too late. Even then, I thought we had her safe away." She bit her lip. "I should have confided in you the reason why Shannon should not attend court."

Giles touched her hand. "Abbess, you had your reasons. And indeed, had it not been for Adam, I should still be none the wiser, is that not so?"

"Even so, I should have foreseen John's predilection for fresh female faces. I should have realised he would notice her."

She appeared so guilty, so downcast, Giles tried to reassure her. "Why should you? I did not spot the resemblance."

"You, Giles, do not search for plots beneath every stone." And as he quirked an eyebrow at her, she said, "Very well, but not in the way John does."

"I still say it could not have been foreseen. Now though, Abbess, our immediate priority is to keep Bardolf from speaking to your nuns or lay brethren. Like as not, he'll winkle information out of them as easily as shelling peas."

Hildegarde pressed her fingers to her temples, closed her eyes and was silent for a moment. "I shall speak to my prioress immediately and call for three days of silence. I do not often invoke the rule, however, I shall say that after so much recent levity, we need to compose our hearts again before our Lord.

"Perhaps you would be good enough to loiter here, Sir Giles, in the corridors near Shannon's chamber. I shan't be long. This is a secluded part of the abbey, so it's doubtful anyone will come upon you. If they do, distract them, ask foolish questions, send them on pointless errands if you must, but make sure Shannon keeps that door closed."

"Do we tell Shannon?" Giles wondered aloud.

"I think not; no need to fret her. She knows the need for subterfuge. We must decide how best to move her without attracting notice. I need to think on this."

She left him standing in the corridor, trying to look as though he was not on guard, and slipped quietly into Shannon's chamber. She was asleep. Hildegarde regarded her for a moment, watching the rise and fall of her chest, then touched her hand lightly.

Shannon opened her eyes, blinking owlishly at first until she recalled her surroundings. The dark shadows beneath her eyes had cleared a little, and if the frown of pain still lingered between her brows, at least the sleep had given her respite.

She glanced up smiling, until she saw the nun's expression.

"What's wrong?"

"My dear, if we needed to get you home sooner than anticipated, would you be able to use your, um, mobile to call a friend to collect you once you get through the beech tree? Or," she struggled to remember the word she wanted, "a taxi?"

Shannon's face fell. "I thought we were going to wait until my ankle was better. I thought I'd have a few more days to spend with Giles and Isabella."

Hildegarde eyed her steadily. "Circumstances have changed. There would likely not have been the opportunity to see them again in any case. Now, however, I really think it would be for the best..." Her voice tailed off; she did not want to alarm Shannon. Surely, the girl had had enough upsets in the last few days.

Shannon chewed her lip and then grimaced; Hildegarde kept her face impassive. "Well?"

"Anyway, I might have to wait until my ankle is better. The battery's probably dead by now. Do you have it?"

Hildegarde fumbled beneath her habit and brought out the mobile. Shannon looked startled. "I thought they didn't have pockets in the twelfth century."

"They don't. I, however, do." She held out the phone, and Shannon took it, switching it on. It flickered for a moment, then died.

"Nope, the battery's dead. I can't charge it from here, can I? And I don't think I can walk." She swung her legs off the bed and put her weight gingerly on her bad ankle, yelping and collapsing back onto the bed. "No. I can't. We'll have to wait until it's better."

Hildegarde tried to stay composed, but, beneath her calm exterior, she was reeling. She left Shannon, returning to her own rooms, where she summoned Ursel to join her, explaining the latest problem.

Ursel's brow creased, and she sat quietly. Hildegarde started to speak, but Ursel held up her hand. "Wait. I'm thinking."

Hildegarde subsided, then sat in an agony of impatience. Her own resources had been drained by now, her ingenuity all but exhausted. There was naught for her to do until Ursel spoke again, so she closed her eyes and prayed for inspiration.

The silence in the room felt heavy. Hildegarde opened her eyes again and saw Ursel watching her, eyes bright.

"Mother, how would it be if Sir Giles and Lady Isabella took their leave at first light tomorrow, before this Hamo is about? Rohese could be one of their party."

Hildegarde sighed. If only it could be that easy. "Dear Ursel, if Hamo is indeed a spy, will he not be watching for just such an eventuality? And if he sees Rohese leave with them, do you not think he will take note? I do not wish to bring John down upon Sir Giles."

The hazel eyes crinkled until they were mere slits. "I think, dear Mother Abbess, Hamo may well find he sleeps long into the morrow and awakens with a bad sickness. Nothing dangerous, just something that will confine him to the infirmary. I'm sure Brother Anselm will kindly isolate him to make sure the 'sickness' is not passed on."

Hildegarde was speechless. Ursel nodded and continued. "And I think, with so many men and maids about, no one would notice if Lady Isabella happened to have acquired an extra maid. As long as Rohese can be assisted to a horse, she can quite well ride pillion. It will pain her ankle sorely; however, needs must."

"It's a good idea, Sister Ursel, but I'm afraid it won't work. Rohese will not be able to summon help once she gets to her own time. The device she brought with her – her mobile, as she calls it – will not have sufficient power to contact anyone. I had thought of going back with her and staying until she could obtain aid, but, now Bardolf is here, how shall I return without being seen? And if Sir Giles goes, how will he contrive it so his party do not notice his absence? For we don't know how long it will take her to obtain aid."

Ursel looked taken aback for a moment, then said, "And how if Brother Bernard...or wait, we do not wish to have any unusual absences, I suppose. Then, how if we confide in Father Dominic?"

"Father Dominic?" Hildegarde was horrified.

"Ah, Mother, you're thinking he will be shocked." She smiled. "I imagine you'll discover our Father Dominic is a lot more able to cope with the extraordinary than you'd expect. And of a surety, he does love adventure, does he not?

"He may seem an unlikely repository for secrets, for certès, but you may be sure he knows how to keep a still tongue in his head, and he's already proved you can trust him, hasn't he?"

Hildegarde had to agree, although she still felt somewhat doubtful. "Yes, Sister, but this…this is so fantastical, and–"

Ursel cut in. "Fantastical, yes; however, you are not considering the man. He may be a priest, my lady, yet have you not seen beneath the cloth? You've heard his tales of pilgrimage often enough; have you not noticed the gleam in his eyes? And he has not been travelling this many a year. If ever a man was hungry to add to his experiences, I should say Father Dominic has that hunger."

Hildegarde was amazed. She'd thought she knew the priest, had thought herself to be good at seeing below the surface. She considered for a moment, recalling the conversations she'd had with him. Ursel was absolutely correct; how had she missed it? "Sister, you never cease to counsel me well."

Ursel's wrinkled apple of a face creased even more at the praise from her Abbess. "And, since he regularly goes about outside the abbey, his absence would attract little or no notice. So, Mother, when shall we speak to him?"

Hildegarde raised her head as a bell began to toll. "Oh, I think immediately after Nones, dear Sister, don't you?"

Father Dominic proved a little more difficult to speak to than they had anticipated, since he was determined to remain with Hamo. Eventually, Sister Ursel took more direct action, going to him, telling him his presence was needed elsewhere.

To judge by the relief on Hamo's face, her interruption was very much appreciated. Ursel repressed a chuckle, knowing the reprieve would be only temporary, for Brother Anselm had been taken partly into their confidence and informed of the necessity of keeping this particular 'pilgrim' busy in conversation. He was bearing down on the unfortunate Hamo even as Ursel drew Father Dominic away, leading him not to the infirmary as he had expected but to the Abbess's quarters.

Father Dominic could scarce believe his ears when the Abbess poured out her tale to him. With his love of intrigue, he recognised this as the answer to his recent prayers.

For the last few years, he had been unable to find reason to travel far beyond the shire, and now, this! The greatest of all adventures, save only death. For what other man on earth would ever see so far into the future?

This was the stuff of legends, of romantic tales; even the stories he had devoured, the books he had collected in his small but cherished library, had not spoken of the future.

Dominic felt lit from within and mentally rubbed his hands together in gleeful anticipation before taking note of the worried faces observing him. He made haste to reassure them. "Dear Mother Abbess, you were right to ask me. I should be delighted to aid you."

This was too easy. A niggle of worry prodded Hildegarde. His acceptance was far too quick. Had he really comprehended her? Truly? "Father, you do understand that I speak not of Bolohovenia but the future, do you not?"

He nodded at her, beaming cherubically.

"And you believe me?" This was surely too easy.

"My lady Abbess, you are the most truthful, most sensible woman I have ever known. Indeed, I have the greatest respect for you. If you say this thing is so, then it is so."

Hildegarde was still dubious. Did men from this century really dive straight into fantasies like…like characters from Enid Blyton? Doctor Who, even? How could this little man believe her so easily? For certès, he was a rarity. Furthermore, she was beginning to have second thoughts, to wish she had never involved him. It was one thing to face the possibility of being stuck in the future herself – that would be daunting enough – but to involve someone else! She shouldn't even have considered it. It was wrong of her. She must dissuade him. She *must*. She would manage the thing without risking anyone else.

She looked hard at him. "And you do realise the dangers?" She was finding it more difficult to believe him than he had found it to believe her.

He nodded enthusiastically. "My one regret, dearest lady, is that I will not be able to speak of it to another. But, Abbess, this is the most wondrous adventure. To be a traveller in itself is a marvellous thing. This – to travel to another time, another century…" He broke off and sat there, his face cast Heavenward, eyes bright, cheeks flushed with excitement.

Hildegarde tried again. "And what, dear Father, if you are unable to go through? And if you do, what then if you cannot return? For we do not know for sure whether it's possible."

He seemed a little taken aback, but then smiled again, and Hildegarde could almost see the cogs inside his mind beginning to turn.

"My lady, we will not know at all if we do not try. And if we can help this young woman, you know we must. Is that not our calling? To serve our Lord by serving our fellow man? Did our Lord not say it is a blessed thing to lay down one's life for another?"

Hildegarde could only nod helplessly. His reasoning was unarguable.

Father Dominic continued, "And if I'm not able to reach this future time, then there is no more to be done. Yet if I can go there, it seems probable that I will also be able to return."

Hildegarde found she was beginning to wring her hands and placed them flat on the table before her. "But how shall we know? You must not return here immediately. That would be most suspect. So how shall we know whether you are here and waiting to return to us or lost forever in a future about which you know nothing? Are you truly sure you wish to do this?"

Father Dominic waved his hands. "Dear lady, I'm convinced our Lord will not desert me. If He takes our visitor safely back to her own time by my hand, of a surety, He will keep me from harm and bring me home."

Sister Ursel, who had been listening but saying nothing, chimed in. "And, my lady, if he is unable to return," she paused, giving Hildegarde a meaningful look, which made Father Dominic regard them both quizzically, "mayhap there is one other who can assist him.

"Father, let us say that if you have returned safely to our time, you continue on to Sir Ralph and Lady Maude, and from there send a messenger to us. If not, I would suggest you stay by the tree in that other time. If we don't hear from you by the morning of the day after tomorrow, there is one other who can come to your aid."

Father Dominic still appeared puzzled for a moment but was soon lost in his own excitement again and sat rubbing his hands as though he couldn't wait to get started.

Hildegarde gave up trying to convince him. She had been prepared for denials and disbelief, for long arduous explanations, not this, and it had caught her by surprise, taking her breath away and leaving her slightly disorientated. The die was cast; nothing she could say now was going to dissuade him. The thing was out of her hands. And Sister Ursel was no help.

Ursel had noticed her confusion, for she nodded and stepped into the breach. "So it's settled. Father, we thought to make sure this Hamo would be unable to rise early on the morrow."

"You wish me to make him drunk? Hmm, well it may suffice; however, it may be that he would suspect we had diverted him. Now, if we do not wish to leave a trail which would lead back to us–"

Ursel interrupted him. "Those were my own thoughts, too, Father. I have a small nostrum here which, if he were to drink unwittingly, would not just render him senseless tonight, but would also require him to spend a few days in the infirmary. It will do him no harm yet would, for certès, give him no desire to be poking his nose into our concerns."

Father Dominic's eyes gleamed as he took the small flask Ursel was holding out, and the pair of them continued with their plans.

Hildegarde rolled her eyes. These two were natural conspirators, while she was beginning to feel like an amateur. Very well, she would leave the plans to them. Leaning her chin on her hands, she listened in awed fascination as they discussed the best course to take and hoped against hope that all would work out. Now she had started this, there seemed no hope of stopping it. She claimed to believe in miracles – now her faith was to be put to the test.

CHAPTER TWENTY-TWO

Hildegarde had not gone back to her bed after Matins, instead slipping silently into Shannon's chamber. Shannon was in a deep sleep, making no sound except for an occasional small snore. Hildegarde watched her fondly for a moment before placing a hand firmly over Shannon's mouth to muffle any noise she might make on awakening, which had the immediate effect of making the girl's eyes open wide with shock.

Once Shannon was awake sufficiently to understand, Hildegarde removed her hand and, placing her finger to her lips, turned to light Shannon's horn lantern with the candle she had brought, for it was still dark. First, however, she closed the shutters. There should be no prying eyes about at this time, but just in case, she had no wish for anyone to see flickering lights at the windows.

She was grateful for the thick stone walls and heavy door that muffled sound so well. Glad, too, she'd had the foresight to choose a room which was set away from the other guest chambers where their wealthy guests slept. Still, they must be quiet.

Shannon sat bolt upright in bed. Hildegarde bent over her, whispering in her ear, "My dear, the time has come. I'm afraid you must leave now." Shannon raised her eyebrows questioningly. Seeing her expression, Hildegarde prayed silently, *Dear Lord, let her not be difficult.*

"What? You mean right now? In the dark? I really wanted to see Giles and Isabella again at least once more, just to say goodbye. What's the rush?" She put her hand to her mouth, her eyes grown huge with sudden fear. "Auntie, has something happened? Am I in danger?"

Hildegarde had been hoping to avoid this, yet now, there seemed to be no alternative. "Child, I already told you it was unlikely you would see them again. Were you not listening?"

"Yes, but I thought just a quick goodbye would be okay–"

Shannon's pout was evident, but Hildegarde forestalled any further grumbling. "Well, you will not see Isabella; Giles will have to suffice. The case is now urgent, for it seems Prince John has sent someone here, probably to find out more about you."

Shannon paled, her face eerie in the candlelight. "But why? I thought once I'd gone, he'd just find someone else."

"Shannon, dear, when you changed into that green gown belonging to Alys, you bore a striking resemblance to your mother, for she wore similar colours when she arrived."

"I was like Mum? Really?" Shannon smiled, pleased for a moment, then became more serious as Hildegarde continued.

"Very like her. And I noticed John watching you. He seemed as though he was trying to remember something. I think your appearance may have sparked off a dim memory of Marion. It may be that he just wants more information about you; nevertheless, we do not wish to take any more risks, I think.

"Come, Shannon, it's time to get you back to the future." She paused, confused, when Shannon suddenly smothered a giggle. "What is it?"

Shannon's eyes were creased in merriment. "Nothing, just a topical joke."

Hildegarde looked blankly at her, and Shannon sobered again, eyes wide, expression sombre, then said, "Won't this man see me leave? If he's a spy, I mean."

"No, for we took certain precautions."

"You mean you drugged him?"

Hildegarde repressed a wince. "Not precisely. However, he has been taken care of."

"What if someone else sees me leave?"

"No one will be aware of you, for Giles and Isabella will be leaving then. There will be so much bustle just before Prime, no one will notice if you leave at the same time."

"You mean I'm going with them? So I will see them. Won't the others realise I'm there?"

"You will be leaving with them, certainly, but I promise you, you will be quite unrecognisable, even if anyone should see you, which I very much doubt. You will be riding behind Father Dominic."

Shannon gawped, amazed. "Father Dominic? You're kidding me!"

Hildegarde smiled. "Yes, I was surprised too. It seems our priest is a man of adventure and action who has no difficulty in accepting the most unlikely of truths. I very much fear he has read too many stories. You know how fantastic medieval tales are."

"Well! I'd never have believed it! And he'll take me to the tree?"

"Indeed. Now, how is your ankle?"

Shannon put her foot gingerly to the ground, gasping as she tried to stand. Hildegarde passed her a crutch. "What if you use this?"

She tried again, getting cautiously to her feet, leaning heavily on it. "I can just about stand. I don't think I could walk far without help though." She sat down again, her forehead furrowed. "What am I going to do? My mobile's dead. The tree's too far away from the road or the abbey. I might have to wait hours before anyone comes near enough for me to call for help."

"Which is where Father Dominic comes in."

Shannon stared at Hildegarde, baffled.

"It seems, child, Father Dominic would fit well between the pages of any tale of adventure. He is not only willing to help you, he's bound and determined none else shall. In fact, he's positively champing at the bit. I'll admit, I'm quite astounded to discover how excited he is; I have obviously underestimated him."

"You're having me on! Seriously?"

"I confess, I found it hard to accept also. Yet, believable or not, it's true, so Father Dominic will escort you through the beech tree and wait with you whilst you obtain assistance. Will it be possible for your mother to collect you? Will she have recovered from her surgery?"

"Well, she should be, though actually, I'd rather get a taxi. Then, she won't even need to know where I've been." Shannon gave Hildegarde a challenging look. "She doesn't need to know, right?"

Hildegarde would have preferred Shannon to be open but could see her point. "Very well," she conceded. "And now, I have an outfit that I have purloined from our charity chest. It's perfectly clean." She held out a dark brown tunic and Shannon's own grey undershift. Shannon, as she expected, wrinkled her nose. Hildegarde gazed back impassively. "I assume you do wish to be unrecognisable?"

"Oh, all right then. And I suppose I have to wear my wimple?"

"Certainly, and we will cover it with this hood." She held out a wrinkled thing in beige with a short liripipe. Shannon screwed up her face again but took it. "And don't forget to wear whatever you came in beneath it. I was worried the good Father might be shocked; however, I do believe he will even take modern fashion in his stride. The man was born to be a time traveller."

Shannon giggled quietly. "He's not Doctor Who in disguise, is he?"

Hildegarde grinned. "At this point, I would be prepared to believe anything. Now, let's get you dressed."

"It's a good job Amice went home yesterday."

"Indeed it is, so I shall be your maid now. Come."

Once dressed, Shannon looked down at herself. Her normally slender figure had been hidden beneath the all-encompassing folds of a garment made for someone of twice her girth. The wimple was fitted low on her forehead, and Hildegarde had contrived to even cover the tip of her chin with it, pulling the hood down closely over her face. She felt as though she was wearing a burqa or whatever it was. Certainly, nothing except her hands and the middle part of her face from her eyebrows to just below her mouth showed.

"That should do it, surely. I don't even think *I'd* recognise me."

"Very true. Remember, you are just a humble pilgrim's wife, not anyone of importance. Slouch a little. You are not quite a peasant, perhaps, but you must, for certès, not seem to be a lady.

"Now, I can't risk bringing you something to eat. I don't want to be seen abroad before Prime."

"That's okay. I'm not hungry."

"Well then, just before Prime, I shall open this door, and Father Dominic will escort you to the outer courtyard where he will get you seated on his mule. Isabella and Giles will be making such a disturbance as they leave, we are hopeful no one will notice you even if they should be about."

Shannon pressed her lips tightly together for a moment. "I'm going to miss wearing my gowns." She stroked the fabric of the one she was trying to fold. Hildegarde retrieved the garment from her, folding it perfectly, with the economy of movement she had perfected over the years. "I'm going to miss you, too, Auntie." Her eyes were suspiciously moist. "I suppose I'll never see you again." She paused. "Probably."

"God forbid, child! Of a surety, you've given me more worry in recent days than an entire convent of nuns has given me in more than thirty years." She softened the words with a smile. "Though I confess, I shall miss you too. However, I shall think of you often and keep you in my prayers."

Shannon twisted and hugged her around the waist, burying her face in the dark cloth then, pulling away, gazed speculatively at her. "Still, you never know. And, I know some of this visit was horrible, but, you know, some of it was fantastic. Meeting you, the sisters, Giles and Isabella, and that gorgeous little boy. Oh! I suppose he's my ancestor, too."

"He may be, or he may not. We do not know how many children they will have or how many will survive. For now," Hildegarde's eyes softened, "I should just think of him as a little boy, if I were you. Certainly, that's how I see them. Not as my ancestors, just people in their own right. Although, they do feel like kin once you know, do they not?"

Shannon nodded.

"Now, are you ready to go? Do you have everything?"

"Where's my mobile?" She started to rummage through her bags, threatening to undo Hildegarde's careful packing. Hildegarde caught her hands to stop her as she tugged it out.

"It's here. I have it. If Mum ever finds out where I've been, she'll kill me. She's going to be so angry."

"And do you blame her? She might never have seen you again. She warned you of the dangers."

"I suppose."

"Still, be that as it may, has this break helped?"

Shannon nodded again. "It really has. I don't give a stuff about Jackson now. Sorry," she added, as Hildegarde winced.

"So, shall we get you moving?"

Shannon frowned. "It's going to hurt."

She started to rise; Hildegarde forestalled her. "Child, wait for Father Dominic. He'll assist you along with Sir Giles. Once mounted, you'll ride with the others. They will veer off from the main party when you near the tree. Sir Giles will take the mule, and Father Dominic will get you through the beech and find someone whose phone you may borrow – I imagine everyone has these mobile things, yes?"

"Yep."

"Good. Now, wait here; I shall return in a moment."

Giles was pacing the garth, half hidden by shadows. He raised his head as though he'd sensed Hildegarde's soft tread and moved towards her. "Is she ready?"

She raised her finger to her lips. Better not to speak out here.

Leading him across to the building which housed the guests, she opened a little-used door at the rear of the guest-house – an alternative way in, which avoided the necessity of passing other chambers. The short hall it opened into which led to Shannon's room was dark and slightly dank but held far less risk of their being heard.

Shannon was resting on the bed, her foot up. She hadn't noticed his arrival, and he hesitated, observing her, studying her features. Hildegarde was right; how had he not seen it? She was not identical to Isabella, yet there was a definite similarity, and...he stared! That ring! Was it his or not? He had to know.

"Rohese?" She opened her eyes, startled for a moment, then gazed up at him, and he flinched. His mother had looked thus the last time he had seen her. She was dead within the month; it had been his final memory of her.

Shannon quirked an eyebrow. "Sir Giles, or, er, should I call you Grandfather?"

Despite himself, he grinned. "Just Giles will do since, although you are kin, I'm in no way old enough to be your grandsire, lass."

"I know. Weird, isn't it?"

And there it was, the other resemblance. Marion! He must have been purblind.

"And my name's Shannon, but you'd better stick to Rohese."

"Shannon, you blow my mind." He couldn't resist it, and her eyes sparked with fun. She had courage and spirit like her mother.

Hildegarde touched his arm; they needed to move. But first... "Shannon, may I see your ring?"

She handed it to him wordlessly. He slid it onto his little finger, where he used to wear his own before giving it to Isabella. It fitted as though it had been made for him. Pulling it off, he studied the inside; he could just make out the inscription his father had had engraved. The words were worn away now; however, the marks he could see corresponded with what he knew should be there. It was true, then.

He caressed the worn smoothness of the ring before handing it back to Shannon. "Take care of it. It does my heart good to know you cherish it."

Hildegarde interrupted. "Sir Giles! We need to go." Then she paused. "Wait one moment. I nearly forgot." She pulled something from the hidden pocket in the skirt of her habit. "Isabella asked me to give you this – it was her mother's – as a parting gift."

Shannon took the little thimble, exclaiming in delight. And indeed, it was exquisite. Tiny deer chased around it, and a small bird was engraved on the top. "Oh, it's beautiful. Thank her for me, please. I wish I could see her again. And Dickon."

At that moment, a gentle scratching came at the door. Shannon jumped. Hildegarde opened it, and Father Dominic bustled in. The Abbess looked at him, then turned to Shannon. "Does he appear as the priests do in your world?"

"Um, I think so. Or a monk, anyway. Close enough to pass, I suppose."

"Then, that will have to do. Now, Father, have you your pilgrim clothes?"

His eyes twinkled. "I do indeed, good Abbess. Might I change into them here? Mayhap in the room where we spoke with Sir Giles?"

"Certainly. You remember the way?"

He inclined his head. "I have an excellent sense of direction, my lady."

And off he went, carrying a bundle which Shannon assumed was his disguise. "He's a nice little man, isn't he? Mind you, he got on my wick when I first met him."

Hildegarde gave her a rueful smile. "I'm afraid I still find him quite irksome. He has a good heart though, and after this, I shall certainly see him in a new light. Also, at least he'll have some fresh tales to tell."

"Yeah, you can probably recite the others by heart, now, can't you? I bet he's told you the same things loads of times." Shannon grinned, then her face tensed. "Auntie, I know I've been laughing, but this is serious isn't it? I'm a bit nervous. Do you think I'll make it home? And will you all be okay? The spy won't cause you trouble, will he?"

"I would almost, were I not a nun, put money on you arriving home none the worse for your adventures apart from a bad sprain. As for Hamo, I trust he will be so grateful for the care we take of him, he'll not consider us complicit in any way.

There is little he can do if you are gone when he recovers."

"What about John?" Shannon was chewing her thumbnail. "What if he comes searching for me? And won't everyone want to know where I've gone?"

"I shall make it known that your father's men came in secret to collect you. He is a high-born lord, after all." Shannon giggled. Hildegarde smiled again and continued, "He wished you to return most urgently, by secret means, due to political problems in Bolohovenia. And may God forgive me for the lie."

"Well, it isn't exactly a lie, is it? I mean Dad would want to get me out secretly if he knew where I was and what had happened. So you aren't exactly lying."

"I fear I am stretching the truth until it's almost unrecognisable, but," Hildegarde held her hands out in exasperation "what else can I do? As for John – we will make shift somehow. We have our Lord's protection and that of our habits."

Hildegarde turned to Giles, who had been standing near the door watching them with an indefinable expression. "Sir Giles," she caught his eye and corrected herself, "well, Giles, then. Are you clear about your part in this?"

"As I see it, my part is to allow Roh...I mean Shannon and Father Dominic to accompany us, then, a short way after we pass the tree, to leave

Isabella and my household to continue to Oakley. I escort them to the woods near the tree, take the mule they will be riding and return to my mesnie.

"It seems, the pilgrim sold the mule to me when he had no further use for it. I believe I shall donate it to the abbey. No one will question me, I assure you. I sometimes have a look about me which discourages questions – do you not recall, Abbess? And certainly, no one will connect this rather stout and devout pilgrim with the flighty young woman who accompanied us to the abbey." He flashed a grin. "In truth, I doubt I would myself."

Hildegarde took Shannon into an embrace. "You see, Shannon. Try not to worry, my dear. At any rate, you can do nothing about what happens here. Now, I must go to Prime. I will not come to see you off; it will be safer if I distance myself."

Shannon's face fell, and Hildegarde kissed her on the cheek. "It has been a delight to come to know you, child; I'm afraid this is goodbye though, for you must not come again. You do know that, do you not?"

A tear glinted at the corner of her eye, and Shannon gave a sniff and mopped her own eyes. "I'll miss you so much."

"As I will miss you. But, Shannon, how blessed we are to have even met this once."

"I suppose." She gave another sniff and threw her arms around Hildegarde, then Giles, who stood helplessly for a moment before putting one arm about her, patting her shoulder.

"Now, I must go. Make haste, and be very quiet until you reach the courtyard. There should be enough confusion there for you to go unnoticed. Even so, it would be better if you do not speak, lest any should recognise your voice." Hildegarde opened the door and left, casting one backward glance over her shoulder, raising her hand in a tiny wave, before moving noiselessly down the corridor to the cloisters.

At the same time, a very stout pilgrim came plodding over from the opposite direction. Giles turned a snort of laughter into something resembling a sneeze. Father Dominic, already inclined to plumpness, had clearly rolled his habit up beneath the tunic he now wore. An enormous girth topped hose and boots, and he was girded with a belt which his 'belly' overhung in rolls. A pilgrim hat with metal badges on completed the ensemble, casting a shadow over his face. Even had it been light, he would have been unrecognisable. He placed a finger to his lips when Giles sneezed and looked around surreptitiously.

He's like Secret Squirrel, thought Shannon, biting her lip hard in her attempt not to laugh.

With various vague hand signals, he indicated they should leave. He put an arm around Shannon, helping her to her feet, and he and Giles crossed their hands to make a seat for her. She perched gingerly and placed her arms around their necks, balancing her crutch across her lap as they made their way as quietly as possible to the courtyard where men, maids and horses milled in increasing confusion.

Giles set her back on her feet, and she leaned heavily on the crutch with Father Dominic on her other side, helping to take her weight.

Isabella, already mounted, was in the midst of the chaos, directing and redirecting, changing her mind and making as much difficulty as possible. As she caught Giles amazed expression, she gave a roguish wink, so fleeting he nearly missed it.

Giles was more than amazed; he was impressed. He had not known she had it in her, and the wink nearly threw him into a gust of laughter. He controlled himself with difficulty, led a mule over to Father Dominic, then cast himself into the deception, arguing with Isabella, redirecting his men and generally adding to the near riot that was taking place. Certainly, all attention would be on them. No one would notice the fat pilgrim and his stout wife.

During the confusion, Father Dominic took the opportunity to slip, unnoticed, through the gates. Sister Berthe eyed them as though trying to think who they might be, but Giles had been watching. Reacting instantly, he nudged Troubadour into the path of two of his squires, which made them drop the coffer they were carrying.

Berthe, still scrutinising the pilgrim and his wife, was distracted by his roar of fury, and Isabella berated the squires in a raised voice such as Giles had never heard before. It did his heart good, this feeling of complicity. He regarded Isabella with deepening respect, bordering on awe. She caught his look and gave him a wicked grin – another first. Until now, she had smiled often, sometimes even laughed; this grin was full of mischief, and something more – partnership.

His heart lighter than it had ever been, he indicated they should allow the chaos to fade and get underway, and she nodded. Somehow, within minutes, the upheaval had been calmed, the wain and pack-ponies reloaded, and order reigned, as Giles and Isabella, riding shoulder to shoulder, headed their entourage away from the abbey with ne'er a glance behind them.

As they neared the bridge, they spied Shannon and Father Dominic plodding slowly ahead of them. Isabella made a small choking sound, instantly quelled, and raised a delicate eyebrow at Giles, face brimming with humour. He murmured something beneath his breath which brought another little snort of laughter from her and called, "Good pilgrims, which way do you ride? Do you wish to join us and accept our protection on your journey?"

Father Dominic, who was turning out to be a consummate actor, answered him in meek, grateful tones, "Aye, lord, that we would. My thanks for your kindness." And halting the mule, waited until they were past, pulling in to the rear of the group. Isabella inclined her head towards them, nodding graciously, every inch the fine lady, and Father Dominic touched the brim of his hat respectfully.

For a while, Shannon didn't speak at all. Neither did Father Dominic. In truth, their silence gave them even more the resemblance of a long-married couple.

Shannon clenched her jaw and tried to ignore the pain the jogging was causing her ankle. Soon, oh soon, she'd be home and safe. To her surprise, Giles dropped back to join them, saying, "Have you pilgrimmed far?"

Father Dominic replied with enthusiasm. "Yes, lord, to Walsingham, Saint Albans, and Holywell and very many others betwixt and between." His voice had taken on a rougher edge, the priestly inflection quite gone.

"You must have seen much of interest."

"Aye, sire, that we have." And, in the same rough tone which sounded nothing like his normal voice, the priest started to tell the story of his travels. Shannon was astounded. These were, in essence, the same stories he had told her, yet they sounded completely different. He never missed a beat, yet there was nothing in them to make anyone who had spoken to him at the abbey recognise him from the tales he now narrated. It was cleverly done, and she mentally applauded him, whilst thinking how much Hildegarde would have appreciated his acting skills. Not a lie did he tell, yet none of his truths sounded as they had at the abbey.

As they passed the woods, the clearing where the tree stood came into view, and she readied herself for turning off, expecting Father Dominic to leave the group. To her horror, they did not. She tensed; he must have got it wrong. Leaning forward, she said under her breath, "Father, the tree – it's over there. We need to go back."

Shannon had expected him to quietly turn back and was shocked when he called aloud, "No matter, Wife, do not concern yourself." She was mortified when one of the squires riding ahead of them gave a snigger.

She sat bolt upright, rigid with apprehension. What was happening? Tugging at his arm, she was further abashed when he admonished her in belligerent, coarse tones, calling her a shrew. He turned then and whispered, "Just trust me. We have it all worked out." Silenced, she could do no more than wait.

The company continued on their journey, and Shannon, feeling desperate to get home now, almost ground her teeth with impatience. What was happening? Why didn't they turn?

They covered a few more miles, with Shannon constantly looking over her shoulder in fear of pursuit, until, at last, Father Dominic called out, "My thanks, my lord, for your company this far. Our way lies in a different direction now."

He touched his hat in respect again, and Giles said loudly enough to carry down the line, "Do you have far to go?"

"Nay, lord, only a few miles."

Giles cantered back to Isabella, and in the same loud voice said, "My love, I'll give these good people an escort to their village. I am eager to hear more tales of their pilgrimage." Ignoring the startled glances from his household, he leaned over his mount, kissed Isabella on the mouth, winked at her then, wheeling Troubadour around, called, "Guy, Miles, Fulke, I trust you to see my lady safe to Oakley. I'll rejoin you as soon as I am able."

Shannon managed to catch Isabella's eye and saw a slim, white hand raised so briefly in farewell that, if she'd blinked, she'd have missed it. Then, the two mounts were turned and moved off to the west, following a path which led away from the river but, to Shannon's frustration, still not towards the beech tree.

Father Dominic sensed her anxiety and turned his head slightly, not murmuring now, for they were out of hearing. "Patience, Shannon. This is merely a ruse. We will turn back shortly."

He felt the tension drain from her as she slumped slightly in the saddle. Poor child, this must be hard on her nerves as well as her ankle; he would not try to guess which was troubling her most but instead, conversed with Giles as if this was the most normal thing in the world for him to be doing.

As they rode, Giles looked at Shannon with an unreadable expression. "Shannon, I only wish we could give you shelter at our manor, wish there was time for us to get to know you as our kin; however, you might not be safe there. Your mother will tell you, John and I love each other not. If he could do me an ill turn, he would. As it is, I have a hold over him, yet if he connected you with me…" he tailed off with a sigh, then gazed at her as though trying to imprint her on his memory. "Know that Isabella and I will speak often of you and forever be in wonderment that we should have spent even this short time with you.

"Will you tell your mother about your time with us? About Isabella? I think she might wish to know." He chuckled. "Or mayhap I overestimate my importance to her."

Shannon hurried to reassure him. "Oh, no. I'm sure she does think of you often, only…"

He gave her a shrewd look. "Only you do not wish her to know you disobeyed her?"

"Mm. Sorry. Maybe one day, if I ever get up enough courage to confess, then I'll tell her all about you, Isabella and Dickon. I think she'd like to know."

"And Shannon, I should be angry with you for your disobedience to your mother. As a grandsire, of sorts, I have the right." He tried to pull a stern face but failed, and she giggled. "Lass, I admit, this is one gift horse whose mouth I shall not examine. It's too much of a miracle, and now we have you away safely, no real harm is done. Although," and his voice took on a harder note, "do not ever think of trying this trick again, for you may not come out intact if you do. Neither I nor the Abbess, or even the good father here, may be around to save you next time."

Shannon grinned, and he scowled at her. "I mean it, Shannon. Give me your promise now. For, had you come to injury or death, how would your mother feel? And we would have to risk ourselves to get word to her, for we could not leave her unknowing of your fate."

Shannon squirmed. He was right. "I promise, then. To be honest, I think I've had enough of your century now. I've had fun, and it's been exciting, but truthfully, I can't see me doing it again." Then, she laughed. "Is that good enough, Grandad?"

He laughed with her, then said, "Mind your manners, Mistress," his light tone belying the gruff words.

Shannon swallowed the lump in her throat and blinked back tears. The time for the final parting was near, and then she'd never see any of them again.

Father Dominic cleared his throat. "Sir Giles, I think we are sufficiently far away to return to this tree now. I do not know exactly in which direction it lies; will you take the lead, my lord?"

"Gladly, Father. Shannon, I know your ankle is likely feeling sore, but the Abbess tells me horses are not used so often in your time. If you are unlikely to ride again, should you like to gallop? I promise you, it will feel exhilarating. And it will cut down the length of time we take."

Shannon considered. Her ankle did hurt, but she hadn't enjoyed her previous gallop; she'd been too afraid. Like most girls, she'd gone through the 'I want a pony' period when she was young. It might be fun. "Go on, then."

Giles and Father Dominic kicked their mounts, which responded instantly. Oh, it felt as though she was flying. It hurt her ankle like crazy, and she knew she shouldn't, but Giles was right. It was exhilarating. They galloped for a short while before dropping back into a walk. It was enough. Her ankle was agony, but she wouldn't have missed it for the world. As a way of ending her adventure, it was pretty amazing.

They travelled in silence now; Shannon was gritting her teeth again, dreading when she had to try and walk. The relief when she saw the beech eased the sadness that she would never see her medieval family again.

Giles had been watching her closely. He'd suggested the gallop for more reasons than speed alone, for how hard it was to say the final farewell. It had been difficult enough with Marion, and that had been before he knew she was kin. Noticing how close Shannon had been to tears, he had thought to distract her. It seemed to have worked well enough.

He led the way to the woods and out again to the clearing where he had watched Marion break away and run to the tree, remembering the feeling he had as she started to vanish. And more than that, remembering his brief view of the abbey standing ruined. The horror had stayed with him a long time, though now, he felt only pleasure when he thought of the future, of his family, out of reach yet living.

When they arrived at the tree, he halted, aware of the same sense of loss he'd had when Marion disappeared that final time. Troubadour snorted as though the emotion of the moment had touched him too, and Giles leaned over, patting him, then dismounted.

Father Dominic was also dismounting, and Shannon glanced at the ground, doubtful he could assist her as easily as Adam had. She needn't have worried. Before Father Dominic could aid her, Giles had reached her and was lifting her gently down, taking her weight.

The priest unhooked her crutch and passed it to her, and she leaned on it gratefully. Father Dominic unbuckled his belt and immediately lost several stone in weight as his habit fell to his feet beneath his tunic. He removed hat and tunic, passing both to Giles, who was struggling to keep a straight face.

"I'll give these into your keeping, my lord. When I return to this time, I shall travel to Oakley before I go back to the abbey. It will add colour to my tale if I do not return too early and can account for at least some of my time. I know your brother and doubt not he will accord me a welcome. Might I ask you to bring those," he indicated the clothes Giles was stuffing into his saddlebags, "to the abbey next time you pass that way? For even if you are still at Oakley when I arrive, it might be better not to give them to me there."

Giles nodded, took Shannon's hand and kissed her cheek. "Fare you well now, lass. We shall speak of you often." He turned to the priest. "And, thank you, good Father, for this. You will always find a welcome at Thorneywell, that I promise."

Father Dominic nodded and took Shannon by the arm. "Well, Mistress Shannon, shall we see whether I can pass through this wondrous tree of yours? I cannot imagine what it will feel like."

Giles spoke before Shannon could answer. "I remember all too well. It feels like passing through pottage. And, Father, I feel I'd best warn you, lest you are as shocked as I was. The abbey is in ruins in the future."

"Ah well, we all come to ruins in the end, do we not. I expect that, in the Heavens, Sparnstow Abbey still stands tall, giving glory to our God." He eyed Shannon dubiously. "Mistress, do you wish to go into your own time dressed as you are?"

Shannon started, then laughed. "I'm such a ditz! I'd forgotten what I was wearing. Thank you, Father. Mind you, is it safe to change here?" She thought for a moment. "I know, I'll get rid of the top layer and this horrible wimple. I think I'd better sit down for that, though. Oh, and by the way, I'm not quite sure whether you'll pass as a modern priest in that get-up. You might need to become Brother Dominic. Will that be okay?"

"Indeed, it will be perfectly, er, okay. Do I have the word aright, Mistress?"

"You've got it. Also, don't call me mistress; It has a different meaning in my world. Shannon will be just fine."

She pulled off her hood and veil, then hoicked the top layer of her clothing over her head, revealing the grey undergown beneath. "Um, Father, I mean Brother, will you be shocked if I show my arms? I mean, I'm not sure I can get away with this. It's a bit, well…"

"Drab?"

"And then some."

"It's not something to which I am accustomed, yet I understand it does not mean in your world what it would in mine."

Wow! she thought, *he's a quick learner.* She looked at Giles. "I suppose you aren't so easily shocked anyway, being a man of the world and all that?"

Giles laughed. "Indeed, Shannon, I'm but a sober husband now, yet you have it right; I am not easily outraged. And, as soon as I see you both safe through that tree, I must head to Oakley, for I don't wish to be long behind them. Make haste now, lass."

Shannon screwed up her face, then tugged the undergown off and sat there, arms almost bare, feeling as embarrassed as though she was sitting before them in her underwear. She stole a glimpse at their faces. Both men were studiously averting their eyes. Relieved, she pulled the wimple over her head, then shook out her plait, letting it hang down her back. Better to leave it braided. The sight of her there in what they would think of as her shift, hair loose, would make all three of them feel even more awkward.

She struggled to rise, and Giles bent down, lifting her easily to her feet. Then, Father Dominic took her arm with one hand and her bags with the other, and they were ready. She stole a glimpse at his face. Was he afraid? No, his eyes were sparkling. "Shall we go, Fa...Brother?"

"With the best will in the world, Shannon. God speed you, Sir Giles, and see you safe home."

"God speed you, too, Father." He clapped the priest on the shoulder, kissed Shannon again, then, taking the reins of both mule and horse, waited for them to walk through the tree.

Shannon took a deep breath, leaned heavily on her crutch and was about to put one hand on the bark, smooth not rippled in this earlier time, when Father Dominic said, "Wait, Shannon, what is that?"

"What?"

"That buzzing. Is there a wasp nest in the tree? Are we at risk of being attacked by a swarm?"

"No, Brother, it's just the tree. It does that when it's ready, I think."

He blinked and said, "Well, if the tree is ready for us, mayhap we had best not keep it waiting." Putting his arm around Shannon, he took her weight and led her forward. She closed her eyes and held her breath as she pushed her way through, feeling the liquid warmth of it as it wrapped itself around her.

A few seconds, a plop, and they were out. She opened her eyes, looked at Father Dominic, pulled away and plunked herself down on the grass to take the weight off her ankle. "Ow! It aches."

Father Dominic remained standing, eyes shut, saying nothing, rather like a zombie. As she watched, wondering if he was okay, he opened his eyes, took a deep breath and gazed around him. His first sight was of the abbey. He stared silently, then said, "Well, Shannon, if anything was needed to bring home to me the passing of so many years, this was it. Tell me, for I forgot to ask the Abbess, what year are we in?"

Shannon hoped he was ready for the answer, but when she told him, he beamed from ear to ear – literally. She had never seen a grin stretch so wide. He rubbed his hands together, saying gleefully, "The year of our Lord two-thousand-and-twelve! Well, well! Most gratifying."

Shannon shook herself mentally, unable to believe he was taking it all in his stride. Then surveyed the car park where, this early, there were no cars. She hoped she wasn't in for too long a wait. What time was it? She'd left her watch in her bag. Around seven? Oh, great. Two or three hours yet.

"Father, I mean Brother, I think we're a bit too early. No one's going to be here for quite some time. If you could help me get over to the abbey, then, when anyone arrives, I can ask them for help; you don't have to stay with me. You can go once you've got me to the gatehouse."

He hoisted her back to her feet, gave her the crutch, put his arm around her again, and helped support her as she limped painfully to the abbey entrance.

It seemed as though it took forever. Shannon was biting her lip to stop from crying with the pain by the time they reached the bench at the gatehouse. Father Dominic settled her there and sat beside her as she hunched over, gasping, tired and hurting. All she wanted to do now was go to bed with some painkillers. Forget breakfast! She felt sick with pain and exhaustion. She closed her eyes, breathing deeply, trying to summon enough strength to last until she reached home. When she opened her eyes, she realised Father Dominic was looking rather too settled.

"Brother, you don't have to wait. I'll be fine, honestly. Go on. You get safely back to your own time." She just hoped he'd be able to, if she wasn't with him. She'd feel happier once she'd seen him go back through the tree.

He didn't move, his gaze still on the ruins.

"Brother! I said I'll be fine. You can go home now."

He turned his head to answer, and her heart sank at the expression on his face. "Indeed, I cannot, Shannon. I promised your aunt and Sir Giles that I would see you safe. I will not leave you here alone."

"Yes you can. Honestly. Tell them I said it was okay. This is my time, I'll be fine; you go. Anyway, I need to know you can get back through. If you don't go now, I'll worry."

He remained stubborn. "Shannon, no. I have given my word; let there be no more arguments. Now, you say no one will be here for some time?"

She shook her head mutely.

"Then, I will set your fears at rest. Observe." He rose and strode away from her, heading straight for the beech. As she watched, he turned, waved and plunged into it, and she breathed a huge sigh of relief. *Thank goodness.*

Her relief turned to horror as he reappeared, walking back towards her briskly. "There," he said rather breathlessly as he seated himself. "You need have no more worries. Now, I will wait with you, and you can tell me more about your time."

After what felt like hours of his questions, which actually weren't that easy to answer, Shannon was feeling wiped out when he suddenly grabbed her arm, saying hoarsely, "Shannon, what is that noise?"

She listened for a moment but could hear nothing. "What noise?"

"That…" He trailed off, looking as though he could not find the words. Shaking his head, he tried again. "Can you not hear it? Truly, I do not know how to explain it. Hark?"

Shannon listened again, head on one side, then realised what he was talking about. "Oh, that. It's just a plane. Look."

He followed her finger and swallowed hard, then grabbed her arm again. "A plane? It looks like a dragon. See! It breathes smoke. Should we not conceal ourselves?"

She shook her head, yawning. She was so *not* going to do this now. "Fath…I mean Brother, I'm not even going to begin to go into detail, but it's not dangerous. It's just one of the ways we travel."

Dominic looked at Shannon with desperate pleading in his face, and she rolled her eyes as she gave him a brief explanation, which she could tell left him far from satisfied. Tough! She'd had enough; she wanted to go home. She looked up, relieved, as a few cars drove in.

Beside her, she heard Father Dominic gasp as he leapt to his feet. "And those," he said, pointing, wide-eyed, "what are they? They gleam like the sun and move like low flying birds. And…and…" his face was wreathed in smiles at this new wonder, "they have people inside."

"Um, they're called cars, Brother. We travel in them, too. They have seats inside and someone to drive them. Like…like a sort of covered cart but much faster. And, when I can find someone who has a phone, that's how I'm going to get home. All you have to do now is get me over there where they are. It's called a car park. Are you okay with that?"

"Okay? Dear child, it's wondrous. The colours! The speed! The grace! They move so smoothly." He stopped, gaping some more as one drew to a halt, spilling out a family of four, with two teenaged girls dressed in – Shannon groaned – shorts.

"But their clothing! Are those young women harlots?"

"No, Brother, they're very respectable."

"But their legs!"

"Brother, there is nothing wrong with showing your legs in our culture."

He tore his gaze from them with an effort and then glanced modestly away, trying not to peer at them again. "Well, well. I confess, I am not easily shocked, yet..."

Shannon decided to take charge. The family would have mobiles; they'd help her. If she left it to him, he'd be here for ages, and she was beginning to wonder if he might not become a problem. "Brother?"

He ignored her, turning to stare once more at the abbey. She cleared her throat and said again, louder this time, *"Brother!"* He started and looked down at her. "Can you help me up, please? I want to get home now, and you need to leave. Come on, you've been a huge help; I couldn't have managed without you, but you really don't need to stay."

She was talking to herself. At the sight of a man in a sort of uniform, who was jangling a bunch of keys in his hand, Father Dominic had gone rushing towards him. The man seemed as though he was about to open up the abbey grounds. She sat there, fuming and worried, hoping Dominic would behave himself.

She need not have bothered; the priest was leading him back to her, beaming. The man fumbled in his pocket and held out his phone. "The monk says you need to borrow a mobile. Here you go."

Shannon almost sagged with relief. "Thanks. Do you know any local cab companies?"

He held out his hand, and she gave him back his phone. He dialled a number and, while waiting for a reply, asked her name and where she was going, then spoke for a few moments before putting it back in his pocket. "Sorted, love. It'll be here in about fifteen minutes. That do you?"

"Yeah. Thanks a lot. Cheers."

"No worries." He turned back to the gatehouse, opening up the entrance. A few other people – probably more staff – had drifted over, and the family in shorts were holding out money, eager to get inside.

Shannon yawned again. She was so tired, she reckoned she could even sleep on this hard bench. She gritted her teeth. *C'mon, Shan, you can do this!* Her determination was slightly undermined by another enormous yawn but she turned to Dominic, trying to sound brisk. "Brother, come on. Help me get to the car park." Then, she could send him back to where he belonged.

She held out her arm, and he hoisted her to her feet again, where she wobbled slightly. He put his arm round her wordlessly, and she had the feeling he was in a bit of a trance. Well, it wasn't really to be wondered at, was it?

Limping across the grass, even using her crutch and with Dominic's help, her ankle hurt like anything, and she was relieved when she could sit down again. She was less relieved when the priest made himself comfortable next to her.

"Honestly, you can go now, Fa...er, Brother. You really should."

He looked at her, one eyebrow quirking up. "Is there so much danger here then, Shannon? You made it sound as though it is much safer than my own time. Was that an untruth?"

"It is. I mean, it's safer for me, but..." Bother him! She was tired and cross. She'd been awake for hours. Her ankle was hurting, and she didn't want the worry of Father Dominic.

"Then, I will stay to see you safely into your taxi," he said implacably. Shannon ground her teeth almost audibly and gave in to the inevitable.

CHAPTER TWENTY-THREE

"Here it is! Help me up, please."

As the cab came to a halt, Dominic stood up, easing Shannon gently to her feet. The driver got out. "Taxi for Shannon Hart?"

"Yes, please. That's me."

"Oh dear. You been in the wars, love? Want a hand?" He held out his arm, to be brushed aside by Father Dominic. Shrugging, he opened the back door for her, and the priest helped her in. She started to wave to Dominic as he turned away, then stared in disbelief as he went behind the car, appeared on the other side and clambered in beside her.

"In truth, this is more difficult than mounting a horse," he muttered, as he folded himself into the vehicle.

Shannon gawped at him. "But you…but… *No!* You can't come."

"My dear Shannon, you did not think I would miss my only chance to ride in one of these wondrous things, did you?" He settled in, smiling complacently as the driver revved the engine.

"Well, fasten your seatbelt, then," she hissed, showing him how to do it, glaring at him in outrage.

He fixed his the way she showed him, then sat back, ignoring her, gazing out the window, eyes shining, face nearly split in two with his grin as the taxi pulled out of the car park. As the car picked up speed, she was conscious of little gasps and grunts of pleasure coming from him.

She ferreted in her bag for her purse, hoping she'd have enough money to send him back. No way would she allow him into the house. He'd be a dead giveaway to Mum, and she couldn't begin to explain him to Chloe and Dad. It was *so* not happening. Surreptitiously counting out notes, she watched the meter go round, holding her breath. At least Father Dominic was staying quiet. She leaned back and closed her eyes.

After what felt like an interminable drive, the taxi pulled up at home. Shannon kissed the priest on the cheek. "Thank you, but that's enough help, now. Here." She pushed some coins and notes into his hand. "This is to pay the fare for your trip back." She looked at him severely. "You *will* go straight back, won't you? Can I trust you?"

Father Dominic still appeared breathless with amazement and delight. She supposed he'd never thought to experience such speed, such excitement; and all from a comfortably padded seat. He nodded his head at Shannon.

"No, that's not good enough. Promise me!"

"I promise. Now, God bless and keep you, Shannon. It has been a wonderful experience; I thank you for allowing me to accompany you."

She withdrew her head and muttered, "As if I had a choice!"

Ignoring her comment, he called, "But wait, how shall you walk? Can you manage alone?"

Could she? She'd manage if it killed her. He was not, absolutely *not*, going to end up meeting her family. She poked her head back through the window, gritting her teeth against the pain and forcing a fake smile. "Yes, it's much better now," she lied and withdrew again, then leaned into the front of the cab, paid her own fare and instructed the driver to take him straight back to Sparnstow. "He only has enough cash for that. It will cost the same as it did to here, won't it?"

Father Dominic chuckled to himself, aware that Shannon was less than pleased with him. But to miss such an opportunity? It would have been rank ingratitude to God. He settled back to enjoy the return trip.

"You all right in the back there, guv? I mean, Brother. Or is it Father?"

"Perfectly well, thank you, my son."

The engine revved, the car pulled out, and he watched as Shannon dumped her bags by the gate, then limped down a short path to a well-built home. As were all the properties here, he observed. And every one with glazed windows. Were they all wealthy merchants? Or mayhap glass was not so rare and expensive in this era, for even the more meanly-built dwellings had them. And he had seen no hovels at all.

As Shannon turned to wave, the door opened, and another young woman, looking much like Lady Isabella, threw her arms round her. Dominic craned his neck. The taxi turned a corner, and they were lost from sight.

Sighing with pleasure, he watched the structures flash by. And such structures. Ugly, yet large and so different. Father Dominic rubbed his hands together gleefully. But then, he realised it would surely take no more than one siege engine or mangonel to bring the downfall of most of them, for they all shared a weakness. So many windows and such large, clear panes. Light, yes, it would be as light as day inside these, but the glass could be so easily broken, and that would favour an enemy.

He drank in everything he saw, storing it up to tell the Abbess and Sister Ursel.

Gazing up into the sky, he watched as another of the dragon things, no – what had she called them? planes? – moved overhead, with its smoky breath trailing behind it. He would have liked much more information about that, but the poor lass had been so weary. To her, these things were as nothing. He supposed it was difficult to explain something which in her world was so commonplace. The frustration was great, but he would have to bear it, for he could ask no one else.

The trip ended all too quickly, and Father Dominic felt a flash of disappointment as the abbey came into view. Deflated, he struggled to unfasten the seatbelt, his shoulders slumping at the thought of his adventure ending so soon. He tugged at the door; nothing happened.

Seeing his difficulty, the driver got out and opened it for him. "All done, Father. Here you go."

The priest held out the money Shannon had given him. The driver shrugged. "Nah, go on. You were doing her a favour. You can say a prayer for me, instead, eh? My name's Dave."

"Most kind. Thank you, thank you."

"Well, I'm a Catholic myself, and if she'd been my daughter, I'd have been grateful someone like you'd helped her out. Go on, you put it in your church collection." He got back into the taxi,

321

slammed the door and drove away, his arm resting on the open window.

As the car moved off, it threw up a shower of small stones and grit, and a distressing odour assaulted Dominic's nostrils, catching the back of his throat so he almost choked. He clapped a hand over his nose and mouth for a moment, then forced himself to free his face, breathing shallowly, trying to ignore the burning of his tonsils. Faugh! How did they endure such a stench?

He watched the taxi disappear down the road, fingering the money thoughtfully. These wouldn't be any good in his own time, now, would they? And a pity it would be to waste them. He eyed the abbey uncertainly.

As he stood there wondering what to do, a large conveyance drove up. Father Dominic stepped back quickly to avoid the noxious vapour as it swept past him, then watched as a gaggle of women spilled out, chattering like magpies. Their dress looked vaguely like...it couldn't be...they couldn't be nuns, could they? Their skirts were nearly up to their knees. He swallowed. Some things in this time were not so easy to become accustomed to.

One of them turned her head in his direction, smiled, waved and came over to him. "Brother! Are you here alone? Would you care to join us?" Her voice had a hint of an Irish lilt to it. "My name's Sister Jacinta, and these are Sisters Bea, Naomi,

Kathleen, Maresa, Angelica, and, believe it or not, Sister Mary." They beamed, fluttering around him like so many moths.

"We're on a jaunt to see the ruins," confided Sister Jacinta. "We've not been here before, have you, Brother?"

Father Dominic was charmed. He was fairly sure they were nuns, yet not as he could ever have imagined. They wore dark clothing, crucifixes and short veils but no wimples, and those skirts! *But then, I must adapt to the time in which I find myself,* he decided.

"So, Brother, do you want to join us?" Sister Jacinta stood before him laughing. "Or have we frightened you to death?"

"Ah, you speak for yourself, Jacinta." That was Sister Bea. "Give the poor man chance to catch his breath."

Dominic made up his mind. "Sisters, I should consider myself honoured." He held out an arm, which was swooped on by Sister Mary, and started towards the gatehouse. "I know this place well."

"So, we have ourselves a guided tour, Sisters."

They chattered all the way to the turnstile, insisting on paying for his entry, ignoring his protests, barely giving him a chance to speak until he led them around, when they hung on his every word, until his stomach made a loud growl. He flushed with humiliation, and Sister Maresa said,

"Oh, you poor man, you're starving. Jacinta, is there a café here?"

"Isn't that one, over there?"

They bustled over, claiming the largest table, consulting the menu, talking about the food and suggesting a drink which they called coffee. "Or would you prefer tea, Brother?"

"No, no. Coffee will be delightful." He hoped it would.

"Milk, sugar?"

"Everything, please." He might as well include the food and drink in his experience. Besides, he had not had opportunity to bring any supplies, and he must have sustenance for he had many miles ahead of him. He waved his money at them.

"Oh, aren't you a darling, Brother." Jacinta whisked it out of his hand and went to the counter, coming back with a loaded tray of plates and cups, which she shared out. "I hope you like tuna mayo or chicken salad; they didn't have much choice. There's crisps. And chocolate brownies; we must have those."

Dominic picked up one of the things she'd called a sandwich and examined it. Some kind of bread. He bit into it experimentally. The bread tasted like nothing he recognised. Tasteless, utterly without texture and soggy. But the filling! Fish never tasted so good. As for the things she called crisps – he had no idea what they were but crunched rapturously.

The first sip of his drink tasted bitter, and he shuddered involuntarily, putting it down again and ignoring his thirst, until Sister Kathleen said, "It's strong. Don't you want sugar? I've never yet known a brother who didn't love the sweet stuff. Here. And some milk?" She opened a couple of small packets beside his cup, tipped them in, poured milk from a jug and stirred it. He sipped again and found the taste more than palatable, this time closing his eyes in bliss.

Sister Bea nudged him. "Have a chocolate brownie, Brother. They look like they're home-made, so they should be good."

He took a bite and had to stop himself from exclaiming aloud. Never before, in all his days, had he tasted anything so exquisite. Savouring each mouthful, he made it last as long as possible. As he regretfully swallowed the last delicious morsel, Sister Jacinta said, "Now, Brother, tell us all about yourself."

"Dear ladies, I'd far rather hear about all of you." It was the right thing to say. He leaned back in his chair, sipping his coffee, drinking in the experience as they chattered around him.

When they finally pushed aside their plates, he realised they were preparing to leave. A pity – he would have liked another of these marvellous beverages, but he drained the last of his coffee and surreptitiously slipped a few packets of sugar into his scrip. After all, as far as he could tell, they had been paid for, and it would be a shame to waste them.

Then, he saw it – one last chocolate brownie, sitting unloved and unwanted on its platter. He glanced around discreetly before picking up one of the things they called serviettes, wrapping it carefully around the brownie and sliding that into his scrip along with the sugar. His mouth watered at the thought of devouring it later.

Sister Mary caught his eye. "That's the way, Brother. Waste not, want not." He flinched slightly with embarrassment, before he realised she approved of his actions. Not only did she approve, she took the untouched one from her own plate, passing it to him. "Here, take this too. You know you want it, and it's too rich for me."

Dominic's hand hovered, undecided, for a moment. Should he be giving in to such greed? But Sister Mary waved it enticingly before him, and his resolve faltered. He could do penance later – it would be worth it. Mayhap, this was an extra gift from God. Yes, that was it. And, such being the case, no penance would be necessary. He beamed his thanks as he stowed it safely along with the other.

Casting one final glance around the café, so full of delights, he followed the sisters out and led them, all talking and pointing, around the rest of the abbey, indicating where the different rooms had once been.

They listened, charmed, as he explained to them where each room was and what it was used for.

"For sure, Brother, you tell it so well," said Sister Bea. "Better than any guide. You love this place, I can tell. It's almost as though you lived here yourself."

Sister Kathleen chimed in. "I can almost see him here, can't you, Sisters? Where would the priest have lived? Not here near the nuns, eh?"

"Indeed not, Sister. That would never be...er, have been permitted. I...the priest had a separate lodging over there." He pointed to the area of his own abode, which was now just a forlorn heap of stones sprawled across a grassy expanse. "He lives...would have lived near the dorter where the lay brothers were housed with their own kitchens."

"And what about the abbesses? One book I read said they had to sleep in the dormitories with the nuns, then another book told me they had their own lodgings. I never know what to think." This from Sister Mary, the historian of the group.

"Indeed, I believe it varied from abbey to abbey, but here, our dear Abbess–"

"He's doing it again," said Kathleen. "If I believed in reincarnation, I'd say he'd been a priest here in an earlier life!"

A chorus of laughter greeted her remark, and Dominic gave an embarrassed chuckle. "It's only because I have spent so long around its confines that, indeed, I almost feel I did once dwell here. Now…" And he continued with his tour.

Father Dominic waved regretfully to the sisters as they clattered back to their conveyance. What had they called it? A mini bus? He looked at the sky. It must be about Nones. After staring again at the abbey, trying to imprint it on his mind, he turned and headed back to the tree, ready now for his long walk to Oakley. His belly full, his head equally full, he walked steadily towards the beech.

As he neared it, he slowed, cocking his head on one side, listening. Ah, there it was, the sound of buzzing. How alarmed he had been when he first heard that. And how strange the sensation of plunging through a solid object, feeling it turn to something like pottage as he pushed through. He had wondered whether he would choke at first and held his breath, but before he'd needed to exhale, he had stepped into fresh air.

He gazed about him once more, regretful that he could spare no more time to explore this wonderful world, took a deep breath and returned to his own time.

CHAPTER TWENTY-FOUR

Unlike Father Dominic, Hildegarde had not had a delightful day. Unable to know how the thing had gone off, whether Shannon had got home safely, whether Father Dominic had been able to return or even whether Giles and Isabella had been able to get them out of the abbey without being noticed, she had spent hours in a state of tension.

Brother Anselm had Bardolf isolated in the infirmary where, for now, he was still too weak to care what was happening. Hildegarde expected he would feel considerably better quite soon. When he was back to himself, she knew he would be nosing around trying to find out where Shannon had gone. She smiled grimly. *And good luck with that one.*

The Abbess struggled to keep her eyes open, so strained was she from the events of the last two days. She was thankful she'd decided to impose the rule of silence, for although she had kept a firm grip on her temper, it was beginning to fray dangerously, and, without the rule, she feared she would have been snapping at everyone who approached her.

How she got through the day, she had no idea. She had moved mechanically, with a set smile on her face, avoiding people wherever possible; however, it was nearly at an end and now, she made her way to Compline, heavy with weariness.

Once there, Hildegarde carefully surveyed the faces around her, all lifted up in praise. She paused, counting; one was missing. Seeing Ursel, she raised her eyebrows. The older woman nodded. Who was sick? She counted faces again. Aldith. She would leave her in Ursel's care tonight and enquire after her tomorrow. It was unlikely to be anything too serious, for surely Ursel would have informed her.

The Abbess finally began to relax; she must leave it in the Lord's hands, as she should have done earlier. There was naught else she could do, so she must just have faith. In an easier frame of mind, she joined with her sisters in the chants which heralded the night.

After Compline, Hildegarde took herself to her chamber, grateful to be away from questioning eyes and thankful to be alone. Silence could sometimes be a great gift indeed – she ached with exhaustion. *These old bones aren't made for adventures and neither is my peace of mind.*

As she opened the door, she hesitated. A faint noise came to her ears; something was amiss. A shiver ran icy fingers down her spine. She berated herself for her foolishness and peered in cautiously, holding her candle aloft, but could make out nothing. *My imagination is overwrought.* Forcing herself to relax her shoulders which were creeping towards her ears, she was closing the door behind her when she heard something which sounded like a muffled sob low to the ground.

She turned quickly and moved silently around the desk, still holding the candle, starting when something wrapped around her ankles. Peering down, she made out the shadowy form of a woman – surely not one of the sisters. But if not, who then? She put down the pricket and bent low. The shrouded head raised itself to her, face haggard, eyes reddened and swollen. She almost didn't recognise Aldith. *What now? Forgive me, Lord, it seems I cannot keep the silence tonight.* Ah well, He would understand; He always did. *And, grant me patience and kindness, Father.*

"Sister, whatever troubles you? Are you ill?" The young nun was always so composed – almost smug. Hildegarde could not imagine what had happened to cause her such distress.

"Oh, Mother! Sweet Abbess, forgive me. I meant no harm." Aldith shuddered and moaned, then wrapped her arms more tightly around the Abbess's ankles, burying her face in Hildegarde's robe as she wept, her whole frame shaking. Hildegarde was aghast, the nun was verging on hysteria. As the Abbess struggled to maintain her balance, Aldith finally let go and started to wrench her veil and wimple from her head, tearing at her cropped hair.

The Abbess pulled the distraught woman to her feet and manoeuvred her into a chair. Aldith fought her and threw herself back onto the floor. "Scourge me! Punish me! Imprison me! I cannot bear the guilt."

With difficulty, Hildegarde hauled her back up, this time holding her upright. Aldith's head sagged, and she kept up her litany of woe. There was no help for it. Hildegarde shoved her over to her inner sleeping chamber, forced her to sit on the bed and slapped her. Aldith's jaw dropped open, and she gaped at Hildegarde with stricken eyes, but at least her terrible wailing had stopped.

"Sister Aldith, I have no idea what you are talking about. What has brought you to this state, child?"

A mistake. Aldith started to weep again, streams of mucus running from her nose. Hildegarde poured water from her ewer into her laver, dipped a linen towel into it and began sponging her face. "Sister!" Her voice rang with authority – nothing else would break through this storm. "Sister, listen to me. If you don't stop crying *this instant*, I will empty this ewer over your head."

Aldith stopped abruptly, hiccuping and choking, watching Hildegarde with wild eyes. The nun was in no state to speak, and Hildegarde had no intention of starting her off again now she had reduced her to silence. She heard the outer door open. What now?

"Praise be to our Lord Jesus Christ, Mother. May I speak?" Ursel's voice came whispering in the dark.

"May He be praised, indeed, Sister. Please do speak." There was a time for rules and a time for compassion. This could not be done without words. "Come in. Mayhap you can shed some light on the matter."

A cloak-wrapped form came silently into the room. "So that's where you went, you foolish girl."

Hildegarde turned. Aldith didn't move, just continued to tremble and moan. Thank the Lord she had stopped pulling at her hair.

Ursel sat on the bed next to Aldith, placing one arm around her. Aldith promptly turned her head into the old nun's shoulder and clung like a child.

"Stay with her. I'll fetch some syrup of poppy. I doubt aught else will calm her. But what–?" She broke off as Ursel put her finger to her lips. "No, of course."

Hildegarde lit the lantern, moving it to a niche in the wall near the bed, pulled on her fur-lined, cloth night boots, then picked up her candle and walked softly to the infirmary, peering at Ursel's remedies by the flickering light until she found what she needed.

Pouring a little into a cup, she hesitated before adding a few drops from another small bottle. That should settle her. Padding back, she wondered where she herself would sleep. They really could not carry the young nun back to the infirmary, neither could they leave her alone. Hildegarde sighed. It looked as though she would take her rest on a pallet tonight. And she would be the first to wake to Aldith. Faced with the challenge of dealing with more hysterics on the morrow, Shannon now seemed the lighter of the two responsibilities.

Opening her own door noiselessly, she slipped back into the room, handing the cup to Ursel who gave it to a now subdued Aldith.

As the potion started taking effect, Aldith lay back on Hildegarde's bed, curling up like a foetus, moaning as though in pain until she dropped into a heavy sleep, whereupon she started to snore instead.

"We may speak now. She will not waken soon." Ursel covered the young nun with a blanket and turned to Hildegarde.

"Did you find out what has upset her so?"

"Aye," said the infirmaress grimly. "And well she might be upset. It seems Sir Giles' young knight," she curled her lip in disgust, "had fooled the witless wench into acting as go-between.

"She'd been keeping watch while he dallied with Rohese, warning him when you or Lady Isabella came near so he could slip away unnoticed. To make matters worse, she'd been telling him where he could find her."

Hildegarde drew in a breath sharply. Whatever she had expected, it was not that. "But how did he convince her? And Sister Aldith, of all people!"

"He told her he'd had a vision of our Blessed Lady; said she'd appeared to him, telling him he was destined to wed Rohese. According to him, the forces of evil were conspiring against this. Of course, the stupid girl swallowed his tale." Ursel was furious. Hildegarde could almost see steam rising from her. "Had her opinion of herself been lower, had she been less inclined to think she had been favoured by visions herself, she would have sent him on his way."

So that was how he'd done it. When Aldith recovered, she would have to be disciplined – there was no help for it. Even if she'd learnt her lesson, and Hildegarde was pretty certain she had, this breach could not be ignored. For Aldith's sake. For everyone's sake.

Still, tomorrow's troubles could not be solved tonight. She and Ursel dragged a pallet into her room and, after bidding the infirmaress goodnight, she knelt and committed herself and Aldith to God, before she sank thankfully onto the makeshift bed. Despite Aldith's snores, she was soon asleep.

For Shannon, the return to her own time had been almost too abrupt. She was still feeling slightly disorientated. If she hadn't been so tired and her ankle hadn't hurt so much, she'd have liked to wander around the abbey ruins, just to say a final farewell and allow herself to adjust slowly.

As she turned to go indoors, she gave Father Dominic one last wave and said a prayer that he might stay out of trouble and go home. She would have felt happier if he had gone back before she got into the taxi. His flat refusal had confused her; now, she wished she'd been firmer. *But what could I have done? I couldn't force him back through.*

While Shannon was still waving and groping for her key, the door opened and Chloe stood there. Her face was blank with surprise at first; Shannon was supposed to be away for at least three weeks. Then, her questions tumbled over themselves when she saw the crutch, and the bandage on her sister's ankle. "Shan! What have you been up to? What's happened to your ankle? Why are you home early? Oh, never mind, I'll get your bags. Is that all you took? You travelled light. I won't be a minute. You go on in and sit down. Fancy a cuppa?"

Shannon was overwhelmed by the onslaught. Her head ached. She didn't have her story quite straight yet, and for a moment, the peace of the abbey was a lot more appealing, but then, Chloe wrapped her arms around her in a bear hug, and she realised how much she would have lost if she had stayed back there.

Her eyes were moist, and she sniffed before freeing her arm and dashing the tears away with an impatient hand, wondering how she could even have considered leaving them all.

She hugged Chloe back, then disentangled herself from her sister, ignoring most of her questions. "Yes, I'd love a cuppa, but can you make it coffee instead of tea? Good and strong." She'd need it if she was going to find enough answers to satisfy them. Her imagination was going to be stretched to its limit, much as it had been at Sparnstow.

An involuntary yawn stretched her mouth so wide, she felt as though her jaw would crack. All she really wanted was her bed. Shaking her head to try and clear the fuzziness that filled it, she leaned against the wall, grateful for its support.

Chloe was out on the path by now, picking up the bags she'd left by the gate, and Shannon heard her mum's voice float out into the hall. "That's not Shannon, is it? What's she doing home so early?"

As Mum called out again, she felt a pang of remorse that she'd barely spared a thought for her during her operation.

"Yep, Mum, I'm home early. Long story. Be with you in a mo."

She leaned on the door handle and took one last look down the road. The taxi had gone. She grinned. It had been pretty funny really when Father Dominic insisted on coming with her. Her face must have been a picture. She hoped she could trust him to go home, but she had a sneaking suspicion that… Oh well, it was up to him. He was probably much more capable of taking care of himself than she gave him credit for.

Leaning heavily on the crutch, she limped into the house, slipping Giles' ring from her finger and into her pocket before her mother could see it. She must remember to sneak it back into Mum's jewellery box as soon as she could and hope it hadn't been missed. Maybe she'd ask if she could wear it sometime – but later. Much later.

As she passed the mirror in the hall, she glanced at her reflection. When Mum had come back from the past, Shannon had felt a difference in her. *Do I look the same?* she wondered. *I don't feel it.* She shook her head again, trying to get her mind completely back into the right century, then opened the door to the front room, went to hug her mother and prepared herself to tell as many lies and half-truths as she must.

CHAPTER TWENTY-FIVE

A few weeks after she had started working at Sparnstow Abbey, Shannon, dressed as Rohese, had just finished with her second group of tourists. She switched off her microphone battery pack, waved across at Emma who was also on her break and talking animatedly to the new archer, Will, and was heading for the café when a voice hailed her from behind. It wasn't anyone she recognised, but she guessed it to be another of the students earning a holiday wage as a tour guide.

"Lady Rohese, I fear I am late to make your acquaintance, but right ready to welcome you now I've returned."

What a fool. She turned, and the laugh that had been ready to bubble out of her died on her lips as she gawped in disbelief at the young chestnut-haired knight standing before her, his lips parted in a grin of welcome, green eyes sparkling with fun. Her hand flew to her mouth, and her legs felt as though they would buckle under her. "Adam? But, but…" She trailed off in confusion.

He took her hand, bowing over it and kissing it before she tugged it away. "My lady, forgive me."

Forgive him? It *was* Adam then. But how could it be? Her head was reeling, and she held her hands to her face, confused and trembling, unable to believe what she saw, clammy with shock.

"Hey, chill! You look like you've seen a ghost. Here, sit down before you fall down." He shoved a chair her way, and she subsided onto it before her legs gave way completely.

"Adam? *Adam?*" A pulse throbbed wildly in her temple, black specks danced before her eyes, and her heart was racing so much, she wondered vaguely if she was having a coronary.

"That's me." He grinned cheerfully. "They told you about me, did they? Don't believe a word of it." He gestured to his chain mail, and she realised it was a cheap imitation. "They tell me wearing this get-up was your idea. Nice one. I like it, and the tourists really go for it, don't they? My tips have doubled."

Shannon couldn't trust herself to speak, couldn't think, couldn't move.

"So where do you come from? Uni? Which one?"

"C…Cardiff," Shannon stuttered. "I start in September. And you?" she asked, fighting for control. This was impossible.

"Manchester. I've been working here in the holidays for a couple of years. I was away on a break. That's why you haven't seen me before."

"A c…couple of years?" Shannon pinched herself. This wasn't happening. And she was sounding like an idiot. *C'mon, Shan, think! Get your brain connected.* "You, er, you have dressed for the part. Is your name really Adam?" *Please, no. It can't be, it just can't!*

"Nah, I'm Craig." He grinned. "Can't call myself that though. Not sure there were many Craigs back then. Had to pick a medieval one."

Yes, but why that one?

Shannon finally got a grip on herself. The world had stopped its wild dance around her, and she was beginning to be able to think straight. She made her shoulders relax, felt her heart steady, and the pulse that had throbbed so hard she could barely see was fading now. *Think, Shannon, think. C'mon, make small talk.* So what if he looked like Adam de Grosmont? Of course he wasn't. As she opened her mouth to speak, Craig waved to someone behind her and got to his feet, saying, "Sorry, gotta go. My next lot have arrived. Can I catch you later? You coming for a drink after we close?"

Shannon grinned. What a fool, thinking he was Adam. But, oh, he'd shaken her up for a few minutes. And yeah, why not go for a drink with him. Just because he looked like Adam didn't mean he'd behave like him.

"Mm hmm. Yeah, that'd be nice."

"See you later, then." And he was gone.

Shannon stood up. There was just time to get a coffee before her next group of tourists arrived, and she'd kill for a chocolate biscuit.

That evening, Shannon sauntered down the lane to the Sparnstow Arms, tagging along behind the rest. Until now, she'd not joined them at the pub.

Craig was way ahead, laughing with a couple of the lads. Out of costume, dressed in jeans and tee-shirt, Shannon found it easier to disassociate him from Adam.

Emma glanced round, noticed Shannon and dropped back to walk with her, linking arms and towing her along to catch up.

They barged into the pub gardens laughing and jostling, ignoring the sidelong glares of a couple of old men under an apple tree, who muttered darkly into their pints about waking the dead.

Pushing and shoving, they took possession of one of the long tables. Emma dragged Shannon onto the end of the bench with her, thrusting a menu under her nose.

"What do you fancy, Shan? Ooh, there's a special on the board. Come on, let's go and see what they've got."

Shannon hung back. "No, you go. I'm happy just to choose from here."

She ordered fried chicken and chips, and the waitress moved down the bench, pointedly tapping her notebook with her pen as the others dithered and argued.

Meal eaten, the temperature cooled, and, as the sun started to go down, they began to drift away in ones and twos. Shannon sat there, running her finger round the rim of her glass as she watched the setting sun start to paint the sky in shades of lavender, red and gold.

Craig got up from his place at the table and ambled round to her, dropping onto the bench next to her and draping an arm lightly round her shoulders. Oh, help. Was she ready for this? She half turned – he did seem different now, but the resemblance was still marked, and it tugged at her like a freshly healed scar.

She drained her glass, and he stood up. "Want another?"

She nodded and glanced away. As he moved to the bar, she realised her shoulders were nearly back up to her ears again and focussed on making them drop back to a normal position, rotating them and feeling the tension ease. She couldn't judge him because he looked like Adam. He seemed nice, and

343

she thought he liked her. Maybe she could get to know him, give him a chance – slowly. She'd had enough of rushing into things.

Craig came back, dumping her glass on the table, splashing the lager as he did so. "Oops, sorry. Here, have a serviette."

She mopped at the table and flapped away a couple of hovering wasps. "So, Adam, I mean, Craig, how come you're working here?"

"Same as you, I expect, and all the rest. Trying to make enough cash in tips to see me through the next year. I love history, so something like this was the obvious choice. And the Americans love us, don't they? Great tippers, not like our lot."

Shannon's interest quickened. "I love history, too."

"Yeah? Do you live round here?"

She shook her head. "Not really."

"So how did you end up here?"

"I sort of have family connections. It's hard to explain." *Don't ask, please,* she begged silently.

"Yeah? Same here. I did my family's genealogy. As far as I can work out – but it's too far back to be really sure – my ancestors didn't live far from here." He stopped and took a long swallow of lager, then wiped his mouth on the back of his hand and continued. "One of them was a right one. He must have loads of descendants round here, most of them born on the wrong side of the sheet, like my family.

"They probably came from Magshall originally, moving here around the fifteenth century. The Lord of the Manor at Magshall in the thirteenth century was called Adam de Grosmont."

Shannon stared in horror, her eyes wide. She was struggling to breathe, but he didn't seem to notice, continuing with his tale. "Apparently, he was a bit of a randy old goat, and it looks as though he had loads of illegitimate kids on his estate. Any one of them might have been my ancestor, so when I came here, I thought I might as well take on the part of de Grosmont. I thought it would give the place a bit of colour, and they reckon the ladies love a villain, eh?" He chuckled. "I mean, villain not villein."

He rose, tilted his head slightly, swaggered a few steps, then turned and bowed, saying, "My Lady Rohese, pray allow me to present Sir Adam de Grosmont, and I counsel you not to believe a word the knave tells you."

He bowed again, took her hand and raised it to his lips before bending to pick a buttercup, which he offered to her as though it were a rose, saying, "A fair flower for a fair maiden."

Shannon sat as though turned to stone. Then, she got up and, without a word, walked to the stream, where she plonked herself down on a flat stone, hugging her knees. Craig dropped his swagger and went after her. Crouching down beside her, he said, "Shannon? What is it? What did

I do?" She turned towards him, and he saw the glimmer of a tear on her lashes before she put a hand up and swiped it away. "Shannon, speak to me. Tell me what's wrong."

Shannon blinked hard. For a few moments, he had *been* Adam. She couldn't speak, just shrugged and sniffed. Craig said again, "Shannon? What did I do?"

Pulling out a handkerchief, she blew her nose violently, then wiping away another tear, she glanced at him again. Adam had gone; it was just Craig, and she was going to have to take him on trust. "You didn't do anything, I was being silly. I just came out of a relationship with someone exactly like that. Worse, he was called Adam and he looked a lot like you. He lied to me – badly. And...other stuff. I couldn't trust him, in the end."

"Oh, hell, Shannon, you must have thought you'd seen a ghost."

Despite herself, she grinned. "You have no idea."

Craig reached for her hand. "Shannon, I really like you; I'd love to get to know you better. And I promise, I'm nothing like Adam, not either one of them. What do you say? Can we hang out a bit?"

Shannon sat there gazing into the distance, feeling Craig's hopeful eyes watching her. What should she do? Could she manage to put Adam behind her? And, why should she allow him to reach out through the centuries and smear his lies on her life in this one?

You can't judge one man by another's sins. Hildegarde's voice came back to her as clearly as if she'd been standing there.

Craig was still looking at her. "How do you feel, Shannon? Can you take a chance? Even if I might be related to him, I'm not a bit like de Grosmont, I promise."

Her eyes clouded, then cleared. Why not? But she wasn't going to rush anything this time. Standing up, she pulled Craig to his feet, then leaned against him, letting him wrap his arms around her. "All right, we'll see how it goes. But you better not let me down. You have a promise to keep."

The series continues with Blossom on the Thorn, the love story of Giles and Isabella. It isn't published yet, but you can read chapter one over the next few pages.

If you have enjoyed reading A Promise to Keep, please consider writing a review on Amazon. It really does make a difference. Thank you.

To keep up-to-date with future books and any offers, you might like to sign up for my newsletter here or on my website.

Start reading book three in the
Out of Time series overleaf.

Blossom on the Thorn

Coming next year

BLOSSOM ON THE THORN

Chapter One

The hunters gave wild yells of glee as they pursued their quarry. At last, cornering it, they dismounted warily, spears at the ready.

The boar's eyes were red with fury. Baldwin's blood sang in his veins with exhilaration as the beast squealed with rage and launched itself upon him. He hurled the spear. His aim was true; the boar shuddered to a halt, blood gushing from its throat, but as it kicked in its death throes, a second one dashed from the undergrowth beside them. Someone cried a warning, another spear flashed, but it was too late.

**

Isabella plied her needle listlessly as the wind whistled through chinks in the closed shutters. The fire flickered as the draught stirred it and cast its smoke sulkily across the room. Her fingers ached with cold, and she longed to cast her sewing aside and move closer to the hearth, but her mother-in-law's sharp eyes were upon her.

Adelaide sniffed. "I told Baldwin chimneys were a mistake, but he would have his way. Girl!" She beckoned to one of the maids. "Stir that fire, and bring hot spiced wine."

Isabella swallowed and hoped Evelina would bring her some, too. The chill had seeped into her bones. If even Adelaide was feeling it, it must be cold indeed. And with no central hearth, very little of the meagre warmth the flames produced was reaching her. Her feet were numb.

"And light the braziers."

Isabella dared to glance at her mother-in-law who was looking even paler than usual, her skin tight to her skull, her lips pressed together in a forbidding line. "Ma mère, are you unwell?" she ventured.

Adelaide snorted. "Is it not enough that this wind gives me the headache? Must I also answer your foolish questions?" Her voice was colder than the ice that formed on the edges of the castle moat.

Isabella dropped her gaze back to her lap, studying her embroidery so Adelaide would not see the surge of hate that blazed in her eyes.

There came a clattering outside the door; raised voices, shouts of alarm, and Matthew burst into the room. Adelaide looked down her haughty nose at him, but at the expression on his face, she rose with a cry of concern.

"My lady!" Her senior woman took an anxious step towards her but stopped as a ferocious glare was directed at her.

"What is it? Are we under siege? Speak, man!"

Matthew hesitated a moment before meeting those fierce eyes. "It's your son, Lord Baldwin." He paused. "An accident…the boar–"

She cut him off, her voice sharp. "My son? He is hurt?"

"My lady…" The man's eyes flickered away and back again. "Lord Baldwin is dead."

Adelaide stood as though turned to stone, her face like bleached linen. She gave a hoarse cry.

So slowly that, at first, Isabella did not realise what was happening, Adelaide toppled towards the floor, falling against the newly-lit brazier. Pandemonium reigned. Matthew caught her and lifted her before the hot coals that brushed the skirt of her gown could catch. Men surged in behind him, righting the brazier, stamping out the flames that had begun to lick the floor rushes. Women screamed and ran hither and thither. Amid the chaos, Isabella had risen to her feet and was now rigid, clasping her embroidery to her, eyes downcast to hide the wild joy that ripped through her.

She was conscious of one thought only. *Free! I'm free!*

Other books by the author include

Fiction

Out of Time (Book 1 in the Out of Time series)

Where Angels Tread

Beautiful and Other Short Stories

Four Christmases

Three for Hallowe'en

Poetry

Rhythms of Life

Jumping in the Puddles of Life

Hopes Dreams & Medals – Volumes 1 & 2

ABOUT THE AUTHOR

Photo by vanessachampion.co.uk

British author Loretta Livingstone lives with her
husband and cat in the beautiful Chiltern Hills.
She started writing poetry but progressed first, to short
stories and now, to full-length fiction.
Her first historical novel, Out of Time, was shortlisted by
the Historical Novel Society for the 2016 HNS Indie
Award.

Loretta suffers from ME, so it sometimes takes her more
time than she would wish to complete books, but she
considers she is blessed just to be able to write at all,
since, a few years earlier, it would have been impossible
for her to write anything of any length.

You can find more about Loretta on her website,
www.treasurechestbooks.co.uk and she can also be
contacted on Twitter or Facebook.

Printed in Great Britain
by Amazon